CROMWELL'S FOLLY

CROMWELL'S FOLLY

A DETECTIVE SAM LAGARDE MYSTERY

GINNY FITE

OPEN ROAD

INTEGRATED MEDIA

NEW YORK

ISBN: 978-1-5040-7748-4

This edition published in 2022 by Open Road Integrated Media, Inc.
180 Maiden Lane
New York, NY 10038
www.openroadmedia.com

For my sons

CROMWELL'S FOLLY

Honi soit qui mal y pense.
(Shamed be he who thinks evil of it.)

CHAPTER ONE

MARCH 29, 2014

Ben Cromwell was murdered in the narrow alley between the casino parking garage and the ramp to the stables behind the Charles Town racetrack. Murdered is the nice word for it. Slaughtered is more apt. Eviscerated. Chopped into pieces scattered in a ten-mile radius from the murder scene that had been carelessly scuffed over with dirt, straw and cedar chips before anyone realized that spot might be critical to an investigation.

It looked like someone really hated Cromwell; maybe several someones. It looked like they didn't care if anyone knew about Cromwell's murder. Most of the body parts were found within a week of the police realizing that he'd been murdered, and not just disappeared on a betting binge into a casino so dark and smoky that individual faces couldn't be made out on the omnipresent camera monitors.

Cromwell had been reported missing by his grandmother, who waited the required thirty-six hours from the evening she became anxious about him to report it. She knew from experience the police would tell her to wait. Even when she reported him missing, she knew the police weren't going to jump on it. Ben Cromwell's absence just meant this time local deputies weren't going to have to pull him out of a bar where he'd started a fight, arrest him for dealing, or haul him off a street corner where he had collapsed in a drunken stupor. To the police, Cromwell was a nuisance arrest, an annoying liar they'd have to cuff and interrogate and transport; more trouble than he was worth. He had been in the regional jail so often the guards who drew duty in the visitors' area knew his grandmother on sight. His grandmother was so accustomed to the visitor's drill that she simply stored her things in the assigned locker, looped the key around her finger, walked into the glass enclosed box, put her feet in the outline on the floor and raised her arms for the ritual wanding and pat down without being told.

Detective Sam Lagarde, who spent much breath telling folks who'd just met him that his last name wasn't laggard, dug around in the dirt with the toe of his shoe at the location where the sheriff had said the murder occurred. It didn't matter that he was messing up the crime scene. It had been driven on and walked on by hundreds of people, a few dogs, as many cats and some horses before local deputies from the county sheriff's office figured out this was the spot where the head they found in a dumpster behind the spa on Charles Street came off a body. *That was some pretty good detecting. There wasn't any blood trail. Any drops of blood right here were contaminated or could have come from a hundred other sources.* The Sheriff would never have found this spot if a stable hand hadn't accidentally dropped her glove here. She stooped to pick it up and found the guy's right pinky sporting an emerald and gold ring engraved: *Forever Yours.*

Strange that the murderer didn't notice the finger with the ring was missing. The murder must not have been about robbery or even money. What robber would have left a ring that looked like it was worth a grand? Lagarde imagined a large box of heavy-duty contractor cleanup plastic bags brought to the butchering. It was an organized project. Well planned. Nothing spontaneous about it. Pieces of Cromwell must have been carted away in all directions at the same time. Lagarde could imagine body parts flung into dark green bags being tossed into dumpsters all over the county. Something was bound to get lost in the flurry. They were still missing his left foot, his left ring finger, and the rest of his right hand. Maybe someone was keeping souvenirs. Maybe they needed to widen their search of dumpsters.

First the county sheriff's office had been called in to help the Charles Town police department that was flagged by the 911 dispatcher who took the shaken spa owner's call. Charles Town, a city of slightly more than five-thousand people, was not ready for a crime like this. Laid out on eighty acres by George's younger brother Charles Washington in the late eighteenth century, there were sleepy days when the town often seemed as if it hadn't changed since Jefferson County was still part of Virginia before the Civil War. To compensate for local inexperience, the state police were added to the murder investigation team, as if they were any better at reading drops of blood like tea leaves.

Truth be told, local police did not want this job. Their hard-pressed staff had enough to do with small time thieves, shoplifters, and drug dealers. The state had the forensic lab and it was clear they were going to need all the pieces they could uncover to solve this crime. The DNA work alone to match the body parts so they could be sure they had only one victim was making the FBI lab in Maryland to which they sent the samples work overtime. The Bureau of Criminal Investigations, part of WV State Police operations where Lagarde was assigned, took charge of the case.

Lagarde caught the case because it was his turn, pure and simple. Nobody in their right mind would have volunteered for this. There wasn't a great deal of pressure to find Cromwell's killer, or killers, but the Captain made it crystal clear to Lagarde that he had to solve the case. He was the right guy for that. He had a reputation for being dogged, if not particularly brilliant. Dogged was okay with Lagarde. Dogged got you to retirement, which at sixty, he was definitely looking forward to enjoying very soon.

Lagarde squatted, turned his eyes away from his feet, and looked slowly around the area. The stables were low, narrow fifty-foot long clapboard structures painted a light yellow with simple gabled roofs hanging out beyond the walls of the stable. Wooden awnings that were propped up at an angle, if a horse was stabled there, covered the windows every fifteen feet; a few were open today. There were several alleyways, one between the two sets of eight stables on each side, and one on either end of the series of buildings, which were wide enough for two horses being led by grooms to pass each other without touching. The entire area was fenced in and a cement ramp led from the casino parking lot into the enclosed area. The stables supported year-round thoroughbred racing on the track at night. Most horses came for a race or two and the next morning were walked into their trailers and hauled out to the next track or back to the farm. A few owners stabled several horses here for longer periods. The purses at this track weren't big, but gamblers could still lose their shirts and owners could lose their horses. Only seventy-five miles from Washington, D.C. and Baltimore, Maryland, the Charles Town racetrack was a place visiting gamblers put their money down on a horse every night. Not for nothing, there was a pawn shop right across the street from the track.

For no one to have seen the attack, Lagarde reasoned, it must have been night, late at night, well past the time horses were put up in their stalls, after night racing and trainers and stable hands had gone home. It would have been darker in this area, a spot that didn't benefit from either the casino parking garage lights or the quieter lights around the stables. Someone would have had to wait near the closest stable, flush up against the wall, watching for the guy to walk down the ramp into the fence-enclosed area to jump him. Or maybe someone lured Cromwell to the spot. Otherwise, why wouldn't he just go to his car in the garage? Maybe he parked in the stable employee parking lot because he was cheap. Maybe he was meeting someone here. A car parked in the area would not have aroused any suspicion. The police had yet to find a cell phone or Cromwell's clothes, or a wallet. If someone took his clothes, why not the expensive pinky ring? Was it a drug buy gone bad? Some kind of mob hit? Not the kind of crime they were accustomed to in this town. He added to the list of his questions. There were no bullets in the pieces of the victim they had located so far. That meant the murder was up close and personal. Someone had been covered in Cromwell's blood. What did the killer do with his own clothes, the weapon? The medical examiner said there were no signs that Cromwell had been strangled before being carved up. And the carving had been precise, done by someone who knew their way around the right tools. When they found the trunk of his body, all his internal organs were missing; had been gutted like a hunter would gut a deer after a kill. Cromwell was surprised, overcome, knocked down. There might have been a scuffle. It happened somewhere between 3 a.m. when the casino night shift went off duty and 5 a.m. for there to have been enough dark to cover the butchering and to cut down on the possibility of witnesses for the open air murder. It would have taken a while for one person to completely dismember Cromwell.

Lagarde was glad they'd found the head, though he was sorry for the young woman who found it in the dumpster when she took out the spa's trash. She apparently screamed for an hour, and was still shaking when he talked to her three days later. They had been able to run the dead guy's head shot and find him on the motor vehicle database. The address on Cromwell's driver's license was no good. The sheriff had a deputy run up there to notify next of kin. Some family named Goode lived in that trailer up on the mountain, and they had no idea who Ben Cromwell was. But they were renters, and it was likely Cromwell had stayed in the trailer before they moved into it. A quick check of criminal records showed that Cromwell had been picked up for possession with intent to sell a few times and did a two-year stint for burglary at the state pen. He'd been a regular at the regional jail, six months at a time on and off for violating his various probations. It was likely he had gotten away with a few other bad acts that no one could pin on him. None of the many addresses on his sheet panned out. The guy must have been shacking up with someone.

It was two weeks before they put the grandmother's missing report together with the murder victim. The deputy who did the notification told Lagarde that Cromwell's grandmother had put her hand to her chest, exhaled quickly, and said, "So that's that. I knew it would come to something like this." She didn't shed a tear, the deputy said.

Sam Lagarde stirred the dirt with the tip of his latex-gloved finger, more to help him think than to find anything. He touched something hard, metal. He looked down, carefully cleared the area the way an archaeologist might clear dirt from an ancient pot shard at a dig, and saw an earring, a gold hoop with a self-closing back. His first thought was that a woman lost it in some passionate clinch in the dark. Then he thought again. Maybe what he had on his hands was a crime of passion. He held the earring up to the light. Sun glinted off a beveled surface. The earring had a certain heft. *It's expensive, solid gold. Not exactly the kind of jewelry a lady would wear to a murder. Unless she was so rich that this was her weekend warrior accessory.* He would have to conjugate a whole other set of verbs. This murder was not about a gambling debt or drugs.

CHAPTER TWO

APRIL 2013

Ben Cromwell was the kind of handsome that made women stop in their tracks and emit a sound from deep in their diaphragms, something like, "Woof." They watched him from the corners of their eyes. They watched as he walked by them. They watched his tight, high, round ass as he walked away. Transfixed. Transported to the state of "yes, take me, whatever you want" in spite of the loud shrieking warning in their heads from the part of the brain that put two-and-two together when the so-called conscious mind wasn't paying attention.

When Cromwell smiled, perfectly formed lips revealing perfect white teeth, women waited, their breath held, to get a glimpse of his tongue. His green eyes seemed to shimmer when he smiled. Women thought it a privilege to be on the runway of that smile, at least for their first few months, at least until they'd bought him a television, Xbox, thousand-dollar bike, leased an apartment or car, or bought him some other bauble he had to have and then discovered he'd pawned it for cash he said he needed for something they didn't need to know about. Until he threw them out of the double-wide they'd paid for, drove off in the car they bought him and hung up on them when they called to confront him . . . they usually stopped paying for his phone service after that.

But for the brief few months of bliss, until he told them to kiss off and leave him alone, they thought they'd died and gone to heaven. He interrupted their work with his calls, "Hey, there, sweet thing, thinking of me?" he'd say. "I've been thinking about you." They'd leave wherever they were, in the middle of a shift, mid-brief, with a backlog of patients waiting, and run to meet him wherever he wanted—parking lot of the hospital, in the custodian closet at a hotel, the bathroom behind the bar—and breathlessly shimmy out of their panties, wet with longing for his mouth and breath and unsheathed dick. He stayed with no woman longer than six months; most for far less. Later, after abandonment, or after the test, his women hated themselves. The smart ones hated themselves earlier, around the second time he hit them up for cash, because he was a little short and wanted to buy his grandmother some roses for her birthday. Some still thought they could tame him, given more time. Some, years later, were still waiting for him to come back.

Evelyn Foster met Ben Cromwell in the hospital when he was recovering from pneumonia he contracted during the induced coma the resident put him in to get him through detox. Evelyn knew all of this when she approached his room. She had checked his electronic patient files. She had all the facts of his life in a nutshell right in front of her. This was his fourth admission to this hospital in two years. Overdosed, AIDs crisis, Detox—those were the admitting causes. His records said everything about this patient. Her only purpose in going into his room was to get his signature on a Medicaid application, since he had told admitting, between long lapses of consciousness, that he had no residence, no job, and no family locally. He said his parents were dead and he had no siblings or other living relatives.

There was some light coming in through the curtains, but the private room was dark. The beige walls and white linoleum floors seemed to disappear in the dusk. Cromwell was lying back on the pillows, his eyes closed, breathing calmly. Evelyn noted how long his black eyelashes seemed against his pale cheeks. He opened his eyes and looked straight into hers. He smiled slowly. It seemed to Evelyn, absurd as it was, that the light came on in the room.

"What's your name, pretty lady," Cromwell asked, "and where have they been hiding you?"

Evelyn looked down at her chart. Her cheeks pinked. She shouldn't be so easy. She fumbled for the pen she kept under the clip on the board. "Mr. Cromwell, I've brought you the Medicaid paper-work. It's all filled out. You just need to sign right here by the X."

She turned the clipboard toward him, pushed the bed tray closer to his chest so he could rest the document on the tray to sign it and offered him her pen. He slid his finger over hers as he accepted the pen.

"You smell good," he said. "In fact, you are the best thing I've smelled in two weeks." He smiled again then looked down to sign the paper.

His signature's large and looping, like the signature of someone with great confidence. "It's Chanel." He looked confused. "The perfume," she said, "it's Chanel. Chance, it's called."

"I'll take that chance," he said and grinned at her. "You're the kind of woman that makes me want to get out of bed and take a shower," he said. The comment didn't make any sense but somehow Evelyn's heart missed a beat. Was he saying that she alone could save him, restore him to life? Of course, that *was* absurd.

"Thank you, Mr. Cromwell," she said, hugging the clipboard to her chest. "If you want, I can help you find resources you'll need when you are ready to leave the hospital, connect you to DHHS." She was rushing through her usual spiel. "That's part of my duties as the social worker here. You can come down to my office on the first floor when you're ambulatory and we'll talk about what you are going to do next." She backed out of the room.

Evelyn leaned against the wall in the corridor. She seemed to be out of breath. Her cheeks were hot. Her hands trembled. Nurse Evans looked up from the desk and said, "You'll want to use that antibiotic cleaner on the wall right there."

Evelyn looked down at her hands. What was Evans talking about? She hadn't given Cromwell any care. Then she noticed the sign on the door that indicated that anyone dealing with this patient should wear a mask and gloves. She shrugged and walked slowly through the double doors at the end of the corridor. She was likely never going to see this patient again. There was no reason to worry about contagion of any sort. After all, no bodily fluids had been exchanged. The thought made her flush again. She took the stairs down to her office to work out the sudden surge of energy that coursed through her limbs.

CHAPTER THREE

MARCH 30, 2014, 10 A.M.

Sam Lagarde believed he should get better acquainted with Ben Cromwell's grandmother. Remote as it seemed, she might know something, have a name on a piece of paper, have met someone recently who threatened Cromwell. Maybe the guy borrowed money from someone he shouldn't have, someone who had now approached his grandmother. All Lagarde was looking for was a lead. It wasn't his intention to make friends.

He pulled into the parking space marked "Visitor" in front of a row of relatively new townhouses north of Martinsburg. Falling Waters was the name of the unincorporated area. Close enough to I-70, Hagerstown and Frederick to attract young professionals at the start of their careers as well as retired transplants not yet ready to give up their favorite shopping haunts in suburban Maryland. Lagarde surveyed the area around the grandmother's end unit. These weren't the cheap tin-box-looking row houses gobbled up by the new slum lords looking to turn them into instant rentals. This was a nice solid house, three-stories, brick, with a one-car garage and neatly trimmed boxwood and azalea bushes. There were sheer curtains in the front bay window. Lagarde wasn't sure what he expected, but it wasn't this middle-class abode. Again, he found himself recalibrating his view of Cromwell, as if by association the victim's own personality had changed. Based on this neighborhood, Ben Cromwell was an innocent victim felled by bloodthirsty villains. If Lagarde was starting from square one on his victim, he'd be looking for motive.

Lagarde had to admit he belonged to the tribe of police officers who thought that low-life criminals came from low-life criminal families, setting aside for a minute the ultra-rich, one-percenter criminals whose ability to avoid capture and prosecution was completely different from regular folks. Whether it was nature or nurture, rich or poor, crime seemed to run in families. At least, that's what he believed, what his experience taught him. Sure, there was the occasional rich kid with an aberrant psychosis, a sense of entitlement, and powerful parents who kept his misdeeds covered up for as long as they could, but for your everyday crime, you could often look at the parents and see the seeds of the deed. He could be wrong, but he didn't think so. It remained to be seen which kind of criminal did this murder. He rang the door bell and stepped back to look around the neighborhood. *Very quiet. No one hanging around outside. No garbage piling up in front of anyone's house. No rusting cars up on blocks in the front yard. 'These were people who kept themselves to themselves,'* as his own grandmother used to say.

The door was opened by a slender white-haired woman wearing jeans, a long green sweater, and a yellow silk scarf looped twice around her slender neck. She wore yellow socks, no shoes. Her ears were not pierced. She wore no jewelry of any kind, Lagarde noticed, not even a watch. If she was wearing makeup, it was very subtly applied. If Lagarde had a notion that a family member was involved in the murder, this woman was not the one. Lagarde guessed that she could not be Cromwell's biological grandmother. Even if she had her own child at twelve, she wouldn't be old enough to have a thirty-year-old grandson. At least, that's how he figured it. Lagarde doubted the woman standing in front of him had reached what he liked to call his own 'heavy middle age.' *Her hair must have turned white prematurely.* He introduced himself.

"Mrs. Wilson? Beverly Wilson? I'm Detective Sam Lagarde." He held out his credentials to her. She looked down at the photo and badge he presented and nodded. "I'm investigating the murder of your grandson, Ben Cromwell."

Lagarde had learned a long time ago not to beat around the bush. People would deal with their emotions and there was always something to be learned by watching them react to the facts. He did not hold out his hand for a shake, but rather inclined slightly, something like a bow but not quite.

"Oh, yes," she said. "Come inside. Would you like a cup of tea? I was just going to have one."

She stepped aside, held the door open for him and closed it behind him. She gestured to the stairs, indicating he should go up. It seemed almost as if she expected him. On the main level, she pointed to the flowered chintz-covered chairs near the green velvet sofa in the living room. Lagarde selected one, surprisingly comfortable. She walked into the adjacent kitchen, opened a cabinet and took out a red mug to match the one already on the counter. Lagarde noted that the counter was black granite. The cabinets appeared to be hardwood, not composite. The house was very clean.

"Are you particular about your tea or will black tea do for you?" she asked.

"Whatever you have is fine," Lagarde said. He noted hardwood floors covered with colorful wool rugs both in the living room and dining room that opened on the other side of the kitchen. Looked like the dining room might have been an add-on, what the builders called a bump out. The living room was uncluttered. A few original paintings hung on each wall. There were few knickknacks and no personal photographs in the space. On the coffee table was a red blown glass vase with glass stems and leaves snaking out of it. The piece looked like it came from an old Star Trek set of an alien planet populated with oddly shaped, brightly colored succulents and tropical flowers. An image of Captain Kirk embracing an alien beauty in a skimpy garment rose in his mind. He quickly dismissed it. *Stick to your inventory*, he scolded himself. A quilt hung on the wall going up the stairs. The house looked like a model home to him, or as if someone lived here only temporarily.

"Cream or lemon?" she asked.

"Nothing in it," he said.

Beverly Wilson brought out the mugs on a teak tray with a plate of delicious looking chocolate covered cookies. *There was no way she actually ate cookies like this,* Lagarde's mind wandered, looking at her slender legs as she sat down on the sofa and crossed them.

"These are the cookies that Ben liked," she said, as if she had heard his comment. "Might as well use them up."

Lagarde marveled at how little emotion she showed as she said that. He took a sip of his tea and lowered the mug to a coaster on the glass coffee table centered between the two chairs and the sofa.

"Ben was living with you?" he asked. "Are his parents dead?"

"Oh, no, they're alive," she said. "They live in Maryland. Ben just used to tell everyone they were dead to get the attention, or get something, or maybe get even with them. They are just dead to him. When they stopped giving him money and cars, he started saying they were dead."

Lagarde began to wonder if there was something clinically wrong with Mrs. Wilson. Maybe she was sedated. She was too unemotional. It was as if she were talking about someone who wasn't remotely related to her, someone she had read about in a newspaper.

"After you've been hurt a lot, Mr. Lagarde, you learn how to keep your feelings to yourself," she said. This time, there was a slight tremor in her hand as she put her mug down on the table.

Lagarde was becoming accustomed to the idea that she could read his mind. "Was he living here with you?" he asked again.

"Well, I wouldn't call it living here. He usually called me once a week. Sometimes he came for a few days when he couldn't find anyone else to impose on. He ran out of friends' couches a few years ago. I keep, kept, a room for him."

Lagarde watched her face as she seemed to think about whether to say more. People had difficulty with silence, he knew. They would fill it with chatter that sometimes was useful.

"He doesn't have a key to the house though," she continued. "He has to, had to, call me and ask first, and I have to be here the entire time he's here. This was just a failsafe, so he wouldn't freeze to death sleeping on the street. You can look at the room, if you want. I did have it cleaned recently, including the carpet. You can look through whatever he left, though, if it will help you. I haven't done anything with his stuff."

She stood and led the way up the second set of stairs. On the landing she pointed to the room and stood by the door as Lagarde went into the bedroom. There was a double bed, stripped down to the mattress, a small dresser, a night stand with a lamp, and a closet. The walls were painted a muted platinum color; the trim a creamy white. As she had said, the room was cleaned. Even the white blinds on the two windows that faced the townhouse backyard were sparkling. Lagarde wondered how dirty it had been, what the cleaning removed. He opened the closet.

CHAPTER FOUR

DECEMBER 1999

It was one in the morning a few weeks before Christmas when Ben Cromwell, at age fifteen, decided to rob his parents. It was the first time he had thought of it that way. Before this moment, he had only thought he was taking what he needed. He needed money, some for dope and some to buy that heavy silver chain he'd seen at the pawn shop the other day when he took in his father's video camera to get a few bucks. Man, he would look so cool in that chain. He looked in the mirror over his dresser just to verify that the chain would enhance his handsome looks. Yeah. That was the thing. He needed it. That was all.

The parents were fast asleep; their bedroom door locked. Even if they heard him moving around the house, they would think he got up to get a drink of water. *They are unbelievably 'slow.'* He'd been pulling dollars out of his father's wallet and his stepmother's purse for years and they never noticed. They had no clue. Well, maybe his stepmother had a clue, but his dad never believed her. He overheard his dad telling her she was psychotic. He knew they were talking about him. His stepmother's voice had that low, intense, shaky quality to it, as if she were spitting out bullets. He had no compunctions about taking their cash, but tonight he had need for more cash than they carried; he had an itch he just had to scratch. He was headed to Baltimore, to a part of the city called Mondawmin Mall; heard they had the best deal on crack there, guys just standing on street corners handing it out to whoever drove up. He and his posse were going. They figured they would get enough to party and then sell the rest around town. Make back their outlay. It would be an adventure, like his father was always telling him he should have, just not in a canoe carrying a backpack and going miles into nowhere where nothing ever happened.

He grabbed his back pack and walked up the darkened stairs from his bedroom in the finished basement to the living room. He grabbed all the CDs in the rack by the player. His stepmother had all this classical music, folk singers, blues and jazz crap. Some yuppies would want that. He opened the closet in the hall and took his father's Minolta camera and long zoom lens. His father got this camera when he was young. There were dozens of boxes of photographs taken with it. *Time to get a new one, Dad.* Cromwell's pack was now heavy. He heard his friend Carl's car idling next to the house. He walked through the kitchen, opened the side door, threw his pack in the back of the car, and whispered to Carl, "Hey, man, give me a hand in here. Got a few things that won't fit in my pack."

Together they took the computer off the desk in the office, the television in the living room, and the turntable. Cromwell looked around. *Too bad the bitch kept her jewelry in the bedroom. I'll have to come back for that. Next time.* He'd need to stay away long enough for his father to get frantic about his being missing and then the guy would practically beg him on bended knee to come home. He could count on that. One thing he had learned: the suckers always beg.

CHAPTER FIVE

AUGUST 2013

The first time Violet Gold ever set eyes on Ben Cromwell was when he sauntered up to her desk in the Legal Aid office. He was wearing a worn leather jacket, his checked shirt outside his pants, over-sized chinos, and some very fancy red leather shoes. His dark hair was buzz-cut short and she saw the tattoo on his left ring finger, a Chinese symbol he later told her meant love. Much later, when she looked it up, she discovered the symbol stood for chaos.

He sat down in the plastic chair in front of her desk, handed her the intake form he'd filled out, and without introduction said, "I want to sue my parents."

Violet leaned back in her chair, a movement she forced herself to execute because she wanted to lean forward. Sitting in the chair opposite her was the handsomest man she had ever seen in her life. Her brain, synthesizing quickly the way she was trained to do in law school, took in classic features and model-thin body . . . and a spark of something else more dangerous. *Those eyes.* She looked down at the paperwork to regain her composure. On the form, Cromwell had written that he was twenty-nine, lived alone, had no job and no means of support. His last job was as a waiter at a local restaurant two years earlier. He was not in school and apparently had no education beyond high school and a few classes at the community college. She wondered if he was claiming his parents had abused him when he was young. Perhaps he'd been in therapy and had what psychologists called recovered memories.

Violet said, "Why do you want to sue your parents?"

"Failure to support me," he said flatly.

She had to hold back an inclination to laugh. She looked at the piece of paper. "You are twenty-nine, right?" she asked.

"Well, yeah, that was the age I was when I got this idea. I just turned thirty a month ago," he said.

"So you're thirty-years-old."

"Yeah, yes. thirty."

Violet amended the paperwork with his correct age. She didn't let herself notice that the man in front of her lied and didn't flinch when caught. "When did they stop supporting you?"

"Maybe a year ago, a little longer, I think. My stepmom is the one who talked Dad into it. Someone told me I could sue her for alienation of affection. He was sending me regular money every month before then and paying for my rent, phone, electric, clothing and food. You know, all the necessities, and now he's not giving me anything. I mean, he's responsible for me, isn't he?"

Violet leaned forward across the desk and looked at Cromwell carefully. She needed to ask the next question gently. She didn't want to upset him. "Have you been declared incompetent or unable to care for yourself by a doctor or a court?"

She wasn't sure she had worded that question simply or clearly enough. She felt a great rush of sympathy for him. A young man who was developmentally disabled thrown out by his parents with no support, no provisions made for his care, it was beyond cruel.

"No, nothing like that," Cromwell said, seeming angry at being asked the question. His green eyes flashed at her. "I graduated from regular high school—I wasn't in the class with droolers—and I got good grades in those classes I took in community college. There's nothing wrong with my brain. But they're my folks. They have an obligation to take care of me, don't they? Like, all of my life, right?"

Violet sighed and sat up straight. "I'll have to research this," she said. "Off the top of my head, if you are not physically or mentally disabled, I'm not sure that your parents are legally required to support you once you're an adult."

Cromwell seemed crestfallen. He looked down at his hands, looked up at her like a puppy dog that had just been shamed by its master. "I am sick," he said, his voice tightened as if the admission cost him something. "I'm trying to get disability from social services." Tears welled in his eyes. His lower lip quivered. It was all Violet could do to not reach out and stroke his cheek. "I don't know what I'm going to do, then. Where am I going to sleep tonight?"

"You mean you don't have anywhere to sleep tonight?"

"No. I'm totally out of cash, and not a single one of my friends has any place for me. I've already been on the phone to everyone." He put his hand, with its long fingers, over his face.

Violet looked around the office, trying to put together a plan for this man who was only a few years older than she was, for whom life just hadn't worked out right.

"Okay, I'm going to call Cheryl Sykes at the Rescue Mission and get you a bed for tonight. They have some rules, but I don't think you'll have a problem with them. The mission is only a few blocks from here. You can walk there and get yourself situated."

"No, I can't go to the mission," he said.

"Of course you can. It's clean. There are people there. You'll get a meal and a place to sleep and Cheryl will put you together with social services. They can help you get a job. You can stay at the mission for six months while you work and put aside money for a room of your own."

"No. I'm not going to the mission," he said. He stood up, and turned away as if to walk out of the office. "If that's all you can do, then we're done."

"Why can't you go to the mission?"

"They steal your stuff there. They have fights. I've been there before. It's bad."

Violet thought she would weep. In her short time at Legal Aid since graduating from law school and passing the bar, she thought she had been told every kind of problem caused by poverty, ignorance or intentional harm. Obviously not. How could his parents just abandon him? What sickness did he have? Didn't they care what happened to him? Somehow, now, she felt personally responsible for him. His plight stirred something in her she had never felt before.

"Tell you what," she said. "Go wait in the public library until 5 p.m. and then come back here to meet me. We'll figure this out together." She felt better immediately. His face had brightened at her words. He smiled at her as if she were the best thing since sliced bread and he knew which side to butter.

CHAPTER SIX

MARCH 30, 2014, 10:30 A.M.

Sam Lagarde pulled the duffel bag off the floor inside Ben Cromwell's bedroom closet. There were four clean, ironed shirts on hangers in the closet. On the shelf above the shirts were several shoe boxes. Giuseppe Zanotti was one of the brand names printed on a box. Another box had the name Wings + Horns on it. Armando Cabral was stamped on another. *No Nikes for this guy.* He would have to research those brands but he was pretty sure that there was no way a guy like Cromwell, who had no job or evidence of a trust fund, could afford them. Cromwell had either stolen the shoes, someone's credit cards, or made very bad use of large sums of money—possibly from drug sales—money that could have paid a few months rent somewhere instead of scrounging off his grandmother. The boxes did give Lagarde another lead, though. He should show the guy's photo around some high end shoe stores and see if anything popped up. Like a murderer or two. *Would someone kill for a pair of shoes?*

Lagarde looked over at Mrs. Wilson. She seemed to be lost in her own thoughts, and a little sad. But maybe he was just reading into her quiet composure. She didn't say anything. She had stopped reading his mind.

"Did you buy him these shoes?" he asked.

"Me? No. I have no idea where he got them," she said.

"Do you mind if I look through this bag?" Lagarde asked.

"No. Go ahead. It's just his junk. The things were in the dresser. He brought the bag in the last time I saw him. I was going to give everything to Goodwill when I was ready. I only got as far as putting it all in the duffel bag."

This was the first time Lagarde sensed that she might be grieving for her grandson. Lagarde spilled the contents of the bag out onto the bare mattress. It would be easier to look through the stuff that way and there would be fewer surprises, just in case Cromwell kept pet snakes. Lagarde pulled a pair of light blue Nitrile gloves from his pocket and put them on. He quickly itemized the most obvious items: an iPod, a cell phone, three thumb drives in an unopened package, a Samsung tablet, three different chargers, the remote from a television not in evidence in the room, one of those Playstation game devices, four rolled up t-shirts, two pairs of jeans, a very fancy bottle labeled No. 1 by Clive Christian in London, an expensive perfume. Lagarde flashed on the expensive gold earring he had found at the site. He had to find that person. He had sent the earring to the lab to see if there was anything they could pick up from it.

Tumbled out onto the bed with everything else was a heavy watch with the name Breitling engraved on the back along with words in French saying it was made in Switzerland. Either Cromwell was an accomplished shoplifter or someone had been very nice to him. Probably the latter. Shoplifting was work and he was beginning to get the idea that Cromwell did not like work. There also were no stores in Martinsburg that carried these items, Lagarde would bet on it. Maybe someone took Cromwell on a little trip to New York City, or they were comfortable with online shopping. Maybe that someone had texted or emailed Cromwell and could be found on the cell phone. He hoped the data on the phone could be recovered and that the SIM card was still in place. The state forensics lab might be able to pull useful information from it, like the last person Cromwell talked to. The other thing that was interesting about this loot, and that was how Lagarde was now regarding it, was that Cromwell had not been wearing or carrying any of it. He was storing it here in his grandmother's house; the way someone else might store important documents or cash in a safe deposit box. *This was his safe house in more ways than one.* Lagarde had a feeling Cromwell never told anyone about his grandmother.

Lagarde picked up a pair of DIESEL stone-washed jeans from the bed and somewhat reluctantly put his hand in the front right pocket. Nothing. Left pocket. Nothing. *Might as well go for broke*, he thought, and put his hand in the back pocket. There was a key. He pulled out the key and examined it; looked like a standard issue post office box key. But which post office? There were several USPS branches between Martinsburg and Charles Town and a few private mail box store front businesses.

"Did Ben have a post office box?"

"I don't know," Beverly Wilson said. "Maybe. He didn't get any mail here."

"I'm going to take this key," Lagarde said. "I'll find the box, if there is one. I'll let you know what I find."

She nodded.

He dropped the key into a small baggie he drew from his pocket and jotted the date, location found, and Cromwell's name on the bag with a pen he carried in his inside breast pocket.

"Do you mind if I take the bag and the things that are in it? There may be more information here that will help me find who committed the murder." He looked at her carefully. "I'll bring it all back."

"It's okay," she said. "I don't need any of it. You can dispose of it. I don't need souvenirs." That last comment sounded bitter to Lagarde. She looked over the things scattered on the bed. "How did he afford those things? He never had any money. He was always asking for fifty dollars." She shook her head. "We didn't give him any cash because he would just get in trouble with drugs . . ." Her voice trailed off.

"Thanks, Mrs. Wilson. I won't bother you anymore right now. I'll call you if I need something else."

As Lagarde added the first shoe box to the duffel bag, the top came off. Inside the box, neatly stacked in rows, were hundred dollar bills. Lagarde opened the other two boxes. More stacks of hundreds. He looked over at Mrs. Wilson. "Is this your money?" he said.

"No, I have no idea where he got it," Beverly Wilson said. Her hand was on her chest, as if she was having a pain. Her face paled. "Where would he get all that money?" She sat down on the edge of the bed. "I've never known him to have money and not spend it immediately." She shook her head.

"I'm going to take it as evidence, Mrs. Wilson," Lagarde said. "Maybe this is what his killer was after."

She nodded, stood and walked out of the bedroom as if Lagarde wasn't there. He heard her start down the steps.

Lagarde put the tops back on the shoeboxes, put the boxes in the duffel bag and walked down the two flights of stairs carrying it. At the front door on the bottom level, he stopped in front of Beverly Wilson who was standing there holding the door open and thanked her again. "Oh, one more thing," he said. "What's the name of Ben's parents?"

"Cromwell," she said. "Robert and Sarah Cromwell. Sarah, Ben's stepmother, is my daughter. They live in Columbia, Maryland. Do you want their phone number?"

"Good idea," Lagarde said. "Would you write it down for me?"

Beverly Wilson walked over to a table in the foyer, pulled the pad she kept by the phone there closer to her and wrote her daughter's phone number. She tore the piece of paper from the pad and walked back to Lagarde at the front door. Handing him the paper, her hand shook just a little. Lagarde took the piece of paper, gave a little nod and walked toward his car. He put the duffel bag in the trunk of his car and put the piece of paper with the Cromwell's phone number in a small plastic bag. He now had her prints to run, just in case there was something in her past he needed to know. He took off his gloves, opened the car door and looked back at the house to see if she was watching him. The door was closed and she wasn't watching him from the window. He felt a twinge of disappointment and shrugged it off.

CHAPTER SEVEN

MARCH 30, 2014, 11 A.M.

Beverly Wilson closed the door behind Detective Lagarde and walked up the stairs to the living room. She had a brightly lit studio with comfortable chairs on the bottom level, but somehow she didn't want to be where Lagarde had last stood. She needed to shake him off. She went upstairs and sat on the living room sofa and put her hands over her face. A few moments passed as she gathered herself together. Her mind re-ran the interview with the detective. *He was a relatively small man, not taller than five-feet-eight, was very trim and had thinning hair that must have been blonde once, piercing blue eyes—pleasant features that would have been called handsome when he was young. His face had worn well and his clothes seemed unusual to her for a detective, more like the horsey set's attire: corduroy slacks, knitted vest, blue work shirt, tan barn jacket with a corduroy collar, and brown work boots. I wonder if he has horses.*

She had liked having horses on the Burkittsville farm she shared with her husband Tom. Known only in the wider world because of the *Blair Witch* movie, Burkittsville's quaint eighteenth century obscurity had been their haven for decades. Tom farmed and she was a farmer's wife. She had loved that life, everything about it—being a wife and friend to a tinkerer, someone who would wake up at 5 a.m. with a solution to a problem in his head, throw on his clothes and head out to his workshop to put pieces of metal, wood or leather together in a way that would make a broken thing work, whether it was a broken tractor, a disintegrating lock on the gate or the furnace. She loved the freedom of having hundreds of acres of her own land to roam and to do whatever she wanted inside their house and in her own kitchen garden. She loved cooking, cleaning and gardening; the chores other women groused about made up the structure of her life. She loved bringing up her children in that home, even though she could see that by the time they were fifteen, both her son and daughter were itching to be somewhere else, anywhere else.

Being with Tom on the farm was the life she craved. It was everything to her and it was all gone. His long, agonizing sickness and death took that life away from her. She could not work the farm alone and she didn't want to bring in some stranger as a partner. It was best to sell it all and move on. At least, that's how it seemed to her three years ago. Now she had a sense that Sam Lagarde could give her a glimpse of what she'd lost.

She knew she was thinking about Lagarde as a way to delay doing what she should do. This would be the second sad call to her daughter in as many days. The first was yesterday when the deputy notified her about Ben's death. She had to tell Sarah and Robert right away, but it was the *last* thing she wanted to do. She had paced her house for a while trying to figure out how to do it. She debated getting in her car and driving to their home in Maryland. She wished she had someone to ask. If only her husband were alive. In the end, she dialed Sarah's landline and just blurted out what she had been told when her daughter answered the phone. In the middle of her third sentence, Sarah had begun sobbing uncontrollably.

Robert had taken the phone from Sarah and said, "Beverly, are you ok? I can't understand anything Sarah is saying. Is something wrong? Can you tell me again?"

Beverly had tried to be very calm. "The police have just informed me that Ben is dead," she said. "The sheriff's deputy said he was murdered at the race track. In Charles Town . . . two weeks ago. He apologized for not telling me sooner. They had trouble identifying him. The deputy showed me a photograph. It was Ben." She paused, exhausted from saying all that.

There was a long silence. Robert said, "God. No. God," and dropped the phone.

It was some time before Sarah came back on the line. Beverly could hear what could only be called howling in the background. "Mom," Sarah said in a barely audible whisper, "I'll have to call you back later."

No wonder Beverly was delaying. She walked into the kitchen, picked up the phone and dialed. "Hey, sweetie," she said into the receiver, "the detective was here. About Ben. Do you want to know anything?"

She listened to her daughter Sarah say no, she didn't want to know anything. Beverly waited a few seconds, in case Sarah wanted to say something else. She had learned how to wait a long time ago, to rein in her desire to fix people's problems.

"What did you tell him?" Sarah asked.

"Nothing," Beverly said. "I answered his very simple questions. I think he was inspecting my house, and me. He seemed to think Ben was living with me. I did tell him that you and Robert are alive. He thought you were dead, for some reason. His name is Sam Lagarde. He asked for your phone number. He will probably visit you."

Her daughter said nothing.

"How is Robert?" Beverly asked.

"Stricken."

Beverly heard her daughter choke back a sob.

"He blames himself. He blames me," Sarah whispered.

"I'm sorry, sweetheart, so sorry. What can I do for you?"

Beverly remembered her daughter's wedding day, her girl's radiance and joy, how handsome Robert had been standing at the front of an old stone chapel in front of solid wooden pews decorated by flowers, light streaming in through the stained glass windows. And then she remembered how his ten-year-old son Ben had walked away from the wedding the minute the vows were finished, simply walked out of the chapel. How Robert ran after the boy leaving his bride standing there alone at the chapel door accepting congratulations from friends and family as if they planned it that way, as if it were the most natural thing in the world for her new husband to be standing on the lawn fifty feet away from her holding onto his son. To Beverly, a malevolent spirit darkened the day for a few minutes. She hoped her daughter had the strength and grace for what would inevitably follow, but never had she imagined the many ways Ben would invent to torture his parents.

"Nothing, Mom," Sarah said, breaking into Beverly's thoughts. "There's nothing to do. We've been waiting for some horrible telephone call for years. Now it's come." Sarah was quiet again for a while. "Did the detective say when they would release the body for burial?" Her voice shook.

"Oh, no, I didn't even think to ask. But he'll be back, he said. He took the things that Ben left here."

"I have to go, Mom," Sarah said suddenly.

Beverly hoped that talking to her mother was not seen as treachery these days by Sarah's husband. "Okay, sweetie. I love you."

"Me, too, Mom," Sarah whispered.

Beverly waited for the click on the other end and hung up.

She stood in the kitchen looking out the window over the sink. The end unit townhouse gave her more windows. That's why she chose it when she downsized from her cherished, Victorian farmhouse. In the far distance she could see the undulating ridge of the mountains, dark blue at this time of day. She would have to draw comfort from that.

CHAPTER EIGHT

FEBRUARY 2013

Ilise Vander stood outside her parent's modest house on Kentucky Avenue, her phone at her ear. This was her fifth call to that bastard. He was an hour late and hadn't even texted. It was cold out; she was dressed for a rave. There were goose bumps on her belly. The gel on her spiked up hair was turning to icicles and her thong was jammed up her ass from pacing. She was typing her tenth text, when there he was, getting out of someone's car, walking over to her like he was prince charming or something coming up in a chariot.

"Hey there, pretty girl," Ben Cromwell leaned down, put his arm behind her back, and scooped her up toward him. He kissed her, gave her a little tongue, pulled back and looked her up and down. "You are definitely the best thing I have seen all day."

"You are an hour late," Ilise yelled at him, shaking him off, backing up, stamping her foot. Her large hoop rhinestone earrings shook for emphasis. "Where have you been? I've been freezing my ass off out here waiting for you."

"Aw, c'mon, don't be like that, girl. I've had a day you wouldn't believe. Got me some dough now, though, and we are going to party. Ryan's gonna drive us over to the warehouse."

"I don't want to go anymore. And wait, is that glitter eye shadow you have on your cheek? Have you been smooching some other girl?"

"No, nothing like that. I just stopped off at my cousin's. It's her birthday. I just gave her a hug with her present."

"You have a cousin in Martinsburg?"

"Nah, down in Maryland. You don't know her. That's why I'm late. You know me, driving sixty miles like a crazy-assed fool to get here so you wouldn't be mad at me; keep my word and all that." Cromwell reached out and took her hand, lifted her fingers to his mouth and kissed each one.

"You know my mother has been watching me out the window. You know she hates you. Now I'm going to have to listen to weeks of her telling me what a creep you are cuz you kept me waiting all this time." She was running out of objections. "I've got to work tomorrow. My shift starts at eleven in the morning. I'll be on my feet all day cutting hair. I can't be out all night."

"No problem, no problem little girl," Cromwell crooned. "I'll get you home in time to take a shower and change your clothes." He put his hand on her ass and steered her toward the car.

Ilise had a bad feeling she would be better off going back inside the house and never seeing him again, but she just couldn't help herself. This was the man of her dreams, after all.

CHAPTER NINE

MARCH 31, 2014

Every once in a while there's a little break in a case that makes the bread crumbs up ahead a little easier to spot. The post office box key he found in the back pocket of Ben Cromwell's expensive jeans came from a Mailboxes Etc. store on Queen Street in Martinsburg. It was the kind of business that gave you a street address even though you only had a box. Lagarde discovered it using old-fashioned shoe leather detecting, which is to say he spotted it by accident driving across town, pulled over, parked and went inside.

Martinsburg's downtown was four blocks long and two blocks deep of brick and stone façade buildings no taller than three stories with many store fronts empty. Some had been turned over into tattoo parlors or bodegas, alongside the courthouse, some federal offices, and a few brave entrepreneurs trying to survive with boutique enterprises like candy, art, pottery and restaurants. More than three times larger than Charles Town, and the largest city in West Virginia's Eastern Panhandle, Martinsburg still didn't register as a blip on the list of small cities in the U.S. A thriving mill town in the nineteenth century, Martinsburg was a city in its last death throes, or at the beginning of a revival. Lagarde wouldn't hazard a guess which way the town was going, but there were streets where he made sure his vehicle was locked when he drove on them.

The Mailboxes Etc. store front looked more like a failing business than a prosperous one. *Windows and floors almost always gave away whether a place was well managed or not.* The front window hadn't been cleaned in a long time and the floor looked like no one had done anything about it since the building was built. Lagarde held up the key he found in Cromwell's pants pocket. "Will this key work here?" he said.

The clerk verified that the key Lagarde held in his hand was theirs. With a little pressure, Lagarde wormed out of him that Cromwell kept a box there. A search warrant obtained the next day gave Lagarde access to the box, which Cromwell apparently hadn't bothered to check in half a year.

Using the high counter in the store, Lagarde quickly went through the box contents. Along with hospital bills totaling more than twenty-five thousand dollars, for care in three states, there were letters from Cromwell's father that were heart wrenching—each one more frantic than the previous one—a few collection notices for past-due rent in various locations, cut off notices for his phone, electric and Internet service, notifications from the community college for classes for which tuition had already been paid, and a letter from one Lila Townsend, M.D. It was the M.D. that was a surprise. Lagarde first thought it was another past-due bill for services rendered, but the letter seemed to be much more personal than that. Lagarde wondered how Cromwell knew her . . . or maybe he was reading into the note. Maybe Cromwell had been doing some work for the doctor, though what he was qualified to do was still unknown.

The note was printed out on her personal stationery with a home address. It said: "We're done. Stay out of my life. I will get a restraining order against you if you come to my house or office again." It was signed Lila. The letter was dated October 18, 2013. The printed address was Lila Townsend, M.D., 4805 Millwood Road, Shepherdstown, WV.

An M.D. could be where the money for those shoes, watch, jeans and perfume came from. After all that overly generous gifting, why was she writing him off? The man really pissed her off somehow. Lagarde cautioned himself; he was jumping way ahead of what he knew.

Obviously, Cromwell had never gotten the warning letter. That afternoon, Lagarde checked the county judicial system database for a restraining order against Cromwell. Bingo. Almost two months before the murder, give or take a few days, Lila Townsend had gotten a judge to order that Ben Cromwell was not to come within fifty yards of her, her house, her car, her office or the parking lot for her office. She would have had to show cause; claimed he was stalking her. He must have been following her on purpose, trying to intimidate or infuriate her, to get her to think that she was helpless against him. Did he get drugs from her and she cut him off? Lila Townsend was next on Lagarde's list of people to visit. But still, he could not imagine that a woman pulled-off that brutal murder in the dead of night. At least not alone.

CHAPTER TEN

APRIL 2000

Ben Cromwell crouched behind the headstone at his mother's grave. The cemetery sloped away toward Ridge Road and you could see a fair distance across Howard County: rolling hills, a few horse farms, some fancy houses he was thinking about visiting. The stone said: "ELAINE CROMWELL 1950–1990." It was engraved with an angel. He had taken many girls to this grave. It was amazing how a few tears, even a sad look, worked on females. Bring some flowers, stand there in front of the grave with his head down, pretend to be talking to his mother, watch them out of the corner of his eye to gauge when to reach out his hand for them. That action was like catnip to them. They would turn themselves inside out to make him feel better. Their reaction must be genetic—some survival of the species mechanism, as his father was always saying—and all girls behaved that way.

Playing on women's sympathy always worked, except with Sarah, his stepmother. Maybe he messed that up. He shouldn't have pushed her away that first morning after his pop came back from the honeymoon. He hadn't really figured women out at that point. Hey, he was only ten. He was standing in the kitchen looking at the assorted cold cereal boxes on the cabinet shelf, trying to figure out which one to eat for breakfast, and she walked in, put an arm around him and gave him a kiss on the cheek.

"You stink," he said. It just came out of his mouth. It wasn't like he planned it. He was fascinated by the effect of his words.

Sarah backed away a few steps, her eyes wide like she was electrocuted. She said nothing and went into the bathroom. He heard the water running in the sink and then the shower. At the time he thought, *That'll teach her.* Now, he realized he had made a tactical mistake at the very beginning of the war between them. Sometimes he admitted to himself that he started the struggle, but he preferred the version where it was her fault. She was to blame. He wanted her to go away. So sure he would win, he tried everything he could think of to make her leave.

Even in his present situation he had to laugh about the time they all sat down to dinner—this was when she was still trying to get them to sit at the table together to eat—and he said, "Whoa, Sarah, you've got worms crawling out of your head. Yech. That's gross!" just as she was passing him the rice. The look on her face was priceless. He kept up the stunt for a while. She didn't touch her head, or anything. He figured she knew there were no worms crawling out of her skull, but he had the pleasure of knowing that she also knew that he had, with little effort, completely screwed up the meal. It was worth it even if she did convince Dad to take him to a shrink. He had the shrink's number right away. She was a woman. Run the same game as with girls: cry about his mom dying, make up shit about Sarah, tell them his Dad abused him. They just ate that crap up.

Right now he was hiding from the State Troopers and trying to make a plan for his next move. Steve next door got a little strung out when Ben climbed in his daughter's second story bedroom window. *When you see it in Romeo and Juliet everyone swoons, but do it in real life and people freak out.* The neighbor also discovered Ben had taken a stash of antique coins he kept in a velvet drawstring bag in a dresser drawer. Ben thought he'd be long gone before Steve missed them. Instead, he called the damn police on him and Ben ran.

He needed a plan. It was too soon to go home. Anyway, the troopers knew where he lived. Sarah called them one midnight a few months ago when she started a fight with him. His dad was already asleep or it would never have happened, her calling the police. Dad would have sided with him and calmed her down or frozen her out. He had this way of turning his back on her as if she wasn't even there. She told the trooper, this giant guy maybe six-foot-seven, that she was afraid of Ben, that he had threatened her, that he was doing drugs. She told the trooper he should search Ben's room. Of course, Ben had to rebut that. Loudly.

"Privacy, and all that," he yelled. "Constitutional rights. This is America, isn't it?"

And she yelled, "This is our house, we pay for everything, we make the rules."

His dad came downstairs in the middle of the yelling, with the trooper trying to be referee. His dad was more upset at Sarah for calling the cops than he was at Ben for anything she said he did. The man always had his back.

Except now, he couldn't go back to the house for a while. This would be the third time since he turned sixteen that he had to stay away for a while, take a little vacation. Ben didn't see what was different about taking his dad's stuff and taking anyone else's, but he sensed that his dad would be mad at him for this. Embarrassed in front of strangers, maybe. Somehow his mom being dead wasn't enough of an excuse to get him out of it. If the cops dug around, it might come out that Steve's house wasn't the first one he'd found his way into. Most people in their neighborhood just left their house and car doors unlocked. It was like an invitation, like they were saying, "Hey, what's mine is yours." That's how he read it, anyway.

Ben shook himself a little. He needed a hit of something, anything. He needed a place to stay. Someone had told him there was this cool, old guy over in Rolling Acres who let kids crash and who was generous with his drugs. That was the place to go to. He just needed the sky to darken to give him a little cover before he headed over there. That was the plan.

CHAPTER ELEVEN

APRIL 1, 2014

Sam Lagarde considered himself a decent man, even if he shed wives after five or ten years, depending on how well they stood up, or how long they could stand him. He liked quiet women, he'd discovered after Mrs. Lagarde number three, women who didn't nag him about a list of things he was supposed to do or didn't ask him an endless series of questions that couldn't be answered. He liked resourceful women who could muck out a stall, feed the horses, cook a meal worthy of a four-star chef, and look like a million bucks on a fifty-dollar a week allowance. He did not think of himself as cold. He was logical. He was a warm-hearted guy when he wanted to be. He would give a woman everything he had, for a period of time. But long relationships were not in his nature. You didn't keep a car for longer than you could repair it without going into hock, did you? You could say he was always alert to the appearance of the next Mrs. Sam Lagarde, sometimes, maybe often, when there still was one walking around on his arm. He thought of himself as a serial monogamist. He wasn't a cheat. He didn't bed the new one until the current one was a former. It was possible that his wives discerned this about him fairly quickly and his unwillingness to change hastened their departure.

He had been without a woman for a year now, the last Mrs. Lagarde having left him to advance her career in LA. She was in costume design. Her one-year marriage to him was a brief interlude in her otherwise interesting life, she told him. Actually, she said, "You are a great fuck, Sam, but there's more to life than that, and being with you is holding me back."

While he was flattered by the glancing compliment, the experience taught him everything he ever needed to know about being with someone one-third his age. It was just those thighs of hers, the straightness of her back astride a horse, how she could throw her leg over the horse's neck and dismount with a little leap off the saddle. Maybe he thought if he could be inside that kind of youthfulness, it would rub off on him. It didn't. Being with her made him feel older, like he was doddering, like her grandfather. Maybe being with a woman his own age, someone self-contained, calm, organized was the ticket. He was seriously thinking about Beverly Wilson. It was not in his calculations that a woman he thought about would not similarly be thinking about him.

Lagarde got his bachelor's degree in the classics at the University of Western Maryland. His major was a clue to how old he was. A quick check of the website of his alma mater, which had now changed its name to something no one would ever know, showed that there was no longer a classics department at the school. *Modernizing was a huge mistake. A university degree didn't prepare anyone for anything other than reading and thinking. If you cut reading and thinking out of the curriculum, what was anyone doing there except drinking and partying?* He had no faith in degrees in computer graphics or programming. That was like spending four years at twenty-thousand dollars a year learning to play games. Clearly, he wasn't adapting to modern times. He would be better off sticking with women who could understand him.

He knew he couldn't initiate a relationship with Beverly Wilson in the middle of investigating who killed her grandson. Most murders were committed by someone who knew the victim, often were related to the victim in some way. But, in spite of that little job-related prohibition, he could be very kind to her, attentive, as the investigation proceeded, so that she would see him as a friend she could confide in. That might help the investigation, anyway. There should be no harm in having tea with her, maybe a lunch, or taking her out to the farm to see his horses. He was stationed at the Troop 2 Command in Charles Town just a few miles from his farm off Paynes Ford Road. Horses usually worked with women. For some unknown reason, women loved them. There was plenty of time for something very pleasant to develop between him and the lovely Mrs. Beverly Wilson.

CHAPTER TWELVE

JUNE 2013

Lila Townsend stood in the cashier's line in the Super Fresh idly reading the scandals on the tabloids' front pages. The stars were having babies, having sex with someone else's husband, or getting divorced, fat or anorexic. One front page teaser declared that Justin Bieber, the Canadian pop music celebrity, had brain damage. *That would explain a lot,* Lila thought, running quickly in her mind through posts on her Twitter feed. She wondered how it was possible to live your life in such glare. *You would have to crave attention at a level normal people couldn't tolerate. You would want someone looking at you, thinking about you every moment. There would be no peace, no space in your life. It must be exhausting.*

She loaded her groceries onto the conveyor, the usual four apples, five oranges, one pound of grapes, a quart of Stonybrook vanilla yogurt, all her usual healthy food plus her one vice—a half-pound of dark chocolate, nonpareil candy."

This was her weekly shopping, in Maryland, across the Potomac River from Shepherdstown, as far from her patients as possible so that she did not have to rack her brain to remember Mrs. Smith's first name, the birth date of a baby she had delivered, or be asked to listen to a fetal heartbeat in the canned vegetable aisle. She craved solitude the way others craved potato chips. She lived alone. She cooked for herself. Usually, she went to the farmer's market for her fruit and vegetables, but this week she planned to sleep in on Sunday. She wished she could find a local market online that would select and deliver her groceries. That would save her an hour and a half every week. Time added up.

She worked long hours, rising at five thirty in the morning to run before her hospital rounds. After that, patient visits every fifteen minutes until six at night in the practice shared with three other obstetricians. Then there were baby deliveries whenever it was her turn on call. Her days left her exhausted but satisfied. This life was what she had trained for. She refused to succumb to frozen meals or fast food, with the exception of a stop at China Kitchen once a week for their amazing fried eggplant with orange sauce. Their crab puffs were also on her list of allowable treats but not more than once every few months. Cooking for herself was not about watching her weight; she kept a steady one hundred and twenty pounds on her five-foot-six frame since college. It was about discipline, observing her own rules, living the kind of life she designed for herself. With or without a partner, and recently without since her husband abandoned her to run off with his surgical nurse, Lila wanted to live well and that included what she ate and drank. She had one glass of wine with her dinner, preferring a velvety red Pinot Noir or a crisp sweet Vouvray, depending on what she was eating. She kept cases of both in her basement wine cabinet. Most of the time, aside from her morning coffee, she drank twice-filtered water kept in a clear glass container in the refrigerator both in her home and at the office. Again, it was simply a matter of balance and discipline.

She asked the cashier to load her groceries into the reusable shopping bags she'd brought along, watching to make sure all of her purchases made it into the three sacks. She paid, thanked the cashier, and walked to the door. She was crossing the parking lot toward her car when a man walked up to her.

"Let me help you," he said, taking the strap of the bag hanging from her right hand.

"Oh, I'm okay. I'm just going to my car." She moved sideways to put some distance between them and held onto the bag. "I don't need help."

He chuckled. "Got it," he said. "You're self-sufficient." He grinned at her and continued walking alongside her.

Lila saw that he was beautiful in a way that one doesn't see in everyday people, at least those who are not in movies or paintings.

His face was symmetrical with startling green eyes, medium sized, finely chiseled nose, almost rosebud upper lip over a full lower lip, and abundant black curly hair. She backed a bit further away, afraid he must want something.

"Okay, I'll come clean," he said. He held up his hands as if to show her he was weaponless. "I saw you inside the supermarket. I noticed how few items were in your basket and I figured you live alone. You're buying for one, right?" He waited for her reluctant, almost imperceptible nod.

"Well, you are just the most beautiful woman I have ever seen and I would have hated myself if I let you walk out of my life without talking to you."

Lila stood there for a minute, mute with surprise. She suppressed a smile and turned her back to him, opening the trunk of her Range Rover Evoque, a gift to herself when her husband notified her that his nurse was pregnant. She had purchased it on an estimate of the hefty alimony her lawyer would secure for her. She put the bags inside the vehicle and closed the trunk door. She turned to him and smiled willingly.

"You are putting me on," she said. "You almost had me. You're quite good. What do you really want? Are you selling something? Asking for donations? Selling magazines to pay your way through college?"

Somehow being close to her car where she could make a quick getaway made her feel safe. He didn't look like a carjacker to her. He was neatly dressed, clean, slender and except for the gold hoop earring in his left ear, seemed relatively normal. He was young, younger than her thirty-eight years anyway. Perhaps that perception of youth came from his seeming unencumbered by worry.

"Really," he said. "I just needed to get a closer look. Your face, your face is perfect," he said and smiled at her as if they were already old friends who had shared their most intimate secrets. "I don't want anything, except maybe your number." He laughed. It was an easy laugh that included her in on the joke on him.

So self-effacing. Who could fail to be flattered by this? It was quite a gambit on his part, bold, brave even. He was putting himself out there for total and complete rejection on the spot. Perhaps there was more to him than a pretty exterior. "What do you do?" Lila asked him.

"Right now, I'm between gigs," he said, as if he were an actor or musician. He looked down at the ground, looked up at her. "I've got some time on my hands," he spread out his palms, the long fingers pointing toward her, like magic wands pulling her toward him. "Would you like to go for a coffee?"

Lila realized he hadn't told her anything, but found herself saying, "Not tonight but meet me at the Sweet Shoppe in Shepherdstown on Saturday at two and we'll talk."

She got in her Rover, started the engine, and pressed the button to roll down the window. He was still standing there watching her. "What's your name?" she asked, leaning out the window.

"Ben, Ben Cromwell, at your service, m'lady." He grinned mischievously and swept his arm up and then down across his body, bowing dramatically.

Lila laughed and drove away, thinking Saturday afternoon could be fun. If he didn't show up, nothing was lost. If he did come, it would be like having an extra crab puff this week. Maybe he was exactly what she needed, a little distraction, a now and again piece of dark chocolate to sweeten her life. And maybe she just wanted to show that arrogant husband of hers that she was still sexy, still attractive to other men. He had thrown her away, discarded the life they'd built together, for a woman fourteen years younger than she. She was thrown a little off-balance, if she was honest with herself, by the divorce. Playing with Ben Cromwell might be just the kind of stretching in the other direction that would bring her back to being fully centered.

CHAPTER THIRTEEN

OCTOBER 2000

The first prick of the needle entering his vein always hurt. Somehow, it hurt more when they were drawing blood than when he was injecting heroin.

He had been negative on the first AIDs test six weeks ago on intake. A second test had been ordered as a matter of course. The whole false negatives and positives thing boggled his mind. Wasn't this supposed to be science? This was part of the battery of tests they gave him for intake at the juvenile rehab facility where the judge had sent him instead of detention or probation for breaking and entering.

His dad had begged for probation, but the lawyer said he couldn't swing it. There were too many people, the cops called them victims, the folks he took stuff from, who wanted to testify that he had broken into their homes and stolen their money and goods. *For the big deal they were making of it, I should have gotten more cash value for the effort.* He saw that look on Sarah's face, a combination of anger, embarrassment and sadness, when he was arraigned. He'd had a feeling the whole court thing wouldn't go well. Breaking and entering was a felony regardless of the value of anything Ben had taken, but Ben was still sixteen. The lawyer recommended that they take a plea, claim it was the drugs that made Ben do it, and see if they could get him into the drug rehab facility instead of going to juvenile detention, which could be grim.

That was the deal, then, six months at this place, which wasn't so bad, and then two years probation, peeing in a cup, keeping his nose clean, going to school. It seemed doable. Ben didn't mind the rehab, same old same old: tell the story about his mom, say what a bitch

Sarah was, pull on their heart strings, claim his dad was a bruiser. People just ate that shit up. He would be a star here, writing down all this shit, writing poems, keeping a journal about his progress from junky to clean. The counselor who led the daily group meeting already told him he should write a book. He had it mapped out, could do this time standing on his head. The chores were easy. He didn't know why any of the other guys made a fuss about making their beds or mopping the floor. Big deal. They had TV, books, lots of time to themselves, and they could shoot hoops. It was like a vacation. Better than hiding in the shed behind the house for three weeks like he did last year, which, he had to admit now, was pretty stupid.

A week after the second test, the counselor called him into his office for a talk. He was holding a report in his hand when Ben walked in. He smiled at Ben.

"Sit down, man," Brian said. "Take a load off."

Ben sat down in the plastic orange chair in front of the desk opposite Brian and looked around the office. It was so-so, for an office, no big deal, but not a bad gig, really. Brian didn't have to dress up for work in a monkey suit. He kept his long hair in a ponytail. He had a little beard. He seemed a lot freer than Ben's father. Maybe Ben could shoot for this job after he got out of here. He was halfway clean now and the bad part was over; he could see a future. Sarah had always been bugging him about that, telling him he was too smart to throw his life away. He figured Brian was going to ask him what his plan was after he got out. He had to write that up like a contract and everyone was going to sign it. Brian told them in group that everybody in their lives had to be aligned on the same goals or it wouldn't work. He thought about telling Brian he should sprinkle fairy dust on it for good measure, but he held his tongue. Brian was an ally. Ben didn't want to piss him off.

"So," Ben said. "I haven't written it yet, sorry."

Brian's face went through some quick contortions and then settled down. "Oh, no, Ben, it's not about the contract. I have to tell you something," Brian said. "It might not go down so well."

Ben imagined all the bad things Brian could tell him—his dad died, the house burned up, the state changed its mind and he was going to prison. Short of one of those, he could pretty much take anything. "Okay," he said. "Shoot."

"This second test, the second AIDs test we took from you?"

Ben nodded, a sensation of his blood freezing in his veins beginning in his face.

"The results are back." Brian paused, looked out the door of his office as if he wished someone would come in and save him from having to deliver this information. "You are HIV positive, Ben. I'm sorry. We'll get you to a physician immediately and get you started on a regimen . . ."

Ben had stopped listening. He could not comprehend what Brian was saying about pills and longevity. None of it made sense. Ben said nothing for a while. He was concentrating on not throwing up. His face went cold, then hot. His hands trembled. AIDs was something he hadn't ever contemplated. It was definitely not a part of the contract he had intended to write. No way did he plan to be sick, to look like a skeleton walking, to have those hideous splotches on his face. He stood up in a rush, a growl starting in his throat, and picked up the chair he had been sitting in and threw it against the wall. Tears spurted from his eyes. "What the fuck!" he screamed. "What the fuck?"

Brian waited without saying anything until Ben was quieter. Then he walked over to him, put his arms around him, and let the teenager sob on his shoulder.

CHAPTER FOURTEEN

APRIL 3, 2014

Sam Lagarde pulled into a parking space in front of the main single story building on Burr Road in Kearneysville that served as the WV State Police Troop 2 Command. It was one of several buildings on the campus, most of them prefab, that made up the local headquarters for the state police. This was repurposed farm land they had built on—flat, rimmed by trees, with a far horizon line in case you needed to see something coming. The county had rezoned the area for an industrial park in hopes of attracting the kinds of large businesses that no longer existed, which made it the perfect location for an operation that needed room for vehicles, a maintenance building, firing range, lab and offices. The headquarters office building comfortably housed the thirty folks who worked out of it in one capacity or another. Sam had everything he needed to do his job. He didn't need fancy to do what he did.

He said hello to Joyce, the redheaded receptionist with whom he had once had a brief but pleasant fling that ended amicably, and headed to his desk.

"Oh, hey, Sam," Joyce called out, "you got a fax. I put it on your computer."

Waiting on the keyboard of his computer was a lab report on the gold earring he'd found at the murder site four days before. It wasn't going to help a lot. The earring was fourteen karat gold; a design frequently purchased at Macy's department store in Frederick, Maryland or many other places. DNA testing on the earring post showed that the last person who wore it was their victim, Ben Cromwell. There were no useful prints on the earring.

Beverly Wilson had no record, at least based on her fingerprints, but she did once work at Macy's about fifty years ago when they fingerprinted all associates. Lagarde had expected as much. He just had to check.

But they had scored on the fancy engraved ring with the emerald left behind at the crime scene on their victim's pinky. Lawrence Black, the corporal assisting Lagarde with the investigation, tracked down the jewelry store that sold it, Bechdel's in Inwood, to one Violet Gold who paid for it with her Visa card.

"A very nice young woman," the jewelry store owner told Black. "Knew her own mind," he said. "Very cute," he added with a wink and a nod.

"When did she buy it?" Lagarde said.

"October 2, 2013," Black said, reading from his notepad.

That made two women Lagarde needed to talk to about Mr. Cromwell. He wondered briefly if they knew each other, if Cromwell found one because of the other. Both Gold and Townsend were easy to locate virtually via an Internet search. Gold was listed with other local attorneys. Her short bio said she worked at Legal Aid of West Virginia in the Martinsburg office. Dr. Townsend was part of an obstetrical practice in Shepherdstown. Professionals wanted to be found—they needed clients. Lagarde wondered again what these women were doing with a guy like Cromwell. It couldn't be as easy as it looks; there had to be more to Cromwell to get women like this, to let him into their lives. Maybe he wrote them poems; hard to imagine, though. Lagarde had difficulty remembering that Cromwell was his victim. The guy was a two-bit crook. Maybe he told these women he was a tennis or golf pro. Or maybe Lagarde was just wrong. Maybe what women wanted was to be on the arm of a handsome man. Maybe women weren't so different from men. They wanted eye candy. They wanted other people to see them with someone who made their blood flow faster. Their own value rose by association. Maybe sometimes women wanted a no strings attached roll in the hay. It was easier in the morning when you woke up sober to see that the face on the pillow next to yours was beautiful.

"Hey, Larry," Lagarde yelled over to Sgt. Black whose desk was about five feet from his. "Did forensics get anything off that phone I found at the grandmother's?"

Larry Black looked up from his computer screen and glanced at Lagarde. Sam could see Larry felt he was just too casual about his work.

"Yeah! As a matter of fact, there were a lot of calls, but they are several months old. Looks like your victim stopped using that phone four months before the murder. Not clear why. Maybe he got another phone with a different number."

Black got up from his desk and brought a ten-page list of Cromwell's cell phone activity over to Lagarde. "The last ten calls he made are all to the same number and the calls are all just minutes apart. Each call lasted less than a minute, like he was leaving a message. Looks like your boy was desperate to get hold of someone."

"Is that his grandmother's number?" Lagarde asked. "Or his father's?"

"Nope."

"Did you try calling it?"

"Yeah . . ." Black paused and raised his eyebrows. "This isn't my first investigation, you know. It's been disconnected."

"Who did it belong to?"

"It did belong to one Evelyn Foster. She called Cromwell pretty frequently from May to October last year and then nothing. She didn't call him back at that phone number after all his attempts to reach her. There's no phone directory listing for her. There are fifteen Evelyn Fosters on Facebook in the tri-state area. You might have to go door to door."

Lagarde groaned. "How about the texts?"

Black laughed. "Oh, yeah, that boy was a texting fool. No taboos for him. There were texts to him going back to December 2012 from a hottie named Ilise Vander, and I've seen just about *all* of her. Whew! Some of those photos wound me up, for sure. She was pretty mad at him there, toward the last days this cell was in service, though. She has quite a vocabulary."

"What do you mean, photos? You can put photos on texts?" Lagarde asked.

Black looked at him sideways. "Where you been, man? Of course you can put photos on texts."

"And what did she send him photos of?"

"Everything, man, everything," Black said. He looked at Lagarde as if he had two heads. "Haven't you ever heard of sexting?"

Lagarde had a sudden idea. He could almost feel the light bulb above his head go on. What if the killer was the boyfriend or husband of one of these women? Jealousy was a fine motive for murder, particularly a rage-filled one. And there was another thought just over the horizon in his mind; he could feel it struggling to dawn on him. Something about a ring from one woman, a letter from another, texts from a third and frantic calls from Cromwell to a fourth. Was the guy seeing four women at one time? No wonder he didn't work. Juggling all those women would have been a full time job. Lagarde felt tired just speculating on it.

"How about email traffic on his phone? Did he use email?" Lagarde asked.

"Not much. Email takes full sentences," Black said. "But there was an email from Lila Townsend telling him to stay away from her. The send date is before the snail mail letter she sent him that you found in his mail box."

"So she warned him in stages. Maybe she wasn't so sure she wanted him to stay away, or maybe she was establishing a date-stamp record." Lagarde rubbed his chin. "Is it possible Cromwell had several women going at once?" he said more to himself than Black. "Any communication from men to Cromwell?"

"His dad emailed him at least once a month. You can see the guy's frustration growing. And there was a single email and text from someone named Marc Delany, who was trying to meet up with Cromwell in September, unclear if he ever did. Maybe he found him after he got a new phone."

Marc Delany, out of the blue, how do you do. One of these ladies had a boyfriend. If anyone ever gave a man a reason to be jealous enough to kill, it was Ben Cromwell.

"How about you find Mr. Delany and see what his story is, if he ever met Cromwell and when, why he wanted to see him and whether he did," Lagarde said to Black. "I'm going to visit some very professional women."

CHAPTER FIFTEEN

JULY 2013

Ben Cromwell stood stock still by the side of Lila Townsend's bed, holding his breath until she stopped turning over in her sleep. It was three in the morning. On the side table next to her bed were her cell phone, the solitaire diamond pendant and chain she wore every day, a man's Breitling watch he admired, and a glass of water. It was the watch he was after. She could get herself another. He hadn't been to see her in over a week. If she didn't wake up, she'd never know he had been there. He figured she'd think she misplaced the watch or lost it. Anyway, she was bound to be insured. She was a woman who had all her t's crossed.

He wasn't quiet enough, though. Lila woke with a start. She sat up quickly in bed, the silk quilt falling from her bare shoulder. In the moonlight filtering through the curtains, Cromwell could make out the round shape of her breasts, the slight roundness in this sitting position of her otherwise flat belly, the dark shadow between her legs. He moved toward her. Lila smiled.

"Oh, it's you," she said. "I was dreaming about you."

She reached out her hand, took his, and placed it on her breast. She lay back on the pillows pulling him toward her. Cromwell ran his other hand up the inside of her thigh. She shivered.

"Do you have protection?" she whispered.

When Lila woke again at five thirty, he was already gone. She wondered, now that the dream had passed, how he had gotten in the house. She called him on the cell phone she'd bought him and asked.

"I watched you when you punched in the key code at the front door the first time you took me to your house," he said.

She admired his memory skills, his candor, his whole Romeo routine. Then she remembered the watch was missing.

"Did you see my watch this morning before you left? I can't find it anywhere."

"Oh, yeah, I took it," Cromwell said, as if his taking it were the most normal action in the world. "I just want to see how it looks on me. I'll bring it back later."

It only took the word "later" for Lila to feel the blood pulsing in her groin, for her legs to feel slightly weak.

On her run, she realized she should change the key code to her front door. I can do that later. She secretly hoped for more midnight invasions.

CHAPTER SIXTEEN

APRIL 2, 2014

Beverly Wilson stood with her paintbrush in her hand in front of the canvas she had been working on all morning. The fat Filbert brush was loaded with cadmium lemon. It hung midair from her hand. Her intention had been to make a block of yellow next to the sap green and cerulean blue, a kind of bridge or intersection, a way of seeing from one color to another. She knew from long attention to color that how people experience color changes based on the company the color keeps. That was the fun of painting, the constant surprise that spontaneous combinations engendered.

She was not the kind of painter who could make the same image over and over, not even a similar image. The same seemed to be true of abstracts. She couldn't bring herself to repeat a happy pattern from canvas to canvas even if she swapped out the colors. That seemed too much like factory work. And then there was the fact that even if she worked out a painting in her head, tried it out on her iPad, and made up her mind to do it just like that, she couldn't. She also couldn't follow a recipe; something else would always occur to her, something better or more interesting. Sometimes this messy process worked; she was satisfied and could call the painting done, and sometimes it didn't. Beverly guessed she had more canvasses that didn't work than did. But that was the great thing about oils, you could just paint right over the failures and start again. Anyway, it was the process she loved, the focus, the falling away of the world until the only thing was her breath, a stroke, a mark, a color.

Today, unfortunately, she couldn't focus. She looked at the gob of paint on the brush, unwilling to waste it and unwilling to put it on the canvas in this state of mind. She put the brush down on the palette and sat in a nearby wicker chair to look at the painting. *Not yet, although it does need that yellow.*

Her mind was on Ben. It had taken a few days, but it hit her this morning—the thought that he would never again turn up at her door disheveled, hungry, sleep deprived, hung over, or the opposite, charming, affable, full of himself and his impossible lies about what he was doing with his life. He would never again exclaim over one of her paintings, "That is the most beautiful thing I have ever seen in my life!"

She realized she would miss him. Perhaps it was as simple as this: there was a person whom she had cared about and now there was an absolute absence, in a blink, gone away, sucked into the black hole of millions of other souls that had blinked out. It didn't make any difference how angry she was with him or how he hurt all of them. There would be no more opportunities to say something or do something that might turn him around. She couldn't fool herself. By thirty, a person is who he is going to be. Still, as long as Ben was alive, there was hope. She thought briefly about Robert and then pulled her mind back from that abyss. Next came Sarah. She would call her today, just to listen and ask if there was something she could do. They really were all connected, and the death of one of them made everything different, even if the world seemed not to notice.

She remembered her first few days in this new home, boxes everywhere, the sense of dislocation, deeply missing her husband and half expecting him to come around the corner and ask her where she wanted him to put the bookcases. Ben called her out of the blue and asked if she wanted help. His call was completely unexpected. She'd wondered if he had been prodded by his father or if this was a way of getting money from her. He never did something for nothing. She told him to come over and together they went to Lowe's and bought azaleas and boxwood. She pointed, he dug the holes, she put in the plants, he tamped down the ground, and together they spread mulch on the bedding. When they were done, she put her arm around him and thanked him. He put his head down on her shoulder. After he left, she discovered that her Kindle was missing, and a bottle of wine. She put it down to a fair trade for work done and never said anything about it to him.

She sat looking at her painting, her hands in her lap. Suddenly Beverly remembered something. The detective hadn't asked, or she didn't think he did, but there was someone who had called her about Ben, a woman, almost six months ago. What was her name? God, if only her memory wasn't failing her more every day. It was at the end of October. She did remember the conversation.

The woman was distraught, sobbing. She said that Ben had been living with her since he came out of the hospital in the summer and things had been fine, he had a job, he was sober, he seemed to be happy and then all of a sudden he was cruel and angry, cursing at her, locking her out of her own home, stealing her things and pawning them, taking off in her car and not coming back for days.

Beverly remembered feeling slightly annoyed by the call. The woman didn't sound like a teenager. Beverly couldn't imagine she would have ever called her boyfriend's grandmother to complain about him when she was young.

"What do you do?" Beverly said.

"I'm a social worker at City Hospital," the woman said.

Then your training isn't helping you. "How did you get my phone number?"

"Ben had your number written down in that notebook he carries, on the inside cover, the one he writes his stories in. The name next to the number is Grandma. Are you his grandmother?"

"Yes," Beverly said. "I am. By marriage, anyway."

"Gosh. He told me he didn't have any family in the area."

"He doesn't tell the truth," Beverly said. "May I ask you something?"

"Yes, sure."

"Have you given him money? You know he does drugs, right?"

There was a long pause. "I, I got him on methadone."

"Pills or injections, administered in the clinic or taken on his own?" Beverly had been down this road before with Ben.

"He was on pills, self-administered."

"Did it occur to you that he was selling those and buying himself the real thing?"

"No. No, it didn't."

"It should have. Is anything of real value missing from your home?"

"My TV and laptop, a couple hundred dollars I kept in my under-wear drawer." The woman sobbed. "I feel like such a fool."

Beverly felt herself relent a little. This was just another poor kid bamboozled by a little glitz and sizzle. *If Ben wasn't so handsome, maybe fewer women would be hurt by him.* "Have you had a test?" she asked, now concerned that this young woman had not been paying attention to anything.

"A test?" the woman said. "For what?"

Beverly wanted to reach across the phone line and shake her. "For HIV. Ben has AIDs, you know, for years. You must know that if he's been living with you. Has he been taking his meds, seeing the doctor?"

There was a deep silence. Then she said, "Oh, God, of course. I do know that. I didn't think I would get it. My first test was negative. I thought I might be immune. I don't know what I was thinking."

"You should get tested again. And change your door locks and get special locks for your windows," Beverly said. She knew from ex-perience that Ben would try to get back in the woman's home at some point. It had been a treasure chest for him so far.

"Thank you," the woman said, her voice barely a whisper, and hung up.

Beverly had felt helpless and angry. How could loving someone make you so stupid? She knew that asking Ben about the woman would do no good. He had breezed in recently during one of his high-energy spells and regaled her with tales of his classes. She always wanted to believe him, but he had taught her what she told the woman, he never told the truth. It was almost as if he wanted the people who loved him to hate him.

It was too much to contemplate. This sorrow for Ben and her daughter were so twisted around that she could not unknot it. She would have to wait, the way she waited for a painting, to see what all of this would turn out to be. She doubted the young woman who had called her could murder Ben, but maybe the information could point the detective in a useful direction. Beverly made a note to call him.

CHAPTER SEVENTEEN

SEPTEMBER 2013

Ben Cromwell sat on the purple sofa in Ilise Vander's mother's house with his head in his hands, his elbows on his knees, his eyes closed listening to Ilise rant, scream, whisper and rant some more. He was waiting for it to be over. He would have left, but her friend from next door, that six-foot-six football linebacker of a guy Marc Delany, was standing square in front of the door blocking his way. He had no intention of getting in a fight with that guy. Ilise had really trapped him here. He thought her text meant to come over for a little afternoon delight while her mother was at work and he walked into this. Man, that girl could lie.

He thought Ilise's reaction was over the top. So she was HIV positive. Big deal. So was he. Now he didn't have to worry about forgetting to use a condom. You just get on the meds, he tried to tell her. Maybe you get a little dizzy and nauseous from the side effects but it's not the end of life. You go for your testing. You lose some weight. That might be good for you. Sometimes you feel like shit, but you deal. But not Ilise. First she was telling him about how she thought she had the worst flu ever and where was he and how she had to go to the clinic all by herself and they did the test. Now she was yelling something about how he screwed up her whole life, she could never get married, never have children, she might not be able to keep her job if they found out, she might as well die right now. Ben expected Marc to cry. He was very pale. He looked like the emoticon for sad.

"Alright, alright, so I screwed up," Ben said. "Hey, I'm sorry."

"Sorry, you're sorry? Jesus, you're a nightmare. I can't get over this. This changes everything. Why didn't you tell me you had AIDs?"

Ben looked over at Marc Delany. The man now looked like he wanted to kill him but didn't want to get his blood on him. Ben had never thought of having AIDs as a deterrent against violence before. That idea presented interesting possibilities. He should let those homeboys who hung out on King Street at night know. Maybe they would leave him alone when he was late paying them their share for the product he sold.

"I might have told you. I think I did. You just don't remember. I would've told you when I first met you. You were so hot." Ben looked up at her. He smiled.

Ilise looked at him with her mouth open. Ben thought if flames could come out of her eyes and burn him up like in a video game, he would be a cinder. Fire was definitely Ilise's superpower.

"I *was* hot? Like, I'm not now because I'm sick?" She screamed again, gripped her hair, stamped her feet. She found her breath. "You know, you are a piece of trash. Get the fuck out of here right now, get out, get out, getouttahere! I never want to see you again."

Ben rose from the couch in a half-crouch, scrambled to the front door Marc opened for him, and left the house. He walked a few blocks aimlessly and found himself at the Legal Aid office in the Martinsburg Plaza. He went in and looked around.

From the front of the space he could see Violet Gold talking to a colleague. Her back was to him. She had a luscious ass. His hands were yearning to touch it. He walked over toward her, perched on the corner of her desk, and said, "Hey."

Violet looked startled. Her cheeks and neck turned bright red as she turned to him. He could see her nipples stiffening under her silk blouse. He loved a woman who was always ready.

"Got a few minutes?" he asked. "I've got something I want to show you. Outside."

Violet smiled. She excused herself, grabbed her purse, and walked out the door with him.

"Where are we going?" she said.

"A little walk. Down to Maple Street. I got a place there," he said. He slid his hand across her ass, up around her waist and over her breast.

She grabbed his hand, laughed a little and moved closer to him. "Hey, not here in the street where everyone can see." She looked back toward her office to see if anyone was watching.

"I just gotta have a little right now or I might not make it another step," he said, pulling her toward him, taking her mouth by force, sucking on her tongue. He could feel her entire body soften against him. She groaned and pulled away.

"Walk faster," she said.

Ben, Violet discovered, was living in an apartment on the third floor of a brick building on Maple Street. It was a nice street, with trees and sturdy buildings that looked reasonably well cared for. The last time she had seen him, he'd said he was homeless. She had let him stay at her house on the couch for three days and then in her bed for a week until she woke up one morning and he was gone. She hadn't heard from him for two weeks. She was glad to see he'd landed on his feet, but she had no idea how he had done it.

She walked up the three flights of stairs ahead of him, his hand sliding up under her skirt, his fingers under her panties. Her breath fled. She felt foolish and crazy and wonderful all at the same time. She had never been wanted like this. He pulled her over to the door and put the key in the lock. Before he opened the door, he unbuttoned her blouse and pulled down her bra exposing her breast. She considered letting him take her right here in the hallway, but she stopped him.

"Inside," she whispered.

He opened the door, pulled her into the small living room and over to the large window that fronted Maple Street. He faced her toward the window, which looked out on a parking lot for the bank across the street, stood behind her and pulled off her blouse, her bra, her skirt and panties until she was standing naked and quaking in the window, for the world to see. He gripped her hips and entered her from behind, pushing her over. She held onto the window sill, gasping. She could see the people parking, going into the bank, coming out. If they looked up, they would have seen a naked woman in the window her head thrown back, her mouth open, seeming to howl at the sky.

They were lying on the floor, his hands still on her, when the door opened. A woman walked in, looked at them, and walked out. A few minutes passed. She opened the door again and walked over to them.

"Get out," she said, looking at Violet. Her entire body was shaking. "Get your things and get out, Ben."

Ben looked at the woman, running his fingers down Violet's belly.

"Sure you don't want to join us, Evelyn?" he said. He turned his body slightly so that she could see he was ready for more. "I've got one more in me . . . and Violet here will do anything."

"Get. Out." Evelyn was crying now. She walked woodenly to the bedroom, gathered up whatever of Ben's she found on the floor and bed, walked back into the living room and threw his things at him. "Now. Or I'll call the cops."

Violet had already pulled her clothes back on and was looking for her shoes. "I'm sorry, so sorry," she was murmuring in Evelyn's direction. This was the worst thing that had ever happened to her. She was not equipped to deal with this situation.

"I had no idea he was living with someone," she said.

"Shut up," Evelyn said. "Just get out."

Violet picked up her shoes and left without looking back at Ben. She ran down the stairs and most of the way back to her office before she put her shoes on. She stopped in the parking lot, opened her car and sat until she was calm. She would call Ben later and make sure he was okay. Obviously, he would need a new place to live.

CHAPTER EIGHTEEN

APRIL 3, 2014, 1 P.M.

Sam Lagarde liked to interview people at their workplaces. If they were guilty of something, and who wasn't, they were instantly nervous and apt to say something that was better left unsaid. It was the sense of being exposed that rattled them. It was the embarrassment, the surprise. No matter what the law said, people were guilty until proven innocent and a police inquiry always rang the guilty gong. It's just the way people were wired. He walked up to the receptionist's desk in Lila Townsend's office and asked to see the doctor. He flashed his credentials. He knew the tittering would start instantly.

The young woman behind the counter looked as surprised as he expected. "Did something happen?" she asked.

"No, ma'am," Lagarde said. "Just need to talk with Dr. Townsend." He handed her his card.

She told him to take a seat. He sat down in a waiting room full of pregnant bellies and watched the receptionist exchange glances with the other young women behind the counter and then pick up the phone and push a button. She turned sideways in her chair as she looked at his card and talked quietly into the phone. A few minutes later, a nurse in a brightly colored smock came into the waiting room and told him to come back. He followed her to an office and she told him to take a seat, the doctor would be with him shortly. Lagarde looked around the office. There was a plastic three-dimensional brightly colored model of a woman's ovaries, uterus and fallopian tubes standing on the desk like a sculpture. He wondered if Dr. Townsend used it as a teaching device for her patients. The rest of the office was traditional doctor, neat and tastefully decorated with landscape prints. No bold statements here. The office was meant to be instantly forgotten. There were no personal photographs in silver frames on the desk. In fact, there seemed to be nothing personal in the office at all. Perhaps Dr. Townsend shared the office with the other docs. Perhaps this *wasn't* her office. There was a small bookcase with piles of periodicals stacked on the shelves. One of them was the *American Journal of Obstetrics and Gynecology*. He had time to note that Dr. Townsend was listed as a contributor on the cover index of the latest issue before the doctor herself, wearing a white coat, walked straight toward him and held out her hand.

"Hello, detective," she said. "I'm Dr. Lila Townsend. Can I help you with something?"

"I think so," Lagarde said, standing up and shaking her hand. He sat down as she walked to her chair behind the desk and sat. She was more attractive and taller than he expected. He didn't expect lady docs to be pretty—red hair, fair skin, a few freckles on her nose and cheeks, blue eyes, athletic looking.

"I'm investigating the murder of Ben Cromwell. You sent him an email and a letter telling him to leave you alone and you got a restraining order against him."

Lagarde watched her. Lila Townsend did not turn pale or startle. She put her hands together on the top of the desk and leaned forward. No nail polish, he noted. No rings of any kind. She looked straight at him. He thought she might have had some practice telling women bad news, like "I'm sorry, you have miscarried," or "You are not pregnant, you have a tumor." Like someone who had been trained to beat a polygraph, her demeanor might not tell him anything.

"Yes, I did get a court order against him," she said.

Lagarde waited. She waited. Finally, he said, "Why was that?"

"I had a brief affair with him and when I broke it off, he wouldn't leave me alone."

"When was this?"

"I met him last June. I broke it off in September."

"So you went out with him? Is that the right way to say it, for four months?"

"I had sex with him," she said. "We went out from time to time."

She wasn't giving him much beyond what he knew from her letter and court order. "Did you love him?" Lagarde asked.

"Not that it's any of your business, but no, I did not love him," Dr. Townsend said.

Lagarde thought that response might be a lie. He might have broken through a bit. "So why did you have a relationship with him?"

"Again, not your business, but I suppose you'd call it lust, or madness."

Lagarde was intrigued by her candor. Her voice was shaky when she said the word "madness." Maybe that counted for something.

"Why did you break it off?"

He was now well past the point where she should have thrown him out of her office. He couldn't tell if she delayed because that might make her seem guilty of something or because she wanted to tell someone about her affair. She seemed like a pretty buttoned up woman to him.

"He stole my car, he forged and cashed two checks in the amount of five-hundred dollars each, he stole my watch and he repeatedly broke into my house." There was some emotion behind that litany of charges against Cromwell. Lagarde assumed there was probably more taken than that, like her peace of mind, her sense of control over her environment.

"Did you call the police about the thefts and the forgery?"

"I laid myself open to them when I let him in my house," Dr. Townsend said. "He brought back the car."

It seemed to Lagarde that she was being "open" with him. She'd told him far more than he expected to get on this first interview. He had to check off a few items more on his list of questions and then he would wrap it up.

"Did you buy him any gifts? Take him on trips?"

Dr. Townsend looked down at the shiny surface of the desk. It seemed to Lagarde this was the act she regretted the most. "I did buy him gifts. He liked fancy shoes and clothes. I took him to New York. We stayed at the Alec Hotel on 45th Street. Do you need to see my credit card statement?"

Lagarde figured that admission cost her something. She was embarrassed to have been so generous with Cromwell. But he could imagine her walking on those broad New York City boulevards on Cromwell's arm, watching women turn to look at her with envy, relishing it. "When was that?" he asked.

"Last July."

"Did he ever live with you?"

"No."

"Do you know where he was living?"

"No. I had an address he gave me, but I never went there."

"How did you get hold of him?"

"I called him."

"Did you know anyone else he knew? Did he ever introduce you to anyone?"

"No. He never introduced me to anyone. Is that all? I have patients waiting."

"One more question. Where were you on March 15?"

"I was in New York for a professional conference. At the Hyatt. I presented my most recent paper on the incidence of acute pyelonephritis in pregnancy with regard to perinatal outcomes on March 15."

Lagarde swallowed. He had no idea what she had just said. "That's it for now. I may have more questions later." Lagarde said. "Here's my card in case you think of anything I should know. I can find my way out."

He stood, handed her his card and left the office, noticing for the first time that she had not shut her office door before the interview. He found that bit of theater as interesting as the rest of her performance. She was demonstrating that she had nothing to hide.

He turned back to look at her, "One more thing. Do you do surgery?" he asked.

"Only those procedures related to gynecology and obstetrics," she said. "It's my nearly ex-husband who's the surgeon."

Lagarde rocked back on his heels. *Her husband is the surgeon. Ex-husband*, he corrected himself. Both items were an interesting piece of news. He noted she had not asked him when Cromwell was murdered or how, nor she had not been shocked about his death. She knew more than she was saying.

CHAPTER NINETEEN

APRIL 3, 2014, 1:30 P.M.

Lagarde sat in his car in the doctor's office parking lot for a few minutes. The office was in the old Shepherdstown train station. *A clever reuse of a building.* Considered the oldest town in West Virginia, at least according to its very partisan citizens, Shepherdstown was home to fewer than two-thousand people and one university all living on less than one square mile. The town was quaint with unusual shops, several restaurants that prepared more than merely edible food at ridiculous prices, an actual book store and a general air of lucky entitlement. Property cost more in the Shepherdstown zip code area than in the rest of Jefferson County, which was why Lagarde purchased his land far from the town. Lagarde liked visiting here but he was glad to go home to Kearneysville.

He called Corporal Black to check in and ask what he had discovered about Marc Delany, the one man who had contacted Ben Cromwell on the phone found in Beverly Wilson's house. Black had been busy.

"I met the young man," Black said, "at his place of work. He's a floor manager at the Bigmart up in Spring Mills, the new one. He worked his way up from stock clerk. He's only twenty-two. Was the high school football captain. He's in the National Guard. Did a tour over in Iraq right out of school. First impressions, he's a good guy, but he's big, trained, and so angry at Cromwell that he vibrates. Seems he's been in love with Ilise Vander, you remember, the hottie from the texts, since he was twelve. Cromwell busted up his fairytale romance with Ilise, gave her AIDs, he said. Delany was practically spitting when he talked about Cromwell."

"Wait," Lagarde said. "You're going too fast for me. Did he know that Cromwell is dead? And did you say that Cromwell had AIDs? Any way to check that without violating patient confidentiality?"

"No, Delany didn't know Cromwell was dead," Black said, patiently attempting to answer one question at a time. "When I started to talk to him, he was all about Ilise and saying what he's going to do to Cromwell, as in bust him up. When I told him Cromwell was murdered, he just shut up, pulled his head in like a turtle. I showed him the head shot and the kid turned white. And here's the other thing: he doesn't seem like a guy who would know how to make those precise cuts on the body the medical examiner mentioned in her report. Those were made by surgical instruments, she said, by someone who knows their way around an amputation. This guy, no way he knows his way around a scalpel, or whatever was used. Delany could have bought a gun from Bigmart and might be angry enough to use it, but there aren't any surgical instruments for sale there."

Black paused for air. Lagarde said, "Got it. Probably not our guy. What else you got?"

"Well, I got curious about all the Evelyn Fosters. There is one who lives in Martinsburg and works at the hospital who might be the first candidate to talk to. Want me to head over there? I'm practically there now anyway."

"Good idea. Go for it," Lagarde said. "I'm going to have a little conversation with Violet Gold, Esquire, at her office. Also, we've got another lead. Dr. Townsend told me her husband's a surgeon, speaking of precise cuts. While you're at the hospital, why don't you see if they've got a surgeon named Townsend who has privileges? Maybe someone in patient information will bend the rules a little and tell you something about Cromwell's health."

CHAPTER TWENTY

OCTOBER 2013

"Hey, Evelyn, this is Ida Farens up here in ICU. We've got a young girl here, tried suiciding using sleeping pills and Tylenol. She came in through the ER around 5 a.m. We pumped her stomach and she's out of danger. We need an assessment of whether or not to send her up to psych to watch her for a few days. Can you come up and talk to her?"

"Sure. No problem. What's her name?"

"Wait, let me check her chart again." Evelyn heard some clicking from Ida's computer mouse as she moved from screen to screen on the patient record. "Ilise Vander. She's nineteen. Her mother is here with her. The mother could probably use a shoulder, if you do that kind of thing. She's distraught. She told me they were her sleeping pills."

"Be right up," Evelyn Foster said. She gathered up a few pamphlets, one for the girl, two for the mother that had information about local support groups and other basic information about suicide prevention. She didn't think the pamphlets did anything, but they gave patients something to hold while they talked, not as good as a teddy bear but better than nothing. She walked out of her office into the hallway and pushed the button for the elevator. *Nineteen, what could have happened to you by nineteen that made you want to give up on life?* Despite the whole teenage angst and romance with death thing, it was rare for a young woman to try or to succeed at suicide. When they did, there was enough heartbreak to go around for everyone. Some event tipped this kid into despair or she was on a very low end of an undiagnosed manic-depressive cycle.

ICU was laid out in a circle with a bull pen in the center. All the monitors for each patient, staging areas for equipment, and the nurses were in the center of the room where they could observe everything. The patient beds with their many snaking lines of fluids and medicines, oxygen, monitoring lines, catheters and feeding tubes, were arrayed in a circle around the bull pen. Privacy was managed with what Evelyn thought were very flimsy curtains that could be pulled around a bed via the tracks in the ceiling. But if you were a patient in here, pretty much you didn't care about privacy. You were too sick for that. Most of the patients just lay back and concentrated on trying to breathe without too much pain.

Evelyn checked in at the desk with Ida, located Ilise Vander's bed and pulled the curtain between the girl's bed and the next patient. There was no one in the bed on the other side. She held out her hand to the woman she presumed was the mother and introduced herself, all the while watching the girl, pale as death, inert, awake but staring at the ceiling, her fingers clutching the blanket at her sides.

"Mrs. Vander?" she said. "I'm Evelyn Foster, the social worker here at the hospital." She offered Mrs. Vander the pamphlets, but the woman waved them off.

Mrs. Vander, around forty, Evelyn guessed, was wearing too-tight jeans and a wrap-around blouse that left little to the imagination with regard to the size and shape of her breasts. *She must have dressed in a hurry. No makeup, her hair matted.*

"I don't want to hear no mumbo-jumbo psychology talk," Mrs. Vander said. "I just want to get my girl home where I can take care of her." She waved her hands again as if that Obi-wan Kenobe trick might work to make the woman standing in front of her do what she wanted. "Please, I'm begging you," she said, "tell them to let me take her home." She dragged her hands through her hair.

Evelyn could see that gray was coming in at the roots. Her daughter's attempt at suicide would certainly hasten that process.

"Well, let's see how this conversation goes, okay? Would you mind if I talk privately with Ilise for a few moments? I have a little checklist," she tilted her clipboard in Mrs. Vander's direction so she could see the innocuous looking piece of paper where Evelyn was supposed to place checks in yes or no boxes. "I want to ask her these questions and then we'll see how she's doing." She didn't really need the mother's consent. Ilise was old enough to consent on her own and to insist on confidentiality. Evelyn was just being polite. "Why don't you go take a break, maybe go get a cup of coffee, freshen up a bit. When you come back, we'll talk."

Mrs. Vander nodded, took her Gucci knockoff bag off the black plastic chair she had dragged over to her daughter's hospital bed, and walked away a little uncertainly on her platform shoes.

Evelyn moved closer to the side of the bed. "Miss Vander?" she said. "Miss Vander, I'd like to talk with you a few moments, if you agree. Do you feel up to that?"

Ilise turned her head and looked through Evelyn, then looked back at the ceiling. "Yeah, whatever," she said.

"Do you understand that these questions will be personal and may affect whether you stay in the hospital a little longer or go home?"

"Yeah. So? What difference does it make where I am?"

Evelyn made a note on her form. "Continued depressed mood," she wrote in the space for observations.

"Why did you take the pills?" she asked the girl.

"I don't want to be alive anymore," Ilise said.

"Have you tried to commit suicide before?" Evelyn asked.

"No. This is my first time." The girl looked at her as if she were totally stupid. "If I had tried before, I'd be better at it and we wouldn't be having this conversation."

Evelyn wrote down that the girl still had a sense of humor, a good sign.

"Do you think if you went home, you would try it again?"

There was a long pause. The girl was thinking. She shut her eyes. Tears leaked from under her eyelids. "I don't know," she said. "Maybe."

"Have you felt this hopeless for many months, or years?"

"No," Ilise said. "Only since that bastard fucked me and gave me AIDs and threw me away like I was a heap of trash on the side of the road."

Evelyn wrote: "Patient has a great deal of anger and is able to express it." She could understand how the girl felt, although her own predilection would be to get even rather than to give up.

"Can you imagine a time when you won't be so angry?" Evelyn asked.

"No. Never." The girl shivered. "I'll hate him forever. He ruined my life."

"Would you like to talk with someone about this experience? That might help you."

"I'm talking to you," Ilise said. "That doesn't seem to be helping."

Evelyn smiled. She liked the girl's spunk. Spunk was proof of life.

"I don't want to talk anymore," Ilise said, and rolled over onto her side, facing the curtain and away from Evelyn.

Evelyn made a few more notes on her paper, stopped at the desk and told Ida she was going to recommend that they keep the girl for observation for three days, give her a chance to talk with the psychiatrist; see what recommendation he wanted to make about a longer-term hospitalization or outpatient services. She caught up with Mrs. Vander in the corridor outside the double doors that led to ICU. She invited her to sit on the padded bench and talk for a minute.

Mrs. Vander wept loudly while she recounted between sobs how she had found her daughter on the floor in the living room, half dead, unable to be awakened, no matter how much she shook her or yelled at her. She had been terrified. "Thank God for the ambulance guys," she said. She wiped her nose with a wadded up tissue she fished out of her purse. "They knew what to do right away." A shuddering sob interrupted her story. "If I hadn't gotten up to pee in the middle of the night, I would never have found her. Must have been God watching out for my baby."

"Do you know what led up to this, her trying to suicide?" Evelyn asked. "Did something in particular happen or has she been depressed for a long time?"

"Oh, yes, I do know. And no, she had never been depressed a minute in her life before. She's always been my happy girl, knew what she wanted to do, was good at it. Anything didn't go her way, she just made lemonade. Had a great boyfriend who lives right next door, a good guy who works hard and cares about her." She stopped to sob again. "And then she met that monster, Ben Cromwell. He just swept her off her feet, made her crazy for him. I tried to warn her about him, tell her he was no good. I should know. If I ever get my hands on him, I'm going to castrate him and shove his balls in his mouth and watch him bleed to death," Mrs. Vander said. She put her hand over her mouth and sobbed again. "No grandbabies for me. He stole my whole future, he stole it."

Evelyn could feel her entire body go cold. "When was this man dating your daughter?" Evelyn asked, although that question had nothing to do with any assessment.

"She's been seeing that criminal since last December," Mrs. Vander said. "Since 2012. That was our Armageddon. Like those Mexican Indians predicted. I told her he was no good. Marc told her he was no good. But oh no, you couldn't tell Ilise anything. 'He's so handsome, Mom,' she would tell me. 'He really loves me,' my poor little fool would say. 'You'll see. No matter how many times he disappears, he always comes back to me. He's gonna marry me.' I tried everything to get her to stop seeing him. I even told her she was related to him, but oh, no. She even visited him in prison. She just had to have her own way."

"Since December 2012, you said?"

"Yeah, does that mean something?"

"And when's the last time he saw her?"

"Right after she got the HIV test results, last month, September. Why?"

"That length of time for exposure, probably the HIV test result is not a false positive," Evelyn said, working hard to push words out of her mouth. "Was she retested?"

"Yes, the doctor called her in to do a blood test after the first one. He said definitely she was positive," Mrs. Vander said. "That's what wiped out my baby. She couldn't hope no more that they were wrong."

Evelyn gathered herself together, pulling her mind back from the whirlwind of her thoughts. Ben had been seeing this young woman at the same time he was living with her. At the same time he was having sex with that other woman. What did he say her name was? Violet. Even after Evelyn took him back, even after that scene in her apartment when he was lying on the floor naked with that woman, he was still seeing Ilise. He had sex with this girl while he was getting Evelyn to steal methadone pills from the dispensary for him. The girl was HIV positive. Evelyn had sex with him after he had sex with the girl. She searched her memory for an encounter when they didn't use a condom. There were several times, she recalled, they had been carried away by passion. "Swept her off her feet," Mrs. Vander had said. Evelyn knew exactly how that felt. She could hardly think in a straight line. She shook her head to bring her back to this moment in the hall with a patient's mother.

She said, "Mrs. Vander, I'm going to recommend that Ilise stay here for another three days and have a chance to talk with the doctor about this experience. It is a harrowing one, something neither you nor I would be able to deal with easily ourselves. And I'll be able to come back and talk with her again also."

She paused. Mrs. Vander nodded. Evelyn stood up. Her legs were shaking but she had to walk away. She shook Mrs. Vander's limp hand and rushed to the stairwell. On the second landing down, she sat on the concrete step, leaned her head against the wall, and allowed herself a few minutes to sob.

CHAPTER TWENTY-ONE

APRIL 3, 2014, 2 P.M.

Sam Lagarde pulled into the grubby strip mall in Martinsburg that housed the local branch of the Legal Aid office. It was pretty clear, Legal Aid had located itself where its administrators thought their clients would be able to get to the office by bus or on foot. He was looking for Violet Gold, he told the receptionist. He showed her his credentials and looked around the office.

They aren't spending any money on fancy furnishings in here, Lagarde commented to himself. At the back of the office, he saw a middle-aged couple in intense conversation with a young man wearing a white Oxford shirt with the sleeves rolled up and a tie. His jacket, Lagarde noted, hung from the back of his chair. He was leaning forward across the desk, listening to them intently and taking notes. If nothing else, these clients were getting respect here, something they might not get in a tonier office. At another desk, a woman was reading something densely typed on her computer screen and taking notes. Lagarde guessed that Legal Aid subscribed to Westlaw so that their lawyers and paralegals could quickly research current law and precedents. Everyone he saw in the office was young, by his reckoning. It made him feel old . . . and tired.

"I'm sorry, detective," the young receptionist said. "Violet quit a few weeks ago. She said she was going to travel."

"You mean, just like that? Up and left with no notice?" Lagarde felt his intuition pick up its ears.

"Oh, she gave two weeks' notice. Best we usually get here. Lawyers are always moving on. Her last day was March 10."

"Do you have a home address for her?" Sam Lagarde's mind was doing some calisthenics. Two weeks' notice might indicate premeditation. Not a crime of passion, a planned attack. That was a whole different kettle of fish. Unless Ms. Gold was simply trying to put as much distance between her and Cromwell as possible, somewhat like Dr. Townsend, but without recourse to law. He would have thought it would be the lawyer who would get the restraining order and the doctor who would run off to parts unknown, but women were hard to understand. Cromwell was apparently not a man you wanted to run into accidentally after the affair was over. Maybe they were afraid that if they saw him they would not be able to walk away.

The young woman looked at him for a minute. She snapped her gum. She twirled the lock of shiny brunette hair that grazed her cheek. She looked across the room. "Wait a sec," she said. "I'll have to ask Harry if it's okay to give that to you." She got up from her chair, walked around the counter and into the only office that had walls in the space. Lagarde had time to contemplate how short she wore her skirt before she walked back out with Harry.

"Detective," the man named Harry held out his hand. "Harry Chaplin, I'm the supervisor here. I understand you are looking for Violet Gold?"

"Yes, Mr. Chaplin," Lagarde did his slight bow routine and showed his credentials. Harry Chaplin nodded.

"I think that Ms. Gold was involved with a man who was recently murdered," Lagarde said and watched as Chaplin blanched and took a step back. "So I need two things from you. Can you give me her home address, and do you know anything about her relationship with a man named Ben Cromwell?"

"I remember a Ben Cromwell," the receptionist said, a beguiling blush blooming on her cheeks. "He came in to see about suing his parents, he told me. He saw Violet." She stopped talking, put her hand in front of her mouth and looked over at Harry Chaplin.

"Please come into my office," Chaplin said to Lagarde while looking sternly at the receptionist. "Thank you, Alice, you can go back to your desk now."

Chaplin motioned Lagarde to a slightly more substantial chair than those in the reception area. Lagarde took it, crossed his legs, put his hands on the arms and said, "So, do you know something about Mr. Cromwell and Ms. Gold?"

Harry Chaplin adjusted his tie knot, squirmed slightly in his high-back swivel chair, and said, "As Alice said, he came in to inquire about suing his parents. We declined to take the case. A few weeks after that, she told me she was seeing him. I think that was more by way of letting me know that she wasn't violating professional decorum. He was not our client, but I advised her against it. Even though we did not take his case, he still came here as a client. I think you have to chalk it up to her being a very young woman, impressionable and sensitive—impetuous, maybe," he paused, apparently thinking of what he wanted to say next in defense of his former employee.

Lagarde thought Mr. Chaplin might have been a little sweet on Ms. Gold himself. Perhaps Mr. Chaplin could have been jealous enough to end Ben Cromwell's life.

"How old is Ms. Gold?"

"She's twenty-four."

"Do you have a photograph of her?" Lagarde asked.

Chaplin pointed to a group photograph of a bunch of young people dressed in a very unlawyerly way in shorts and t-shirts. "This photo is from our office picnic last summer. We do that once a year to build team spirit." He looked at Lagarde as if to receive congratulations on his management skills. "This," Chaplin pointed to a short young woman with curly blonde hair, an angelic face and a sex goddess body, in Lagarde's estimation at any rate, "is Violet Gold."

"What is Ms. Gold like?" Lagarde asked, just to see if Chaplin would give away something during his minor panic that his lawyer training would tell him not to.

"Oh, she's very bright, went to the University of Maryland, passed the West Virginia bar the first time she took the exam, has a great career ahead of her. She might have been a little bored here."

"Bored? Isn't it customary to work young lawyers seventy hours a week? Do they have time to be bored?"

"We don't have that much of a caseload right now . . ." Chaplin said, "and maybe the cases she caught weren't enough of a challenge.

Whatever the reason, after ten months, she gave her notice. She said she wanted to spend some time in Europe roaming around like a tourist. Something about giving herself a little graduation gift, reconsider her options."

"Did she actually go to Europe?"

"I got a postcard today from London," Chaplin said. "You know how long it takes for mail to come from there." He pulled the typical Big Ben view from Parliament Square postcard out of his middle desk drawer and handed it to Lagarde. On the back of the postcard, Violet Gold had printed: HAVING A WONDERFUL TIME. GLAD I CAME. It was postmarked in London on March 16.

Lagarde did some quick calculations and realized Violet Gold had to be airborne on March 15 for the eight hour flight plus the five hour time difference to mail the card in time for the March 16 date stamp. He felt somewhat let down. Unless she mailed the postcard from Heathrow airport the minute she arrived, she was probably standing in a very long security line at the airport at the time of the murder. She'd have to be very organized to pull-off being nearly two places at one time, but Chaplin said she was bright. He wouldn't rule her out right now, although he still preferred his idea about Dr. Townsend's surgeon husband. Lawyers, as far as Lagarde knew, had no idea where to make the cut to sever a head from its shoulders.

Just in case, he asked, "Do you know if Ms. Gold was friends with any surgeons?"

Chaplin looked dumbfounded. He was obviously drawing a blank. "I really don't know much about her private life," he said, "nor would I tell you."

"Thank you, Mr. Chaplin," he said. "That's all for now. Oh, and could you give me Ms. Gold's home address, in case I need it?"

Harry Chaplin wrote Violet Gold's home address on the back of his own business card and handed it to Lagarde. Lagarde thought Mr. Chaplin looked nauseous as he raised his hand in a short salute and walked out of the office. He stopped to thank Alice for her help and left the building. Back in his car, he called Corporal Black and asked if he'd had any luck at the hospital.

CHAPTER TWENTY-TWO

NOVEMBER 2013

"Dad." It was a declarative sentence, not a question.

"Yes?" Robert Cromwell said into his cell phone. He looked at the phone number of the caller on the screen and waited.

"Dad, just wanted to see how you are."

"I've been writing to you, calling and emailing you for the last five months. Did you read anything I sent you?"

Ben expected his father to be pissed. He just had to wait through all the yada-yada.

"You didn't answer any of my many phone messages. You didn't go to those classes at the community college I paid for. You haven't turned up at the doctor when you were supposed to. Where have you been staying? And whose phone are you calling from?"

"Staying with friends, sometimes with Grandma. This is a friend's phone. She lets me use it."

"You stayed with Beverly?"

"On and off, you know how she is. Won't let me stay there for long. Has all those rules."

"You mean rules like you can't drink, do drugs, have orgies in her house or steal anything? Those rules?"

Ben laughed. "Yeah, those. Just like your rules, I know."

"So you called to check on me?" Robert said. "I'm fine. What else is going on? Are you working? Are you sober? Have you been in jail? Are you staying on your meds?"

Ben knew from long experience that the answers to those questions would make his father unhappy or angry. The questions always preceded a long lecture about how to plan his life. He was hoping to get his business done and get off the call before his father had time to launch the lecture. The Lecture, as he thought of it with initial caps, went on for forty minutes. It had gotten so he could put the phone down, play a video game, come back in time for the wrap up. It was like his dad was on autopilot.

"Well, I wanted to tell you my girlfriend is pregnant." He said it like it was great news, with just the right lilt in his voice.

Ben heard his father curse under his breath. He must be at work. It was three in the afternoon on a Wednesday, but Ben had just gotten up and hatched this great plan. Maybe his father being at work would be good, keep him from going long.

"What girlfriend?" Robert said.

"You know that girl I told you about last year, almost a year ago now, the real pretty one who's a beautician. I sent you a photo of us by email. Ilise."

"I remember the photo. I remember telling you that she's too young for you. You do remember that you're thirty years old. That girl is barely out of high school, and now you've knocked her up?"

"Hey, I expected you to be all excited about being a grandpa, but if you're not, so be it. I'll catch you another time."

"Wait a minute," Robert said.

Ben smiled to himself. *Got him.*

"How far along is she?" Robert said.

"She told me yesterday she was three months. She's got a cute little belly. I'm thinking you could make a contribution to our baby fund so we can go get a crib and stuff."

"There's still time to abort it," Robert said.

Ben wasn't expecting this. Wasn't his dad all anti-abortion? "What're you saying, Dad? You want me to tell her to kill my baby?" He brought the right amount of indignant sorrow into his voice.

"I'm saying that you are not father material, and that she is too young to have a baby, and if there are other options, you should be taking them." Robert's voice was about as tense as Ben had ever heard it. *Any minute, the old man is going to snap.*

"Do you realize the baby will be born with AIDs?" Robert said.

"She's Catholic, Dad, so no abortion. Anyway, I heard there are drugs to cure the baby."

Ben had no idea what religion Ilise was, but, hey, she wasn't really pregnant, or at least he didn't think so. He hadn't seen her in a couple months so he might as well make up something good. Speaking of that, maybe he should send her a text. Missing you, something like that. Or better, he could post on his Facebook page how she was his whole life and now she was gone. That should get her to message him.

This whole call to his father, which he now realized was a mistake, was intended to pluck a few hundred dollars from his pop's pocket, preferably by Western Union so that he did not have to see his father face to face. Visits with his father ended badly because Sarah always interfered.

"So where will you live? How will you support your little family? What's your plan for that?" Robert was on a tear.

It was clear now that this conversation was not going the way Ben planned. His father was supposed to be all googly-eyed at the idea of having a grandchild. Ben expected an offer to come and live with him and Sarah, let them take care of the baby, something like that. He had already prepared the little heartbroken speech that he would give in a few weeks about how Ilise had lost the baby and was broken up about it. Time to get out of this mess.

"Hey, Dad, I got another call, gotta go."

"You what?"

"Gotta go, Dad. Catch you next time."

His father was still talking. Ben pushed the end call button on his phone. Damn, the man was getting harder and harder to deal with. Change of plans. He'd just have to visit with Violet for a short time. Invite her over to the trailer she was paying for. Make her dinner, play house for a few days. She was getting too clingy but he could manage her. Pants down, she was still the hottest chick in the tri-state area.

CHAPTER TWENTY-THREE

APRIL 3, 2014, 2:15 P.M.

The minute Sam Lagarde clicked off a call with Corporal Black, his cell phone bleated. He looked at the little screen on his supposedly smart phone. It was Beverly Wilson. His entire world seemed immediately brighter. Even the grubby strip mall seemed to have little points of light beaming from the asphalt and the window of the Legal Aid store front gleamed.

"Hello, Mrs. Wilson," he said into the phone, hoping she would correct him and tell him to call her Beverly.

"Hello, Detective," she said, with no attempt at further intimacy. "I'm calling because I remembered something that might help you in your investigation of Ben's murder. I thought maybe every little piece of information could add up to something."

"Yes, you're absolutely correct," Lagarde said. "And please call me Sam. Otherwise, I feel old." He waited to hear her giggle. She didn't. She certainly knew how to hold onto her boundaries.

"Well, I remembered that a young woman called me, late last October, about Ben. She was practically hysterical. She said she was a social worker at the hospital in Martinsburg. I thought she might be someone you want to talk to about Ben."

"We are, in fact, pursuing that line of inquiry," Lagarde said, now a little too formally. Damn, the woman confused him. "Did she give you her name?"

"She might have, but I have trouble remembering names. Maybe Ethel, Arlene . . ."

"Could it have been Evelyn?" Lagarde said.

"Oh, yes, that was it. Evelyn. She said Ben had been living with her last fall. Really, she seemed to be out of her mind. She was more than a little incoherent. She was calling because Ben was being mean to her, stealing from her, his usual routine when he is desperate for drugs. I tried to tell her not to expect anything else from him. I did tell her to get an HIV test."

"Why did you tell her that?" Lagarde said. This might prove to be a useful conversation after all.

"Well, Ben had AIDs. I presumed you knew that, Detective. He had full blown AIDs. He had it for years. If he didn't take his meds, his T-cell count dropped to zero and his viral load zoomed up. His immune system was wrecked. He was always at risk for fatal pneumonia. Any time he went into the hospital he could have died. He was really quite sick without the meds."

Lagarde was glad most people didn't realize they weren't supposed to talk about someone else's health status. Corporal Black hadn't gotten anywhere at the hospital. Evelyn Foster was on sick leave, the hospital wouldn't give out her home address, and no one would talk to him about any of Cromwell's hospitalizations there except to say that he had been admitted three times in the past two years. Even to get that information, Black had to practically threaten to abduct the woman's first born. He did discover that there was a Sterling Townsend, a surgeon with hospital privileges in an office in the professional building on the hospital campus.

"Thank you, Mrs. Wilson, that's very useful information for us to have. Sounds like your grandson had a tough time." Lagarde was now fishing. You never knew what would hop on your hook if you baited it the right way. Sympathy was as good as any bait he had available.

"Truth be told, detective, he had the time he set himself up for," Beverly Wilson said. "It seems such a waste, though."

Lagarde detected sadness in Mrs. Wilson's voice but he wasn't going to assume anything about her. She did not respond like a normal woman, or any woman he ever knew. Beverly Wilson was a woman without drama. It was disconcerting. If she had feelings, she kept them to herself. He listened mutely for another minute to see if she would say more, but that was it for today. He was hoping to find a way to invite her out to the farm, but this conversation was not the bridge to that. Maybe next time.

"Okay," he said, "I appreciate the information. I'll be back in touch."

"Goodbye," she said and disconnected.

Lagarde recapped for his own benefit: his victim had AIDs, he was living with Evelyn Foster and bedding Violet Gold, Ilise Vander, and Lila Townsend, seemingly all at the same time. There were at least two men, Marc Delany and Sterling Townsend, with either the strength or the skill and possibly the motive to kill Cromwell. It remained to be seen if they had the opportunity. So far, the police had found no weapon or weapons. They had no fingerprints or other incriminating evidence on anyone. They had no witnesses. Basically, all they had was a dead, dismembered body. They didn't have a clear idea of how the murder was committed much less a case against anyone right now. Two people who might have motive had reasonable alibis. All Lagarde had was speculation and conjecture. There were still rocks to look under, though, and he and Black would continue to turn them over to see what might scurry out.

Lagarde's thinking took another turn. *Cromwell had a lot of energy for someone so sick, if he in fact was as sick as his grandmother said. Had he somehow gotten over on his family, convinced them he was sick when he wasn't to get out from under all their expectations?* Lagarde made a mental note to ask the medical examiner to determine whether Cromwell had AIDs or not.

He had yet to talk with Cromwell's parents. He might be putting that off because he didn't want to deal with their grief. But what if one of them, or both of them, had something to do with the man's death, maybe indirectly. At the very least, they might be able to shed some light on Cromwell's last few days. There could be useful clues in that information.

If Cromwell didn't work and he didn't go to school, he was essentially a playboy, living off the women he drew into his vortex, like a black hole from which nothing escaped. Certainly Townsend and Gold gave him some expensive trinkets. Foster gave him a place to live. He was guessing, but it was likely Ilise was the woman it was easy to be with, someone on Cromwell's own emotional and intellectual level, which was to say adolescent, someone easy to manipulate. But if Cromwell really had AIDs, did he care so little for the women having sex with him that he didn't tell them? Now there was another line of inquiry entirely. Maybe Lagarde was investigating the wrong people.

Or were these women so in love with him that they knew about his illness and didn't care? Lagarde remembered how Violet Gold looked in that office photograph in shorts and t-shirt. Lila Townsend wasn't bad either. Both could have any man they wanted. Certainly, Violet could have had Mr. Goody Two Shoes Chaplin with the snap of her fingers. The photos Ilise texted Cromwell made it clear that she was beautiful all over. And Marc Delany thought Ilise was perfect. Lagarde wondered what Ms. Foster would look like when they finally found her. Ben Cromwell preferred beautiful women, or more aptly, he preferred to have a stable of beautiful women the way some people of means collect thoroughbred horses. Perhaps he suffered from a kind of sexual gluttony; maybe there were no limits to his appetite and he didn't know when to stop.

Somewhere in the Googleverse there was a study of this kind of behavior, not Don Juan syndrome but something else. Don Juan didn't kill his paramours, but Cromwell's behavior could. Did he know that and not care? Or was Cromwell deliberately using sex to infect women with a killer virus? If so, he was a modern day vampire, literally sucking the life out of women. Lagarde realized he would be doing some heavy reading this evening. He groaned thinking about it. He had never fancied himself a vampire hunter.

CHAPTER TWENTY-FOUR

DECEMBER 2013

Violet banged on the storm door of the trailer she rented for Ben Cromwell in Shanondale, a community of cottages, trailers, and summer homes nestled in the woods along narrow winding roads that meandered up and down the mountain on the eastern shore of the Shenandoah River. The rent was cheap enough and included utilities. The trailer was the size of a small bungalow—a living room, kitchen with dinette space, bedroom and bathroom—up on cinder blocks on a wooded lot with a gravel driveway. The month-to-month lease was in Violet's name, a small precaution against Ben subletting it without her knowing. She wasn't a complete idiot, she told herself. She had also bought him a disposable phone and a cheap used car to get around in, hoping perhaps that he would get a job. She had spent almost all the law school graduation gift her grandmother gave her on Ben Cromwell. She did not expect Ben to change the locks on the door, but he must have done that since her key didn't work. She had been standing on the small wooden porch for twenty minutes. She texted and called him. It was cold. The ground was frozen, snow covered. Under her winter coat she was wearing only a lace baby doll, a garter belt and stockings. She was very glad she had remembered to wear fleece-lined boots.

Ben invited me to dinner this afternoon. He has to be in there. Maybe he was taking a shower. Darker thoughts, like maybe he shot up with heroin, overdosed, made her anxious. Violet had a few moments of true doubt. What was she doing here at all? Why was she drawn to this loser and what kept her locked in this relationship like her life depended on it? She had so much else going on in her life. If she was honest with herself, her life was just beginning. Anything, everything was possible. For some unexplainable reason she was weighing herself down with this man. Involving herself with him couldn't be explained by how handsome or completely sexy he was. And it was freezing out here while she was thinking about this. The cold itself should be enough to drive her back into her car. Maybe it was a simple as this: she had been protected her entire life by two gentle, loving parents. She had succeeded at everything she tried, even though that success had been within the framework her parents created for her. She wanted something of her own, she wanted to do something difficult and dangerous, to risk herself in some way. *Perhaps*, she scolded herself, *I should have tried skydiving.*

She walked around the trailer looking to see if a window was open, thinking about whether she could hoist herself through one of them. She heard talking, came back around to the front door and banged again. Neighbors were far enough away that they couldn't see who she was, but she was making enough noise for their dogs to bark. Just beneath her consciousness was the thought that she was making a fool of herself in public. Was this what she worked so hard to achieve, standing in the cold in her underwear in hopes of sexual bliss? Reality bloomed for a moment and then shut when the door opened. Ben, wearing only sweatpants stood there looking slightly bemused.

"Oh, hey, I didn't expect you so early," he said.

"You said seven o'clock, didn't you? It's now seven-thirty."

Ben opened her coat and looked at her. "Girl, you look good enough to eat."

He took her hand and pulled her into the warm trailer, yanked off her coat, dropped it on the floor, and turned her around in a circle so he could admire her from all sides, running two fingers across her body as he did it.

Violet felt her anger disappear. She loved the way he craved her body. She put her arms around his neck and rubbed her body against his. She looked over his shoulder toward the dining area where she expected to see the table set for their dinner with candles and flowers, although she thought they might eat later. Someone else's coat lay over a chair. A pair of woman's shoes lay a few feet from the coat, headed toward the bedroom. Beyond that was a woman's sweater on the floor. At the door of the bedroom, she could see as clearly as if the door had zoomed in toward her on a telescopic lens, a woman's bra hung over the doorknob. She held her breath.

"Is someone living with you here?" she said as calmly as she could, feeling that she was swallowing each word like dry bread as she said it.

"Nah, nothing like that," Ben said and smiled at her, squeezing her breast, biting her lip.

"Well, is she here right now?"

"Yeah, she's here, and waiting for you. C'mon. I'll introduce you."

Ben took Violet's hand and led her to the bedroom. With a flourish, he pushed the door open. A girl was arrayed on the bed like a model posed for a painter. She was naked, as if she had just finished making love and was completely relaxed, near sleep, except that she was looking directly at Violet, almost insolently, as if Violet had committed some crime against her and the girl was getting even. Or was it simply that the girl was here first and was holding onto her territory? Could the girl be drugged? Violet's face got hot then cold. Her breath caught in her throat. She remembered with a flash the look on Evelyn's face, as if the bones in her face had melted, when she discovered Violet and Ben on the floor in her home. She realized with a shock that Ben was doing the same thing to her. Violet closed her eyes. She shook her head no and took a few steps backward. Ben dragged her back into the room. He grabbed her around her waist and pulled her to the foot of the bed, holding her face with his other hand so that she was forced to look at the girl on the bed. She closed her eyes again. This was not an image she wanted burned in her memory. But it might be too late; the flash from this bomb had already gone off.

"Violet, this is Ilise," Ben said. "Ilise, this is Violet. You girls have a lot in common." He laughed. "You love me and you'll do anything for me. Right? It's time for a demonstration."

He pulled Violet over to the edge of the bed, grabbed her wrist, and stroked Ilise's thigh with Violet's hand. "See, isn't she soft?" he said, as if he were talking about a pet or explaining the virtues of a product. He kissed the back of Violet's neck, rubbed his body against her.

"Lie down next to her," he commanded. "Touch her."

Violet's stomach clenched. She wrenched herself away from the bed and ran to the bathroom. She didn't make the toilet. She vomited on the floor. She splashed cold water on her face. *I have to get out of here. I'm in danger. This man is dangerous, too dangerous. I'm an idiot. I'm a fool to put myself in this position. I let this horrible game go on too long. I'm addicted to him. So crazy.* Thoughts were like daggers. She wiped her face on the towel in the bathroom and started to run out of the room. She stopped. She turned around. There was one more thing to do. She wanted to help the girl, to help her escape.

At the bedroom doorway, she found her voice. "You don't have to do this," she said to Ilise. "He's just using you. You can leave. I'll take you home. Come on, Ilise, come with me now." She held out her hand, but she stayed as far from the bed as possible.

Ben said nothing and made no move to stop her. He was lying on the bed next to Ilise watching Violet with a strange sideways smile on his face, as if this performance was as good for him as what he had planned. He took a long drag on his cigarette.

In a slow, soft, drugged voice, Ilise said to Ben, "Where is she going? I thought we were going to do a threesome, you said." She rolled over and burrowed into Ben's chest.

"Good girl," Ben said to Ilise. He stroked her hip. He looked over at Violet. "You'll never know what you missed," he said and smiled. Then he put out his cigarette on Ilise's bare hip. The girl moaned softly.

Violet ran into the living room, grabbed her coat off the floor, threw it over her shoulders and bolted out the door. She pulled her car keys out of the coat pocket running for the car, unlocking it along the way, then flung herself behind the wheel, hands shaking so hard she couldn't get the key in the ignition. Finally she started the car and backed out of the driveway. All the way down the mountain she screamed at herself, *How could you do this, how could you do this? Have you lost your mind? You can never see him again. You have to cancel the lease. You have to get out of here, out of this state, out of this country, away from him.* When she reached Mission Road she pulled over onto the shoulder, opened the car door and vomited again. She waited until her mind quieted. She was a fool, maybe worse. But that was over. Never. Again.

CHAPTER TWENTY-FIVE

APRIL 3, 2014, 3:30 P.M.

Sam Lagarde called in to the office and told the receptionist he was packing it in for the day. "Only batting 250 out here," he said. Joyce giggled. At least here was a woman who knew how to make a man feel good. "See ya tomorrow," he said and clicked off.

Driving out the winding country road to his farm, he felt himself relax. There was something about rolling hills and a lot of sky, a tree line, a few horses in the distance, their long necks bent in that elegant curve while they munched new grass that made him feel whole. This was his way of washing his hands of problems, kind of going through nature's car wash and coming out clean on the other side. By the time he stopped the car in front of his two-hundred-year-old house, he was refreshed, ready to pull on his rubber boots and head out to the stable to pitch hay, refill water buckets, pour some sweet oats for the horses and listen to them munch. It was a sound he never tired of. It made him feel connected, linked to a cycle of life that had nothing to do with human want and misery. Lagarde shook his head. What man was capable of doing to his own kind? That was the real mystery.

Lagarde stood at the paddock rail and stroked the neck of the Paint who trotted up to greet him when he arrived. He acquired the Paint for $200 by a fluke at a horse auction. A man was selling his daughter's training horse, moving up to a thoroughbred, and no one would bid on the Paint. Even though there were a million registered Paints in the U.S., horse owners were as snobbish about horse breeds as aristocrats were about mingling with the little people. The girl had given the buyers at the auction quite a show, riding on the horse bareback, backwards, then rising to a stand on the horse at a canter around the arena. People applauded, yet nobody bid higher than the reserve price. Lagarde was standing by his horse trailer when the man led the Paint out of the paddock. "I'll give you $200 for him," Lagarde said to the man. "Sold," the man said. Lagarde lowered the tailgate on his horse trailer and the man walked the horse in and tied him up. Lagarde handed him cash, the man said, "Much obliged," and walked off. The daughter looked back once, her long braid swishing like a tail.

The Paint's name was Jake. Jake was a good ride—not too calm, not too feisty—just steady so a man could see the world around him and not have to walk on his own. Jake could also jump anything that was in the way, having proven that late one afternoon when at a canter through someone else's woods they came upon a discarded claw foot bathtub. They sailed over that tub without a millimeter of hoof hitting porcelain. Jake made Sam Lagarde happy. *Having a horse was like having a friend who didn't talk too much, a friend who just hung out with you and was attentive to your moods.* He could tell Jake whatever he wanted. The horse never judged. Bring him some carrots or an apple, Jake would eat right out of his hand. And he was big enough to lean on. You could not say that about women.

Lagarde leaned his head against Jake's neck and said, "I've got a doozy, Jake, like the world is upside down and inside out. Let's go for a ride and sort it out."

He led the horse to the grooming area in the barn, tied up his halter to the leather straps with clips on either side of the aisle, just in case Jake thought about taking an amble on his own, and brushed the horse down. This was a contemplative process, one that both horse and rider enjoyed. When the horse's coat gleamed, Lagarde pulled on the fleece pad, then the English saddle, cinched it to hold it in place, replaced the halter with reins and a mild bit, cinched the saddle tighter and walked the horse out of the stable, talking to him about his day. Lagarde's one concession to his age was the mounting block he kept outside the stable. He stepped up and threw his leg over the horse, adjusted himself in the saddle, and steered toward the far field and woods beyond at a walk.

Two miles out, Lagarde had a thought that made him rein the horse to a full stop. *All of them, like a coven.* He was a long way from proving that, or proving anything. He turned Jake toward home and walked on.

CHAPTER TWENTY-SIX

APRIL 4, 2014

Beverly Wilson presented herself unannounced at her daughter's home in Columbia, Maryland. It was ten in the morning. It had taken her an hour driving east on Route 70, the highway that ran from Baltimore, Maryland all the way to Utah, to the planned community of nearly one hundred thousand people in what had long ago been rural Howard County. She wondered if the West Virginia Eastern Panhandle would ever be that dense. If so, she might have to move further out. There were more people living in Sarah's "village" than there were in Martinsburg.

Beverly rang the bell. She never entered her daughter's house without permission. Before Sarah opened the door, Beverly had time to note that the daffodils that crowded along the stone path to the house had broken ground and the buds on the Japanese cherry trees were thickening. Red sap was running through the branches of the large Maple tree. Spring would happen no matter what the weather in their hearts. Some days the dissonance was too much to take.

Sarah greeted her with a hug and told her Robert had gone to work. That was good. Beverly wanted to comfort her daughter. She was not sure anything she could do would comfort Robert. His loss was too great. He would never get over the death of his son even if he found a way to keep doing normal activities. Years from now, that howl of grief she had heard over the phone would still be lurking there just below the surface of Robert's every act, thought and emotion. To Beverly, it was ironic that Ben's death was having the effect on Sarah's marriage that the boy couldn't make happen when he was alive. Sarah looked as if she wasn't sleeping or eating. She looked as if she had worn the same jeans and sweatshirt for weeks. Slept in them maybe, on the sofa probably. Sarah worked from home doing graphic design for the last ten years. Her office was in the converted den. The house, once so lovingly arranged by her daughter and filled with flowers, light and color, seemed dark and drab, as if life had discarded it in an attic corner. Robert and Sarah bought this house, with its large family room, den, dining room, five bedrooms, a finished basement and pool in the backyard, with the thought that they would fill it with children and then grandchildren. And then came three miscarriages, each one more devastating than the one before. By the time they stopped trying to be pregnant no agency would place a baby in their home because of Ben's juvenile record. The house, empty of children, echoed with their seeming failure.

Beverly's first act was to open all the drapes and blinds, pull up some windows and let in air and light. She went into the kitchen and washed the dishes in the sink. Her daughter sat at the kitchen table with an untouched cup of coffee in front of her. It looked like what little Sarah and Robert had eaten had been take out. They had not announced their son's death and there were no flowers or cards of condolence, no casseroles in the refrigerator. No friends leaving messages of support. There had been no ritual farewell to the dead to carry them to the next place. They had retreated into a cave of sorrow and huddled there, waiting for something, anything that would help them understand what had happened. They might never understand even if facts were laid out in front of them like a map. Beverly could not understand it either, but she thought it was time to break her daughter out of this prison. *Small steps*, she cautioned herself, *small steps*.

"If I make you an omelet, will you eat it?"

"I don't know, Mom. Maybe. I don't feel hungry."

"Let's try."

Beverly busied herself pulling out eggs, milk, butter, cheese from the refrigerator. She checked the freshness of the rye bread in a clear plastic bag in an open basket on the counter. *Still okay to toast.* She pulled a small frying pan from under the counter, put it on the stove top, and started the process of making what she hoped would be a perfect omelet. Running a spoon around the edges of the firming egg, she tilted the pan and let the uncooked egg run to the sides. In a few minutes, she folded one half of the omelet over the other and tipped the pan so that the entire omelet fell out onto the plate.

"Not bad," she said. Even after fifty years, she always held her breath a little around omelet making.

She spread butter on the toast and put the pieces on the plate. She quickly set the table with Sarah's blue plates, two forks and napkins and put the omelet with the toast and a serving spoon on the table. She sniffed the orange juice in the container she pulled from the refrigerator and poured two glasses and set them down.

"Eat something, sweetheart," she said and sat at the table with Sarah.

Sarah looked up at her and smiled. "Not bad at all, Mom." She took one spoonful of the omelet onto her plate and one piece of toast, then lapsed back into her sorrow.

"Tell me what you're thinking, sweetie. Maybe that will help."

Sarah ran a hand through her hair, sat back in the chair and looked at her mother. "You're a very optimistic person, Mom. I don't think anything will help."

"Try, honey. Say anything."

Sarah was quiet for a while. Beverly ate half the omelet and half of a piece of toast, drank the orange juice, then got up and made fresh coffee. Finding two clean cups to pour it into, she put the cups on the table.

Finally, Sarah spoke, "I don't know why, but I've been thinking about what Robert told me about how Ben's mother died. Did I ever tell you? She died in a car crash. She hit a tree head on and went through the windshield. She wasn't wearing her seat belt. There were no skid marks on the asphalt. She didn't try to stop or swerve. It's like she did it deliberately. The coroner said her blood alcohol level was point three-nine. There were empty bottles of vodka on the floor of the car. He said the alcohol itself might have killed her if she hadn't lost control of the car. Everyone assumed she lost control of the car, except her sister, Robert told me. She kept saying that Ben killed his mother. But that was insane. It was daytime when she crashed. It was a clear day, no rain, a school day. Robert was at work. Ben was in the backseat of the car."

Sarah paused.

Beverly cleared their plates, scraped the remaining food into the trash bin, and washed up. She gathered up the trash bag, tied it and took it out the kitchen door to the garbage can in the garage. Coming back into the kitchen, she poured them fresh coffee. She put her hand on her daughter's back, leaned over and kissed her cheek. She sat down and took a sip of her coffee.

"Ben spent five days in the hospital with a concussion," Sarah continued. "The doctor said something about how he might have frontal lobe damage, although of course Robert had no idea what that meant. He was just glad Ben survived the accident. And here's the other thing, Ben was eight. His blood alcohol level was point one-five. She gave him alcohol. Can you imagine? And the doctor said the boy also had been given a huge dose of valium. I think she was trying to kill him. Robert never said as much, but that's what he thinks. It's like Ben's being murdered now is finishing the job his mother started. It's too horrible."

Sarah was shaking. She wrapped her arms around herself as if to stop the shaking. Beverly walked into the family room, located the red chenille throw she gave her daughter one Christmas, brought it into the kitchen and wrapped it around Sarah's shoulders. She stroked her daughter's head. Sarah's shaking continued.

"I was just thinking today," Sarah said, "that Ben never had a chance. His own mother made him into an alcoholic, took him on her wild rides. All those days he didn't go to school after her death, even after we married, do you think that's what he was doing here at home? That he was replicating what his mother did with him?" Sarah put her head in her hands, tears rolling down her cheeks. "I wish I had been kinder to him," she said.

"I know, sweetheart, I know," Beverly said. She stroked Sarah's arm. She waited. Tears were a good thing. She would wait all day for whatever her daughter needed to say, for however many tears she needed to shed.

CHAPTER TWENTY-SEVEN

DECEMBER 2013

On the fifth day of feeling like this was the worst flu she had ever had in her life and worried that it wasn't flu at all but pregnancy, Violet Gold dragged herself to the phone and called to make an appointment to see a doctor. She wanted someone outside of Martinsburg, far from her parents' circle of friends. Whatever she had, she didn't want it getting back to them. To her parents, she was a paragon of intelligence and industry. She would hate to burst their bubble. She looked through the online directory of gynecologists to find a woman and located a Dr. Lila Townsend with a practice in Shepherdstown, which seemed far enough away from home to keep tongues from wagging. She negotiated with the receptionist for the earliest possible appointment and got a Thursday at 11 a.m. with the caveat that if the doctor had a delivery she would be rescheduled. The receptionist was entirely too perky for Violet's taste.

On the assigned Thursday morning, one and a half weeks since Ben tried to make their duet a trio, Violet, wrapped in several layers of clothing, socks, fleece boots, woolen scarf and hat, presented herself at the doctor's office.

"You're in luck, Ms. Gold," said the overly perky receptionist who took her insurance card and driver's license for identification and handed her a clipboard with three pages of questions to answer, "no deliveries. The doctor should be able to see you in a few minutes. Just fill out the forms and give them back to me. The nurse will call you."

Violet did not smile back at her. Couldn't the receptionist see that she was suffering and that cheeriness made it worse? She took a seat in the waiting room, crossed her legs and propped the clipboard on her knee to fill in the form. She had not had any of the listed diseases. She did have her immunizations. She had never had any surgeries. Her symptoms were deep fatigue, swollen glands, extreme nausea, pain on urination, muscle pain, headache. She checked boxes and wrote in answers and then turned in the clipboard. Shortly after that, she was called into the back by the nurse who weighed her, measured her height, took her blood pressure and temperature, at which the nurse frowned, told her how to pee in a cup and where to put the cup when she was done. After that, the nurse guided Violet to an office and told her the doctor would talk with her first before examining her. That seemed very civilized to Violet. She might like this doctor.

Within minutes, Dr. Lila Townsend walked into the office and introduced herself, shook Violet's hand, sat down behind her desk and said, "I see you're a lawyer. That's wonderful. You must have been a very good student, very determined. We probably have some things in common."

Violet nodded. She understood the doctor was trying to make her comfortable, establish a rapport. She felt like she didn't have time for this conversation. Dr. Townsend seemed to get the idea without Violet saying anything.

The doctor leaned across her desk and said, "Tell me why you came to see me today."

"I've been feeling really awful," Violet said. "And I've been seeing this guy, and sometimes I wasn't home to take my birth control pill in the morning and then I went to work and forgot to take it so I think it's possible I'm pregnant." Violet paused to gather herself together. It took some effort to contain her emotions. She didn't want to sob. The thought of being pregnant with Ben Cromwell's baby made her want to vomit. She imagined herself as Sigourney Weaver with an alien growing inside her, poking through her skin, killing her in a wild eruption of blood and tissue.

Dr. Townsend looked through the form Violet had filled out, looked over the nurse's notes on the chart, and then looked at Violet. "Let's take a look," she said. "I'll give you a thorough exam and then we'll know what we're dealing with. The nurse will show you to an examining room and give you instructions. I'll be in to examine you in a few minutes."

She smiled at Violet, left the office and was replaced by the nurse, who did exactly as Dr. Townsend had said.

Violet hated being examined. She hated the stirrups. She hated having the doctor press on her breasts and abdomen. She hated staring at the ceiling, gripping the sides of the table, pretending she didn't hate these exams. She particularly hated the speculum. She hated being invaded by someone who didn't know her at all. But in comparison to what she had been through with Ben, somehow this exam now seemed benign. When it was over, Dr. Townsend told Violet to sit up.

"Here's what I see right off," she said as Violet shivered in the flimsy paper gown. "You don't appear to be pregnant, but we will test for that in case it's very early days. You do have a massive infection and signs that you might have gonorrhea. The nurse will give you a large dose of azithromycin by injection. You're not allergic to any medications are you?"

Violet shook her head, no. She could not find her voice.

"Then we'll follow that injection up with a course of antibiotics. You must take every one of the pills as directed. Otherwise you won't be cured. Do you understand?"

Violet nodded yes.

"If you are pregnant, you will have some decisions to make. We can help you with that if you wish, and I can certainly be your obstetrician. I am also sending you to have blood drawn to check for other issues, such as HIV and other STDs. We will call you as soon as we have a report back. I'd like you to come back for a follow up visit. If you are HIV positive, it would be useful if you would tell the health department who your most recent partners are. You will have to do that for STDs. Are you willing to do that?"

Violet nodded. "I've only been having sex with one man," she whispered.

"I'm sorry, I didn't catch that. What did you say?" said Dr. Townsend.

Violet found her voice. "Ben Cromwell, he's the only man I have been having sex with for the last five months. I was fine before that." She began to weep.

Dr. Townsend seemed to make a note in the chart. Violet thought she saw recognition in the doctor's face when she said Ben's name. *God, I'll bet other women have been in here with the same story. Of course you're not the first*, she chided herself. She knew the doctor couldn't reveal anyone else's health history.

"Okay, Ms. Gold," the doctor said, her voice so quiet Violet had to strain to hear it, "we will get you through this and, if you are HIV positive, I can refer you to a very good infectious disease specialist who will help you control the disease and successfully live with it for a long time. There are good drugs available today. Being HIV positive is no longer a death sentence. You can live a long, productive life."

Violet took the piece of paper with the prescription for antibiotics written on it, nodded her head in thanks, took her shot without complaint, got dressed and walked to the patient check out window. The nurse gave her the address of where to go to have her blood drawn and a card with the date of her next appointment. The appointment was in January.

The buzzing in Violet's ears would not stop. She could barely hear what the nurse was saying to her. She had come in thinking she was pregnant with that monster's baby. He had impregnated her, alright, with his diseases. She could barely think straight. *Not a death sentence? How could the doctor say that? Of course it was.* It was the death of the life she hoped for, the one she'd planned and worked for. Violet staggered to her car and sat behind the wheel. Maybe she was okay, maybe it was just the gonorrhea that was making her sick like this. Maybe she didn't have anything to worry about. She wasn't pregnant. That was a good thing. Still, it was clear she needed to get away from here, as far as she could go. She would wait for the results of the tests and then, then she would go somewhere that Ben Cromwell had never been. She wanted to go home to her parents and cry in her mother's arms, but that's the last thing she could do. She started her car and slowly navigated her way home, shaking the entire distance.

Dr. Lila Townsend completed her next patient exam, made her notes, and told her office administrator that she needed to run an errand. She would be back in an hour. She put on her coat, grabbed her purse and phone, and went out to her car. On the car dash screen, she punched up the address for the women's clinic in Hagerstown, Maryland. She told the GPS to talk her through the driving directions and pulled out of the parking lot. She drove blindly for fifteen miles, turning when the voice told her to turn. Within half an hour, she presented herself at the clinic intake window and asked for the rapid HIV test to be administered. She had to know.

CHAPTER TWENTY-EIGHT

APRIL 5, 2014, 11 A.M.

Dr. Sterling Townsend's office was in the new multi-story building next to City Hospital in Martinsburg. The reception area was modern, clean, and stocked with the latest issues of *Forbes*, *The Economist*, *Sports Illustrated* and the *Wall Street Journal*. The television was tuned to Bloomberg TV with a continuous stock ticker running below the headlines. *The subtext here was that Dr. Townsend's patients were going to pay through the nose for their surgery. He was an orthopedic surgeon, the kind who should know about sawing through bone, the kind of doctor who would know what implements to use to dismember a person.* Not that he was prejudging the good doctor. This interview was just a check-the-box meeting to determine if Townsend had a motive and was minus an alibi that would affect his having the opportunity to kill Ben Cromwell.

The doctor made Lagarde and Corporal Black wait nearly an hour in a practically empty waiting room. When the doctor finally swept into the reception area, his white coat flapping open in the breeze caused by his long strides, it was simply natural for them to stand to greet him. Lagarde realized instantly that their knee-jerk reaction gave Townsend the upper hand. *Score one for the doc.* Townsend barely glanced at their credentials, as if checking to see if they were who they said they were was beneath him.

Sterling, Lagarde concluded looking around the personal office space the orthopedist led them to, was the showoff of the Townsend doctor duo. Black leather chairs, glass desk on chrome legs, rosewood floor-to-ceiling bookcases all spoke to how well the doctor was doing collecting his fees. The walls were plastered with diplomas, certificates, commendations, and photographs of Dr. Sterling Townsend with famous people he had fixed: Senators, West Virginia University football players, the occasional young person turned fabulously successful actress with long, straight beautiful legs. The wall was meant to impress. The silver-haired doctor gestured to the chairs. Lagarde and Black continued to stand. This wasn't a social call. Townsend sat down in his high-backed chair and relaxed. He looked at the police officers as if inviting them to begin.

"We're here, Dr. Townsend, to ask about Ben Cromwell, a young man who was murdered and cut into pieces in March," Lagarde said without preamble or other small talk that might put the police at further psychological disadvantage. He waited to see the effect of his statement.

Townsend looked blank. Then he looked at his computer screen and tapped a few keys on the keyboard. "I don't see a Ben Cromwell on my patient list either as a primary or referral patient," Townsend said. "I don't know any Ben Cromwell personally."

"Your wife was having an affair with Ben Cromwell," Lagarde said, watching for any change in Townsend's complexion or what he did with his hands or feet, or any minute twitching of his face muscles.

The doctor kept his composure. "What my nearly ex-wife does with her free time is entirely up to her," Townsend said. "We don't talk very much. We are separated, as you must know, and as soon as the divorce is final, I am marrying again."

Lagarde thought that he might have given this master of the universe some ammunition in that divorce proceeding, but that wasn't his problem. "Do you happen to know Marc Delany?"

Again, the doctor consulted his screen. "I did a rotator cuff repair for a Marc Delany early this year, if that's the same person you are asking about," he said. "What does he have to do with my wife or Ben Cromwell?"

"Probably nothing," Lagarde said. "Does that repair mean that Delany would have continuing weakness in whichever arm was affected by the rotator cuff injury?"

"He would probably have full use of his arm within six months of the surgery, which was four months ago," Townsend said, glancing at his screen. "He's a young man; likely to make a complete recovery by his final visit two months from now. Is there anything else you need to ask me? I'm due in surgery this afternoon." Townsend stood.

"Where were you on March 15th, doctor?"

"As it happens," Dr. Sterling Townsend said with a broad smile on his already-tanned face, "I was with my fiancée in Maui for ten days from March 10th through the 20th. We had a wonderful time." His blue eyes twinkled. "Do you need to see some proof of our hotel reservations? I can have my office administrator fax a copy to you."

Lagarde handed Townsend his card. "That would be very useful," he said. "Just have the administrator fax the copy to this number. Thank you for your time."

"Oh, one more thing," Corporal Black said, turning back from the office doorway. "Do you know Evelyn Foster, Ilise Vander or Violet Gold?"

Townsend shook his head no. Then his eyebrows rose. "Wait. I do know an Evelyn Foster," he said. "She's the social worker at City Hospital; very nice woman, very effective, has a good reputation among the staff. What does Evelyn have to do with this murder?"

"We're just following the breadcrumbs, doctor," Lagarde said. "Do you happen to know where Ms. Foster lives?"

"Why, I think she lives in town. She told me once she only has a five minute commute."

"Thank you very much," Lagarde said. "We'll be back in touch if we think of anything else we need to ask you."

Back in the building corridor, Lagarde slapped Black on the back. "Good job," he said. "That should narrow down the Evelyn Foster addresses quite a bit."

Black consulted his notepad. "Let's stop by the Maple Street address. Hospital says she's on sick leave. Maybe we'll find her at home."

CHAPTER TWENTY-NINE

JANUARY 2014

By some lucky fluke of genetics, Lila Townsend was HIV negative. The rapid test results were confirmed by the more thorough blood test. She would have another test in six months. For now, she was breathing easier. Somehow she had sidestepped the gonorrhea also. She did always insist on using condoms in spite of his complaints. *Celibacy is the ultimate solution.* Perhaps this experience with Cromwell had taught her that.

She'd been thinking about what needed to be done about Ben Cromwell. She paced from room to room in her beautiful house. She wrapped up in a warm coat and blanket and sat in one of the teak chairs on her back deck overlooking the Potomac River and watched the water flow by endlessly. She took runs through her lovely neighborhood, down along Shepherd Grade Road and back, her breath hanging in the cold air like the fog in her mind. Five mile runs to jog loose the panic and stoke the endorphins that would help her to think clearly.

She could report Cromwell to the health department, which would lead nowhere. They had no power. He was just another statistic to be compiled. It might be possible to sue him in some way. Except that he had nothing, so winning a civil a suit would be a pyrrhic victory that would maybe be precedent setting but ultimately useless. It seemed to Lila that he was deliberately infecting women, in a kind of slow-motion serial murder spree. At the very least, he should be put away somewhere. Would his behavior be considered mentally unstable enough to forcibly commit him? He certainly was a danger to others, if not himself. Who could she enlist to help her with a committal? Was there a criminal prosecution possible or did the justice system not care about this kind of behavior. Could he be charged with reckless endangerment of human life? Was there such a charge outside the world of the television show *Law and Order* and would a charge like that get him put away for life? Probably not. She had slept with him willingly and so did Violet Gold. They were adults, responsible for their own behavior. No one had abducted them or forced them to have sex with Cromwell at gun point. He wasn't the pied piper. Still, he was deliberately harming them. Maybe they could pin harassment on him, but that would only put him away for six months, if that. There was just too much Lila didn't know. Ms. Gold, however, might know whether Cromwell could be prosecuted for attempted murder, or something—anything—else.

Lila knew that under her seemingly logical approach to solving the problem of Ben Cromwell was a deep desire for revenge. If she were honest with herself, she wanted him dead. Her dreams were colored in blood. He had disrupted her life. Her home no longer felt safe. He seemed to be able to break into it no matter how often she changed the locks or improved her security system. She would come home from work and find something missing. Something obvious like the Chihuly glass flower arrangement, that he couldn't possibly know the value of, would be gone from the foyer table. Once she discovered that he had taken her extra set of car keys she kept on a hook inside the kitchen pantry, causing to have her car re-keyed—a small fortune but worth it to keep him from taking her car again in the middle of the night. He had already taken her gold necklace, a gift to herself for completing a difficult ropes course to master her fear of heights. Her iPad was long gone. The television in her bedroom was missing. The Breitling watch was never going to be returned.

She got a restraining order against him, but she knew that wouldn't keep him away. She worried he would start breaking into her professional office soon. That's where the drugs were. It wouldn't be difficult for him. She came out of her office one evening and found him watching her. He was the required number of feet away from her, leaning against an electric pole, watching her as if she were a deer he meant to shoot. She missed her footing and stumbled, catching herself by putting out her hand on the car nearest to her in the parking lot. It was as if the earth had fallen away under her feet. She was very glad at that moment that she was not the last to leave.

The next step was to call the police and say he had violated the restraining order, report all the things he had stolen. There had to be something she could do, something more permanent than putting him in jail for a year for burglary or stalking. She shouldn't be the one who had to leave the area. He was the criminal.

She needed assistance in figuring it out. She couldn't ask any of her friends or colleagues. This problem would make her a pariah. She would be derided, never again be asked to present at conferences. Her papers would no longer be selected for publication. She would be shunned, not because she had harmed a patient or made a medical error, but because she had lost her mind, because she had a sexual relationship she didn't manage well, and because she had sex with a man almost ten years younger than she. It didn't matter that her male colleagues were forever falling into and out of inappropriate young women's beds. Witness her husband. Women, in this profession, if not all, were held to higher standards.

She dialed Violet Gold's number. Maybe a legal perspective would help. She knew the call would turn up the heat on the simmering anger she felt toward Cromwell but she needed an ally. Who else could she talk to but another one of his victims? She had to tell Violet that the HIV test was positive anyway. Lila knew this call was manipulative; tell the woman she was HIV positive and ask her to help put the perpetrator away for good. She wasn't following the physician's creed, 'first do no harm,' but harm had been done to them. Didn't they have any recourse, any way to answer that? Wasn't there any possibility of self defense?

Violet Gold answered on the first ring. She must have been waiting for the call.

"Ms. Gold," Lila said. "This is Dr. Townsend."

"Yes," Violet said. Her voice was constricted, as if she were holding down a sob.

"The good news is that you are not pregnant." Lila let that fact sink in for a minute. She went on, "The test for gonorrhea was positive, but I think we've taken care of that with the antibiotics." She paused to allow Violet time to absorb that information. "But I'm sorry to tell you that the HIV test was positive."

Violet gasped. "No. Oh, no. Oh, God," she said.

Lila gave Violet a few minutes to calm herself. "I'm going to give you a referral to Dr. Rosen at Johns Hopkins Hospital. He's very good. You'll want to start taking anti-retroviral medication immediately. Don't delay."

"Thank you," Violet said, choking on her tears.

"I want to talk with you about something else," Lila said.

"What, what else is there to talk about?"

"Getting even," Lila said.

There was a long silence. Lila waited. She thought Violet might hang up but she didn't. Lila could hear Violet's breathing change, become more even.

"Where do you want to meet?" Violet said, calm as winter ice over a deep pond.

"You're coming into the office on the 15th, right? We'll talk then," Lila said.

"Yes, of course, alright," Violet said. "I'll see you then."

They disconnected. Lila walked outside on her deck and looked out at the river. No matter the season, the water flowed urgently toward the Bay miles and miles from here, as if it were rushing to meet its fate.

CHAPTER THIRTY

FEBRUARY 20, 2014, 7 P.M.

Violet Gold, Lila Townsend, Evelyn Foster and Ilise Vander met in the coffee bar area of the Target store off Route 11 in Winchester, Virginia, twenty miles or more from where any of them lived and a place none of them frequented. They sat on plastic red chairs at a table near the large windows at the front of the store so they could watch the parking lot. There was a constant hum of people coming and going, talking to each other, ordering special coffees, the sound of cash registers, the sound of old-fashioned commerce before the age of Internet shopping. Their own voices would be jumbled in the mix of sounds coming from everywhere.

During Violet's January appointment, Violet convinced Lila to bring Evelyn into their confidence. It didn't take much. They were sitting in Lila's office where they first met as patient and doctor. The space looked different to Violet now that they were talking as equals. The office was impersonal, maybe cold. Violet told Lila the story of Cromwell's threesome attempts. Lila's well-trained composure broke when Violet told her about Ben stubbing out his cigarette on Ilise's naked hip. Violet thought Lila might faint, she turned pale, she closed her eyes, her hands shook, but she didn't faint. She got angrier. It was as if they were in training for a marathon. Each story was another five miles they had run, could run. Each story was another anguish they mastered to keep going. Hate made them strong and they were stronger together.

Evelyn was 'in' the moment Violet called her at work and invited her to meet with them. Evelyn said she was ready to do something besides weep. She had just discovered that Ben Cromwell took a two-thousand dollar cash advance on her credit card. He had apparently written down all the information from her card and figured out how to move cash from her credit card into his own bank account.

Ilise joined them through Evelyn's intervention. Evelyn told Violet it was good to include Ilise, in the sense that the girl needed to be broken free from the monster by her own doing, not by the magical intervention of some fairy godmothers.

Violet said, "If I was her, I'd rather have this problem solved by a few fairy godmothers," but Evelyn insisted. She coerced Ilise to come to the meeting by telling the girl she belonged with them and that they would take care of her. She did have some misgivings about the girl's ability to keep anything secret from Ben Cromwell, so Evelyn picked Ilise up in the Martinsburg mall and drove her to Target to make sure she got there.

The surprise was Ilise's mother. She pried the information about the meeting from her daughter. She showed up, coffee in hand, just as they began to exchange their horror stories. "I'm Katrina," she said to the group, "Ilise's mom, and I just want the bastard dead."

She smiled at Evelyn. "Glad to see you here, sister. I thought you seemed more involved than just being worried about my girl."

There were three gongs on the store's PA system and an announcement that a fifty percent off sale was on in women's lingerie. They looked at each other and laughed. They took the announcement as a good omen. Maybe they were giddy, too giddy for their own good. They seemed to be drawing a strange energy from each other.

Katrina Vander was the honest one. Lila, Evelyn and Violet still had excuses, concerns and the veneer of all those years of socialization and education to break through. Ilise had her youth. Even now, Ilise seemed to think Ben could be turned around.

Ilise twisted her hair around her finger. "Don't you think if we all just tell him how awful he's been to us, he'll want to change?" she asked naively.

They looked at her and shook their heads.

"He doesn't care about you, honey," her mother said. She unwrapped a stick of gum and popped it into her mouth. There was no smoking in the store. "He made you all into his harem, he made you all sick. What does that tell you about him?"

Ilise looked baffled. She twirled her hair and sucked her finger. "But I love him," she said.

"You can love him when he's gone," Lila said. "It'll be safer that way."

Lila Townsend's expensive haircut made her standout in this setting and even though she had been careful to wear jeans and a sweat jacket they were from designer makers. Lila didn't seem to know the difference, but Katrina Vander noticed. She looked over at Lila and nodded appreciatively.

"Doc here has a point," Katrina said.

Ilise stared at Lila for a minute and then looked down at the table and ran her finger around on the tabletop in a circle as if trying to push that idea into its correct place in a catalog of thoughts that didn't make sense.

They drank their coffees, lattes, and teas and each told their Ben Cromwell story again with new emphasis on the betrayals. It was like a group therapy session, Evelyn said. Good to get all this anger off their chests.

From Lila's viewpoint, telling the stories was like practicing driving a wooden stake through the heart of a vampire. They were rehearsing; they had to find a way to do it for real.

"No one is going to take care of this for us," Lila said. "It's our problem."

"Doesn't he have parents?" Ilise asked.

"No," Evelyn said. "Not according to his chart. He does have a grandmother." She pushed her glasses up on her nose, her cheeks pinked.

"Yes, he does," Violet said. "He does have parents. He wanted to sue them."

They all looked down at their drinks for a few minutes, as if the cure for Ben Cromwell's deep deceitfulness, or their stupidity, could be found in the bottom of their paper cups.

"Is there a class action suit we can bring against him to force him into a state hospital for the criminally insane?" Lila said.

"I've never heard of such a thing. I'd have to research it," Violet said. "Besides, that would take at least six months, maybe more. We'd have to find a doctor who would sign the committal papers."

"I might be able to find one," Lila said.

"You girls are over-thinking this," Katrina Vander said. "We just kill him." She looked at each of them defiantly. "If you don't have the stones for that, at least two of you have enough money to hire somebody to do it."

Lila almost laughed. She liked Katrina Vander. The woman was right. They should just get to the point.

"I think that's going too far. But if we killed him," Lila said, "how would we do it?"

"I can't, I can't kill him," Violet said. "If that's what you're going to do, you have to leave me out." She squirmed in the plastic chair, looked out the window, looked over at Lila as if to see a better suggestion written on her forehead than the one she seemed to agree to.

"You're in whether you like it or not, kiddo," Katrina said. "You're here. That makes you part of it."

Violet thought that technically, by the law, Katrina's assertion was not accurate. If she left now, she was not part of the conspiracy, but she didn't leave. Being together amplified their hatred; it created a magnetic force field that held them all there, made them feel invincible. Or maybe it was simpler than that—she hated Ben Cromwell enough to kill him. Alone, she wasn't strong enough to do anything about it.

Katrina Vander had new information for them, information that made them rethink every moment they had ever been alone with Ben Cromwell; that made them terrified in retrospect that they had ever allowed him into their beds, between their legs, and then closed their eyes and went to sleep. Once she was done with her story, they were ready for the leap to the next level. Their lives, it now seemed to them, depended on it.

And it turned out, Katrina Vander worked in the meat department at Bigmart. She was a certified butcher. She had the plaque. She had some definite ideas.

"I don't mind getting my hands dirty," she said.

CHAPTER THIRTY-ONE

MARCH 5, 2014

"Hey, Grandma," Ben said when Beverly Wilson opened the door of her home. He embraced her and put his head down on her shoulder. He stepped back. "Good to see you. Brought you some flowers."

He handed her daisies wrapped in colorful paper. Beverly didn't ask if he'd paid for the flowers or grabbed them out of the bin and walked out of the door.

"How lovely," she said. "Let's put them in water. Come up stairs. Have you eaten?"

It was one in the afternoon. She guessed that Ben only woke up an hour ago. "I'll make you some scrambled eggs and bacon. You can smother the eggs in ketchup the way you like. I won't cringe."

"That's great, Gram. I'm just gonna put some stuff in my room and get cleaned up. Been sleeping in my car." Ben slung a large duffel bag over his shoulder and headed up the stairs.

As she pulled out a blue glass vase from the cupboard, Beverly made a mental check of what she had left out upstairs in her bedroom. After his phone call, she put her purse with cash and credit cards, keys, checkbook and the box of blank checks, all truly valuable jewelry, and her iPad in the hidden wall-mounted safe in her painting studio. Just to be careful, she changed the code on the keypad. She wasn't a fool. She knew he would outwit her in some way, take something she valued and forgot to tuck away. Sometimes she didn't realize for weeks that something was missing. There was always that moment of deep disappointment when she discovered he had taken something. *He brought that big duffel bag in to take something away with him.* Ben couldn't bear too much compassion. He had to hurt you when he left. He didn't want you to love him unconditionally. Beverly always did her best to minimize the harm from contact with him so that she would be willing to see him again. It was she who had been trained over all these years, not Ben.

She ran cold tap water into the vase, cut off the bottom of the daisy stems and put them in the water. She set the blue vase of white and yellow daisies on the dining room table and stepped back to enjoy the still life. The mid-day light glowed through the French doors in the dining room like a halo around his gift to her.

Beverly knew not to react to Ben's reference to sleeping in his car. That was a hook into a conversation about giving him money. She knew it could be a flat out lie. He could have slept in the Taj Mahal last night and still said he was sleeping in his car. False sympathy wasn't her way. Her goal was to provide a safe space for him for a short time, until he got his legs under him. Generally he left on his own within a day or two. He couldn't bear the quiet confinement of her life. Watching television and eating popcorn with his grandmother was not Ben's idea of a good time. She didn't have a game console. She didn't let him smoke in her house. Two days without some drug coursing through his system was as many as Ben could go. She had tried to make it possible for him to leave as easily as he came, without the scenes he needed to make with his parents; the irritability, the harsh words and arguments he provoked so that he would have an excuse to run away.

She heard him moving around in his room. Then the shower was turned on. When he came downstairs he was clean, his black hair slicked back, clean clothes on. *He was still a handsome boy, in spite of the way he lived.* She did a quick inventory of his skin, not jaundiced, not ashen, no signs of Kaposi sarcoma, the red lesions associated with late stage AIDs. He was thin, but not heroin addict thin. Someone had been feeding him. His eyes were clear. He might be drug free right now; might be sticking to his meds. Beverly felt her shoulders relax. Drug-free meant he was less likely to do something harmful to both of them. She busied herself making his food and then put the plate in front of him with a glass of milk.

Ben bent over and placed both his arms on either side of the plate like a man protecting his food from nearby predators. It was a habit he had developed in prison where stronger men enjoyed taking weaker men's food away. Beverly always cringed when she saw the behavior, but there was no way to train it out of him without making him unhappy and souring the mood.

"So what have you been up to?" she said.

"Not much, Gram, bouncing around from place to place. But I've got this great idea. I think I want to go out to California, you know, where it's warm. One of my friends said I should try out for movies."

He looked up and grinned at her. There was a splotch of red ketchup in the corner of his mouth. She handed him a napkin.

"What do you think of that idea?"

Beverly was accustomed to Ben's sudden enthusiasm for impossible projects. She knew there was no point in talking him out of them based on reason. She also knew he rarely undertook them. It was mostly about the talk, for him, not about accomplishing the thing he was talking about. It was as if imagining something was as good as actually experiencing it. She wondered if that was a universal hangover from video games and constant visual stimulation that everyone in his generation shared. So much of their lives were spent in darkened rooms living virtually, their eyes glued to a screen, their fingers hitting keys, and all the brain chemicals associated with real thrills coursing through their bodies. They didn't need to actually go hang gliding or snowboarding. They had the experience burned into their neurons by proxy. She wished Ben would do something big, different, adventurous that took all his brain power to master; just once in his life, make something real happen that he could be proud of.

"It's warm in Southern California, so if you have to sleep in your car you might not be cold," she said. "I think they have public showers and bathrooms at the beaches."

Ben laughed. "Do you think I could make it in the movies?"

"I think the movie business is pretty tricky to break into. But if you work hard at it, learn how to act, go to auditions, get yourself an agent, do everything you have to do like memorize scripts, wait tables in a restaurant or do carpentry until you're discovered—you're certainly cocky enough—there's no reason why you can't make it."

Ben looked down at his plate. His shoulders sagged. "So you don't think I could."

"I didn't say that. I said you'd have to work at it. There's no magic wand."

"I could do that," he said. "I could work."

"Yes, you could. You're certainly handsome enough," she said. "And work won't hurt you."

That seemed to be the response Ben was waiting for. He grinned at her. "Do you love me, Gram?"

"I do, Ben, I love you."

He nodded and bit into his toast. "I love you, too," he said, bread-crumbs coating his lips.

They worked in Beverly's garden that afternoon, raking out leaves from the flower beds, trimming up perennials for their spring emergence. Ben bagged leaves and spread mulch without complaint. They ordered Chinese take out for dinner and had it delivered and watched *American Hustle*, a streaming video rental, on television. When Beverly went up to bed she felt they had a good day. She hugged him and kissed him on the cheek and left him to watch the TV on his own. Her mind nagged at her that this was risky, but there had to be some small trust that he wouldn't burn the house down. Yet, she did lock her bedroom door.

He was gone when she woke up at seven the next morning. He must never have gone to sleep. She walked around her house looking to see what he might have taken, or what had triggered his restlessness. Instead of something being missing, she found a beautiful blown glass flower arrangement, Japanese in its simplicity but definitely American in its coloring, sitting on the coffee table in the living room. She picked it up and looked at the bottom. It was signed by the artist. Ben could not have afforded the piece. He had obviously stolen it, and like a cat that kills a mouse and brings its owner the head, he left the treasure for her as a gift. She sat down on the sofa to catch her breath.

She walked back upstairs to his room. His dirty clothes were on the floor; he had tracked mud and leaves from the backyard across the carpet and left the wet towel on the rug. She opened the bureau drawers and found an assortment of things that he obviously didn't need or he would have taken them with him, including a phone and an iPod. On a whim, she put the iPod buds in her ears and pressed the button to see what kind of music he was listening to. The first few notes filled her head with sounds so vibrant and full it felt as if the notes were coming out of her heart, her bones, running through her veins. *Amazing Grace* was the song playing on the iPod. It was her husband's favorite song. She listened, weeping, until the last notes died away, then turned off the device, put it back in the drawer, and walked out of the room.

CHAPTER THIRTY-TWO

APRIL 5, 2014, 12:15 P.M.

Exactly as Dr. Sterling Townsend said, the address on Maple Street that Black had in his notebook for Evelyn Foster was five minutes from the hospital campus. It was a nice street, the kind of street young people just getting started in professional jobs might have lived on in the 1950s and '60s. There were grown Maple trees, branches tingling with red sap, getting ready to leaf out. A solid looking bank was busy across the street. Around the corner was the arts center. The buildings, a little shabby from wear but holding up, were brick and stone with large windows. If the rest of the city wasn't falling down around it, you could imagine this street in Brooklyn, New York, where the literati, actors, musicians and artists lived. Evelyn Foster was the name printed on a small piece of paper above the door buzzer for Apt. 3B. Lagarde pressed the buzzer. They waited a few minutes. He pressed it again. No response. He pressed the buzzer for 1B, then 2B.

From the intercom, a man's voice said, "Yeah?"

"Police," Lagarde said. "Would you open the front door, please?" They didn't have a warrant and being polite might work in their favor.

A man in a t-shirt and very dirty, once-blue overalls opened the door. They showed their credentials. He nodded. They walked into the narrow hallway and asked him if the super was around.

"I'm the super," the man said. He pulled on his nose. The action made Lagarde wonder if the man thought it got smaller after he said he was the super, a kind of inverse Pinocchio response. The man scratched his whiskers and then the top of his head.

"Do you live on the premises?" Lagarde said.

"Yeah, right there, number 2," the man said.

"Good, we'll knock on your door if we need you," Lagarde said.

Lagarde and Black started to walk up the three flights of stairs. By the second flight, Lagarde was convinced Ms. Foster must be in very good shape. At the top floor, he stopped to catch his breath before knocking on her door. Black didn't seem to be having any problem with his breathing. *It's easy to resent the young.*

Lagarde knocked on the door of apartment 3B and said "Police" and they waited. After a few minutes, the door was opened by a woman wearing a faded pink terry cloth bathrobe. She looked as if she had not slept well in several weeks. She was pale. Behind her glasses, her eyes were puffy. Her hair hung in greasy hanks. She did not look like a Ben Cromwell collectible. Lagarde looked behind her at the room. There were potted plants near the window that had not been watered in a while. Used tissues littered the floor by the sofa. It looked like she might have been asleep on the sofa, pillows piled up on one end, a blanket thrown over the arm at the other.

"I'm sorry if we woke you, Ms. Foster," Lagarde said, "You are Evelyn Foster, the social worker at City Hospital, right?"

Evelyn Foster nodded. "And you are?"

"I'm detective Sam Lagarde; this is Corporal Black," he showed her his badge. "We're from the Bureau of Criminal Investigations with the West Virginia State Police."

Lagarde watched the pulse at the base of her throat quicken. She paled.

"We want to talk with you about Ben Cromwell. I understand he lived with you at some point."

She nodded and put her hand on her chest.

"He was murdered on March 15th. We'd like to ask you some questions."

Evelyn Foster took a step back. Lagarde thought she was looking behind her as if she hoped there was a chair to fall into. She turned around in a circle.

"Yes," she said. "I do know him . . . he did . . . he was here, for a few months."

She looked bewildered, as if she had suddenly found herself in her pajamas in someone else's home and had no idea how she got there. She opened her mouth to say something and then stopped. She put a tissue against her mouth. She turned around twice more, her right arm leading then trailing the rest of her body. It seemed to Lagarde that she was demonstrating something, pointing to something and then changing her mind.

"I can't talk like this. I'm sorry. Do you mind if I go put some clothes on?" she said. "Please take a seat. I'll just be a few minutes." She walked toward the bedroom.

Black and Lagarde exchanged looks. Lagarde said, "Fine."

When she closed her bedroom door, Black walked around the living room and kitchen to see if there was anything in plain sight that might assist their investigation. Dirty dishes crusted with food were in the sink. The loaf of bread on the counter was sprouting green mold. There was a film of grease, like despair, over the counter. They heard drawers being opened and closed in a bureau, steps back and forth across a wooden floor, water running in the bathroom, and then a single gunshot.

Black was closest to the bedroom door. He put his hand on his gun, released the safety, then opened the door. The bedroom was empty. He walked from the bedroom into the bathroom. Evelyn Foster was sitting naked in her tub with the back of her head blown out against the tile wall. The water rushing from the tub spigot swirled her blood into spirals around her body.

CHAPTER THIRTY-THREE

FEBRUARY 20, 2014, 8 P.M.

Katrina Vander placed her hands together in the form of a steeple on the imitation walnut table in the Target coffee bar, as if she were praying or playing an old child's game of 'here's the church, here's the steeple, open the door, find all the people.' The women watched her hands because they could not look at her eyes, which were burning, brimming with tears that had never been shed.

"I am Eileen Cromwell's sister," she said. "Eileen is Ben's real mother," she added.

Ilise startled, she looked over at her mother. She jabbed her mother in the ribs with her elbow. "His mother? You mean I'm related to Ben Cromwell? He's my cousin? God, mom, why didn't you ever tell me?"

"I tried to tell you so many ways, Ilise, to just stop seeing the bum, but you weren't going to listen to me. Anyway, Eileen and I had different fathers, so you're hardly related."

"Still . . ." Ilise's words and breath trailed off. "Did Ben know?"

Katrina shook her head. "I don't think so, but that's not the point. The point is I knew Ben Cromwell when he was young. He was weird then. Your dad and I used to call him the terrorist—he was so sneaky and mean. My sister used to call me and tell me what was going on in her marriage to Robert. She knew she never should have married him. He went from being a fun loving guy to being all straight laced and go to work every day the minute she told him she was pregnant. She didn't even want to marry him, but he was so Dudley Do Right about it, had to do the right thing by the baby, yada-yada. She got stuck in that marriage. She was suffocating just sitting home, taking care of the house and the kid. But that's not the point. After a while, she used to tell me the stuff her son was doing. It was really eerie, but neither of us knew what to do about it. He used to torture her cat, fold its tail up and put a rubber band around it and watch it run around in circles trying to get it off."

Katrina took a sip of her coffee and looked around at the other women. They were now staring at her as if she were the one who tortured the cat.

"Anyway, Eileen took that as kind of funny, and she was often just a little bit tipsy by the middle of the afternoon, so some things that might not be funny to you were pretty funny to her." Katrina watched Lila turn her head away and look out the window. *You ain't no better than her, you fancy bitch.* "Ben had trouble making friends, so whenever there was a kid who wanted to come over and play with him, Eileen always bent over backwards to give the kids a good time. One afternoon she caught Ben and one of those friends sticking sparklers—you know those little firecrackers you get on the Fourth of July that you light and they shoot off sparks—anyway, they stuck one of those in the cat's butt and lit it. She was watching out the kitchen window. They were in the backyard. She ran out and rescued the cat and yelled at them, but Ben said it was his friend's idea and he didn't want to do it. So she sent the friend home and took Ben out for an ice cream cone. Then the next thing, the cat disappears, just gone and she figures it had enough of being tortured and went off to somebody else's house. Then when she's doing her fall yard clean up, she finds the half-disintegrated cat buried under some bushes with its tail cut off. She said she gagged for a long time. Couldn't even get her breath to scream. She knew it was Ben who did it, she didn't know how, but she knew it. She thought he might have strangled it."

Evelyn put her hand on top of Katrina's, as if to comfort her. "Did Eileen ever tell her husband about this stuff?"

"She tried," Katrina said and flicked off Evelyn's hand as if it were an annoying mosquito, "but she couldn't find the right words and

He hadn't even checked Cromwell's drug connections yet. Maybe they had been going down the wrong alley all this time. Maybe Violet Gold met Cromwell, gave him his ring to get some closure, and went off to Europe without a clue that the man who messed with her was dead. Maybe Robert Cromwell and Beverly Wilson were correct, he should let it go, file the case as unsolved and move on. But he couldn't. Something about it had sucked him in. He felt compelled to find out how Cromwell ended his short life in pieces on the ground near the racing stables.

Driving out of the fancy neighborhood, Lagarde said, "Let's get a real change of scene. Drive by Blue Ridge Technical and see who's got Ben Cromwell's corner now. Maybe we'll pick up some useful information."

CHAPTER FORTY-ONE

APRIL 8, 2014, 11 A.M.

Corporal Black parked the unmarked police car where they could watch the arrivals and departures of students at Blue Ridge Technical School, as well as the two street corners that framed the old warehouse where the school was located. Sure enough, there was a small-time hood in his gangsta wannabe uniform—baggy polyester sweatpants hanging below his butt. To hold them up, he had to walk as if he had shit his pants. The guy was wearing a knit cap even though it was nearly spring. Three rows of ten karat gold necklaces were hanging from his scrawny neck. The outfit was capped by an unzipped sweat jacket exposing a bony chest and a load of attitude. Occasionally, a student with a book bag walked by the guy and, almost without stopping, slipped him bills for a small cellophane packet in a quick-handed exchange that would go unnoticed if you were just driving by.

"Got him carrying, at least," Black said. "I'll take a photo of the next buy and we'll have him dead to rights."

Sam Lagarde nodded. He did not envy the police who had this detail. Drugs were everywhere and it seemed like everyone was doing them. Hell, rich people bought their drugs online and had them delivered by FedEx. Drugs were the real epidemic and nobody had a vaccine. "We're not arresting him for possession with intent," Lagarde said. "We just want information."

"Right," Black said disappointed.

After watching a few more dollars-for-drugs exchanges, they got out of their car and started to walk over to the corner where the guy did his business. He watched them, assuming they were buyers, then he 'made them.' Lagarde thought he might be nearsighted, didn't wear glasses because that was uncool, and didn't realize they were cops un-

Robert kind of lorded it over her. He loved his boy, but he sure wasn't paying a lot of attention. He was mostly working all the time and going on trips for work. She was alone with Ben a lot. But that's not the point."

"Really, Katrina, what is the point?" Lila Townsend said.

Katrina felt heat rising up from her knees to her neck. *Who does this uppity doctor think she is? She got caught with her pants down just like Ilise did. She's no better than anyone else here.* "I'm getting to that," she said to Lila. Lila looked down at the table, sat back in the chair, and looked straight at Katrina.

"When Ben turned eight, he had a friend who used to come over a lot, to hang out and play, sleep-overs, you know, the normal friend stuff that kids do. So it's the summer and Eileen gets them one of those plastic swimming pools, the ones you can put about six inches of water in, jump into, slide around a little, just have some kid fun. Ben and his friend are all excited. They take the hose and fill it up with water right to the top so it's almost sloshing over. Then they strip down to their underpants and jump in. Eileen is watching from the kitchen window. It looks like they're having a great time. She goes and makes them some peanut butter and jelly sandwiches and lemonade and takes it out on a tray to them. She puts the food on the picnic table she's got there in the back yard and calls them over. They come over all dripping wet and she rubs their faces dry with a big towel she brought out. The friend is shaking, like he's cold, so Eileen wraps him up in the towel and rubs his back. Anyway, they eat the sandwiches and take a gulp of the lemonade and then they're ready to go back in the pool, so she lets them cause even if they get a cramp, it's just six inches deep, they could stand up and get out of the water.

"She goes back in the house with the tray so the ants don't start crawling all over the plates. She drinks some lemonade with a little spike added to it and then puts the lemonade away and washes the dishes and when she looks up, she sees Ben sitting on the other kid's back in the pool. The kid is face down in the water. Ben is as calm as if nothing is happening. He's got his fingers in the kid's hair and he's bobbing the boy's head up and down like he's playing a game. This goes on for a couple of minutes and then it hits Eileen that the kid could be drowning. She runs into the backyard and she's calling Ben's name and Ben just looks up at her and gives her this strange look. When she gets to the pool, she yanks the kid out of the water, but he's dead, drowned, gone. She looks at Ben and he says, 'We were just playing horsey, Mom. He wanted it.' She tried to revive the kid, but she couldn't. She called 9-1-1, but they couldn't do anything. The police came. They blamed her, yet chalked it up to an accident. But she knew, she knew that Ben did it on purpose, like he did with the cat, just to see what would happen."

Katrina looked around at her small audience. They had turned pale, their hands were either on their chests, cheeks or covering their mouths. She had their full attention. "Do you get it now?" she said.

"Where was this?" Lila Townsend said.

"Springdale, where they lived before Eileen died."

Lila Townsend wrapped her arms around herself and looked out the window. She was ready.

CHAPTER THIRTY-FOUR

APRIL 5, 2014, 12:30 P.M.

Sam Lagarde's first thought about Evelyn Foster's suicide was simple: *Shit. Now I'll have to do all that paperwork.* He looked at Black, who was on his cell phone almost the instant after finding Foster's head blown out in the bathroom, calling in the incident, pulling in another criminal investigations team so that he and Lagarde could be cleared of involvement in the death. They waited for the team to arrive to make a thorough search of the woman's apartment, document the suicide and take their statements. The team would get an autopsy on Foster, to see if she was on drugs or something else, or if she had any other physical problem that might have been the motive for her suicide. By the time they were done, they would know this woman's life inside out, but Lagarde wasn't sure that knowing anything about Evelyn Foster would help him figure out who killed Ben Cromwell. Her suicide would seem to indicate she was guilty, or complicit in some way in the murder, but maybe their showing up at her door and saying that Cromwell had been murdered was the last straw for her. Maybe she was thrown into grief and couldn't imagine her life without him. Lagarde wished now that they had found her sooner, taken her into the office for questioning . . . but spilled milk and all that.

He stood in the living room looking out the large window at the bank across the street. He tried to imagine Ben Cromwell in this space. It didn't seem large enough for Cromwell. Lagarde guessed Cromwell would have felt claustrophobic here, maybe more so in a relationship with Foster. Any arrangement Cromwell had with the woman had to be pragmatic, not romantic. There was no saved stash of syrupy sweet greeting cards from him, no romantic notes any-where in her desk. There was no indication that Cromwell had ever lived in this space except that Evelyn Foster had just said so. A quick search of email on her laptop showed no emails from Cromwell at all, although the forensics team would go over the computer and all its files completely and give him a report of anything useful. Lagarde recalled that Cromwell had called Evelyn Foster repeatedly, seemingly in a panic, a few months ago. She had not returned his calls, at least on that phone number. Lagarde guessed the relationship, if it could be called that, ended last year in November. The last email Evelyn Foster sent appeared to be to her supervisor at the hospital on March 14th saying she was ill and needed to take a month of sick leave, of which she had six weeks accumulated. The last email she received was from the women's clinic in Hagerstown, Maryland reminding her of a follow up appointment on March 12th. Something was going on with Ms. Foster, something that made her sick enough to stay home from work. But as far as providing any clues for their original homicide case, Evelyn Foster appeared to be a closed door. Whatever she knew about Ben Cromwell's death, she made sure she didn't tell them.

Corporal Lawrence Black walked over to Lagarde and said, "Look at this." Black handed him a letter on Hagerstown Women's Clinic stationery. The letter said that Evelyn Foster was HIV positive and should come into the clinic for her follow up visit and health consultation on March 12. The letter was dated February 24, 2014.

"Where was this?" Lagarde said.

"On the night table by her bed. And there's more. On her phone, there's a message from a doctor's office confirming that she was pregnant, about four months, and asking her to call to set up her prenatal appointments. That message was dated January 21, 2014."

Lagarde shook his head. The woman certainly had a lot on her plate. She already had the gun before they arrived. Maybe this was the day she was going to pull the trigger whether he and Black showed up at her door or not. He looked around her apartment. She had already given up on life. It just took one more little nudge from the goon squad to push her over the edge.

"Got to get some air," he said to Black.

He walked down the stairs and stood outside the building. She must have parked somewhere on this street near the building. He made a mental note to remind Black to have her car impounded and searched. Maybe they would find something in it that was useful. He looked down the street toward King. He breathed in deeply. Maybe fresh air would clear his head. Two thoughts came together: *Ilise Vander was HIV positive; Evelyn Foster was HIV positive.* As far as Lagarde could see, that made the probability that Violet Gold and Lila Townsend were HIV positive better than fifty-fifty. And that might be a motive for murder. The question was, did one of them do it alone or did they know each other and conspire together to get the job done?

Should I go for a ride on Jake, or should I call Beverly Wilson? Both thoughts were like a tonic. He dialed Beverly Wilson's phone number and when she answered the phone he said, "How about going for a ride with me?"

To his great surprise, she said, "Sure. I'm at home. You can pick me up."

"Be there in two hours," he said, suddenly noticing that the forsythia bushes at the front of the bank had bloomed in all their starry yellow glory.

CHAPTER THIRTY-FIVE

APRIL 5, 2014, 4 P.M.

The first thing Sam Lagarde asked Beverly Wilson when she opened the door of her house was whether she had any mud boots. "It gets a little deep out this time of year," he explained.

As it turned out, she did have a pair of rubber Wellies that had a little heel. He noticed the heel with a feeling of happiness. *Just enough for hanging on in a stirrup.* He also noticed she had a barn coat similar to his own and was wearing a soft-looking green scarf. She placed the boots on the floor of the back seat of his car and hopped in the front. Lagarde thought she might be glad to have this sudden reprieve from her solitude. She wasn't talkative but she was alert. He noticed now that her feelings played across the screen of her face and if he was attentive, they wouldn't need words. He wondered how she learned to be so quiet. Most women he knew just yakked and yakked until he wanted to put plugs in his ears. On the other hand, her silence forced him to talk more. Maybe it was a strategy on her part; the other guy had to make the first move all the time with Mrs. Wilson. Maybe that gave her time to assess people. Of course, the minute he had his conclusions drawn, she overturned them.

"Do you have any more information about who killed Ben?" she asked him as he turned off Route 81 onto Route 9 towards Charles Town and Harpers Ferry.

"I have more information but it's like having more pieces of the puzzle that still don't fit together," he said.

"Tell me some of your pieces."

Sam Lagarde decided he liked her directness. It was possible he would like whatever she did. It was very comfortable sitting next to her, both of them going in the same direction, looking out over the passing landscape. They were about half way to their destination driving on the new overpass above what used to be a two-hundred acre orchard for apples and peaches, now cut in half for the very convenient highway from Martinsburg all the way to Berryville, Virginia. Beverly was looking at the acres of trees still bare but getting ready to bloom into a galaxy of pink and white stars.

"It's a shame about the orchards," she said. "Can't really call this area apple valley anymore." She turned her head and looked at him. "So, what do you know?

"We went to talk with Evelyn Foster, the woman who called you, today. She was in a bad way. She committed suicide while we were there. Apparently she was pregnant and was HIV positive."

He paused. That was a lot of painful information to dump on Beverly at once. He looked over at her. She was staring out her passenger side window. Nothing showed on her face but the changing light from the window.

"God, how horrible for you," she said.

That was the last thing he expected her to say. He waited to see if she would say more, maybe defend Ben or claim he had nothing to do with what ailed Evelyn Foster. Maybe express sympathy for the woman. But she went back to looking out her window as if she were sightseeing.

"She's the second woman Ben was seeing who is HIV positive," Lagarde said. "There's a nineteen-year-old who had a relationship with him who is also infected. It's possible there were two more women who are too."

Beverly Wilson put her hand to her mouth. She closed her eyes. She lowered her head. She breathed deeply for a few moments. "You think Ben infected them," she said.

Lagarde exited the highway onto Wiltshire Road, drove a few miles past fields that would be sown with corn soon and turned right onto Paynes Ford Road. This was the view that took his pain away. Beverly looked out the window and sighed.

"How is it possible that the world is so beautiful and so ugly at the same time?" she said.

"Exactly," he said. He drove slowly up the dirt lane and pulled up in front of his house, turned off the car, got out and walked around the other side and opened the door for her. "Put your boots on here," he said. She did as he said, putting her tennis shoes on the floorboard. Lagarde's interpretation of this action was that she had no intention of coming into his house. "Let's walk down to the paddock," he said. "There's a horse there I'd like you to meet."

She smiled at him. For an incredible instant Sam Lagarde had the sensation of floating. That was ridiculous of course. He wasn't twelve, he was sixty. He weighed himself down with similar thoughts so that his feet touched the ground as he walked with Beverly Wilson over to say hello to Jake. It took all his control not to take her hand as they walked. When they arrived at the paddock, she leaned against the rail and Jake walked over slowly, assessing her. He shook his head a little, nickered and then leaned his head down over the fence and seemed to whisper in her ear. Lagarde watched as delight bloomed on the woman's face as suddenly as crocuses opening in early spring. She reached up and stroked Jake's neck. She whispered something to the horse.

"What are you telling him?" Lagarde asked.

"That he's the best antidote for sorrow I've ever met," Beverly said.

Lagarde nodded. Nothing more needed to be said. He watched the woman and the horse get acquainted. He was completely happy. Everything else slipped away.

CHAPTER THIRTY-SIX

APRIL 6, 2014, 11:30 A.M.

Sam Lagarde hated interviews with the bereaved family members. It was like walking into a dark tunnel without a flashlight. You were going to step in something you would prefer not to or get bushwhacked by something you didn't see coming. But he'd put this interview with Ben Cromwell's parents off as long as he could. On the hour drive to Columbia, Maryland from West Virginia's Eastern Panhandle, he thought of all kinds of ways to approach the interview. The minute they'd crossed over the Potomac River Bridge he started feeling uncomfortable, as if he'd forgotten to take something important with him like his wallet or badge. Corporal Black was driving. Lagarde had time to think through everything he knew or didn't know. He was hoping somehow the parents would know something that would help him put this case together. Maybe they knew someone who had a grudge against Cromwell. Maybe he had communicated with them just before he died. Lagarde also had time to figure out what his opening line would be. He discarded ten or twelve versions.

At the door of the house, he introduced himself and Corporal Black, showed his credentials. Sarah Cromwell nodded, gestured toward the living room, stepped aside and said nothing. Lagarde had a moment to notice how like her mother she was.

Lagarde walked into the living room and said to Robert Cromwell, "I'm very sorry for your loss."

Robert Cromwell sat with his elbows on his knees and his head in his hands. He stared at the floor. He said nothing.

"I'd like to ask you a few questions. Your answers may help us figure out who killed Ben," Lagarde said.

"Does it matter?" Robert Cromwell said.

Lagarde was surprised by the question. He couldn't remember a time when another bereaved family member had ever asked that. Almost universally, people wanted to find the perpetrator, bring him to justice, revenge the death of their loved ones. "What do you mean?" Lagarde said.

"I mean, what does it matter who killed him? He's dead. He won't be restored because you put your hands on the person who killed him."

"Well, we don't want a killer running around free. We are a lawful society. We want to take dangerous people off the streets so that they don't harm anyone else." Lagarde felt like he was talking to a truculent five-year-old.

"Then you should have taken Ben off the streets. If your system of laws had been any use, he would have been in jail where apparently he was safer than out in the world."

"Are you saying you think Ben's killer was justified?"

"No." Robert Cromwell shook his head. "I'm saying the whole thing is senseless. I'm saying that if or when you catch his killer, that won't bring Ben back." He raised his head and looked directly at Lagarde. His face was ashen. There were deep circles under his eyes. He looked like a man who had seen his worst nightmare play out while he was awake.

"We have to try, Mr. Cromwell, otherwise we just have tribal justice and anarchy."

Robert Cromwell waved his hand in the air as if to dismiss the argument from the screen of his mind. "Here's what I know," he said. "Ben had AIDs. Ben rarely worked. Ben went on alcohol and drug binges. His drug of choice was heroin, but he'd put anything in his body. Ben never stayed with a cure, not his AIDs meds, not AA, not a shrink. Ben sold drugs when he had them. He stole things and pawned them. He probably had plenty of people infuriated with him, but I don't know any of them. Ben had a series of girlfriends and he almost never told them he was sick. He was a walking epidemic maker. The last time I talked to him, he said he had gotten an Ilise something pregnant and that it didn't matter if the baby was born with AIDs because there was treatment for that now. He was cavalier about everyone else's life and he wanted what he wanted when he wanted it."

He paused for a minute. Sarah Cromwell was standing by the window with her hand over her mouth weeping.

"And I loved him anyway. That's all I know." Robert Cromwell sat back in the chair and shielded his eyes with his hand.

Lagarde nodded. "Thank you, Mr. Cromwell. That's all for now. If I have any more questions, I'll call. We'll see ourselves out."

Sarah Cromwell walked with them to the door. "One more thing, Mrs. Cromwell," Lagarde said. "Do you know when Ben called your husband and told him about Ilise?"

"No," she said. "I didn't know about that at all. He didn't tell me." She wiped her cheeks with her hand. "Sorry," she said.

Lagarde and Black walked down the walk to their car. Black said, "Ilise Vander was pregnant? Do you think Marc Delany knew that?" Lagarde and Black exchanged looks.

"Let's go find out," Lagarde said.

CHAPTER THIRTY-SEVEN

APRIL 6, 2014, 1 P.M.

Winter was finally over. This had been the longest, grayest, coldest winter Beverly Wilson could remember in her entire life. They were teased by sunny days where the temperature never climbed above seventeen degrees and then plunged into day after day of snow and ice. She woke up some mornings to skies so dark she thought she had slept until dusk. Somehow her entire state had been picked up from its normal location on the globe and plopped down where Alaska should be. There were days when it was below ten in Martinsburg and a balmy thirty-six degrees in Anchorage. Something beyond global climate change was going on, at least the way it was being presented in the media. At the same time as the eastern United States was covered in snow since October, California was experiencing a drought.

Beverly knocked the dirt off her gardening gloves and stood up to survey her backyard improvements. She didn't have a lot of space here but she had divided the yard into a round stone patio big enough for a table and chairs surrounded by plantings with a little winding walk of stone pavers that led to the back gate. She filled the yard with an apple, dogwood and pear trees for their spring flowers surrounded by boxwood for their sturdiness and tangy smell, azaleas just because the color of the flowers brought her joy every time they bloomed in the spring, a few low-growing pines, and of course a perennial bed for more color in the summer. She had filled that bed with lavender, irises, tulips, lilies, black-eyed Susan, daisies, colorful flowering plants that would come back year after year without too much work. Planning a garden seemed to her to be the same as planning a painting. It was a composition of complementary colors. She had worried about the bushes she and Ben planted in early March, but it looked like they had made it. It was amazing how resilient nature could be.

She knew her former green friends would shake their heads in misery over her error and list all the animals that were extinct, but she didn't think this climate change was caused by human habitation. There had been alternating ice ages and warming periods in the history of the earth before humans, when there were no factories spewing poisonous particulates, no pig farms. Were humans fouling the environment? No question. Yet the latest item she saw on the dangers of ammonia from farm animals made her lapse into giggles every so many hours for an entire day. But she had washed her hands of politics a long time ago, stopped watching television news almost a decade before, and preferred the serenity of staring at a blank canvas to having the false sense that she knew anything about what was going on in the world or could do anything about it. If she stuck to color, she could keep her sanity. It seemed to Beverly that was the only job left to her.

In the middle of these ponderings, now hoping for rain to water her newly planted bushes in the backyard, the phone rang. Beverly dropped her gloves on the patio and raced into the house to answer the landline phone, another anachronism in the world of instant electronic communication. Her daughter Sarah was always nudging her to terminate this phone contract and just use her cell phone. But Beverly always retorted that on September 11, 2001 all the cell phones in New York City went dead. If there was another attack, she wanted to be able to connect with her daughter. It was worth the forty-six dollars a month, she said to Sarah, just in case. It was her insurance against silence.

She picked up the receiver and said hello. The caller responded with a thin hi. Beverly didn't recognize the voice.

"Who is this?" Beverly said.

"This is Ilise Vander," the voice said, "I got your number from the front of Ben's journal that I took from his jacket," the voice trailed off into sobs.

Beverly rolled her eyes. Not another one of Ben's endless series of discarded women. The boy was dead and they were still calling her. She said, "Yes," in her tersest voice.

"I'm sorry for bothering you," Ilise said, gaining control over her voice. "I just needed to talk to someone, sort some stuff out. Do you think I could come over to your house and talk to you?"

"No," Beverly said. It sounded cold, she knew, but Ilise Vander was none of her business.

"What should I call you? Can I call you Grandma?"

"No, you cannot. My name is Mrs. Wilson."

"Please, Mrs. Wilson, I don't know who else to talk to. My mom doesn't care. I can't talk to Marc. I can't tell anyone what I did. And really, I don't have anywhere else to go. I'm too screwed up to work so I don't have any money for my own place."

"Really, Ilise, this is none of my business. I don't want to get involved with you. I'm sorry that Ben hurt you, but I'm not able to fix it."

"No, you don't get it, I hurt Ben."

"What do you mean?"

"I killed him. Well, we all killed him, but I was part of it."

"You all? I think I don't really want to hear this. You should call the police."

"Please, Mrs. Wilson. I think I'm going crazy. I need to talk to you."

Against her better judgment, Beverly gave Ilise her address and waited downstairs until the girl arrived at her front door. She berated herself for giving in so easily. There was something about the girl's desperation that both saddened and frightened her. If Ilise was capable of killing Ben, then she could certainly kill an old lady. But twenty minutes later Beverly's first impression of Ilise Vander was that she was a waif and couldn't hurt anyone. The girl was so slender she looked like a sapling before it had grown branches. It was impossible that internal organs were stored somewhere in that thin body. She wore no makeup. The strange pink streaks in her hair appeared to be fading.

Over tea, Beverly heard the whole story of the girl's relationship with Ben. Beverly's heart felt like a rag being rung out. How could someone she loved cause so much hurt? How could she love someone who behaved like this? She wondered about herself, her ability to separate out Ben's behavior toward others in order to continue loving him. *It must be a survival mechanism.*

Then Ilise told Beverly what she read in Ben's journal. "He said he was pimping me out," Ilise said. "He said he got drugs in me and then let his boys have me for fifty dollars." The girl sobbed. Beverly handed her tissues.

"I'm not defending him," Beverly said, "but sometimes he claimed he did things he never did. You can't believe what he says. Do you remember this happening?"

"No, but he wrote that I passed out, so I wouldn't know." She began wailing again.

Beverly waited. She noticed that the girl had a habit of pulling on her hair when she was crying. She couldn't imagine any words that would console the girl. "Did you bring the journal with you?"

"No, I left it under my pillow in my room."

"Was there anything in the journal that you think I should know?"

"He said he was playing you, but that you were smarter than he thought you would be."

Beverly grimaced. Ben certainly made it hard to love him. "Did you read the journal before you killed him?"

"No, I didn't have it till after. I didn't tell the others about it. When I took it, I hid it in my clothes. They don't know I have it. We weren't supposed to keep anything of his and we're not supposed to ever talk to each other again. I don't see how it matters whether they know about the journal or not. They hate him enough on their own without it."

"Having the journal in your possession proves that you were the last person to see him, I think, Ilise. It's evidence. It might contain information that will help the police." Even now, Beverly couldn't believe that Ilise, plus whoever the other women were, could kill Ben. It had to have been a gang of depraved men.

"Nobody has to know I have it," Ilise said.

Beverly kept her hands folded together on her lap and listened to the girl talk through her sobs. Ilise seemed to be truly confused, her story was a muddle. There was nothing Beverly could do. It was over. The harm was done, in all directions. But maybe she could help Ilise calm down, figure out what to do next. Somewhere in her mind was the niggling thought that she was being played, but she squashed it. If this were Ben sitting next to her telling her this, she wouldn't believe it. Why did she believe Ilise? Just because she was female? Not a good enough reason.

"Does your mother know you're here?" Beverly asked.

"Yeah, I told her I was coming to see you."

"What do you want to do?"

"Mom says I shouldn't be at home, that I won't hold up if the police talk to me. Could I maybe stay with you for a while?"

"So your plan is to get away with murder?" *Maybe a little verbal shock therapy might jog the girl into finally telling the truth.*

Ilise look shocked, as if she had not realized that what she was saying was that she committed murder.

"My mom says we just put down a rabid animal, that it's not murder."

It was Beverly's turn to be shocked. She needed some time to think. She couldn't see a clear way out of the bind she just put herself in. She now knew something the police should know, even if it was this child's fantasy. But, really, it wasn't her story to tell. The girl should tell them. She should never have let Ilise come to her house and disrupt her life. *When in doubt, do nothing,* she reminded herself.

"I'm not going to hide you from the police, Ilise. If they come here looking for you, I'll tell them you're here." She paused and looked for a long time at the red blown glass pot with glass leaves on her coffee table. "I won't call them right now but you cannot stay here."

Ilise looked up at Beverly. "Sounds like splitting hairs to me," she said.

Beverly smiled in spite of her sadness. The girl did have some spunk. She would need it.

CHAPTER THIRTY-EIGHT

APRIL 6, 2014, 2:30 P.M.

Before Lagarde and Black set out for Ilise Vander's home in Martinsburg, they stopped back at their Troop 2 Headquarters in Kearneysville. They found a preliminary medical examiner's report on Evelyn Foster waiting for them. She had been pregnant and apparently had an abortion recently, within the last month. *That might have been the reason she took sick leave.* The HIV test showed she was in fact positive. She was taking an anti-retroviral medication, probably for the HIV, and also diazepam, "Valium to you," the medical examiner said in the phone call Black made to go over the report. Lagarde could understand why Evelyn Foster wanted to take a drug to treat her anxiety. She would have had plenty of anxiety.

"Having the abortion and taking the meds seems to indicate that she intended to go on living. Otherwise, why go to the trouble?" Black said. "Maybe the gun was for something else. Maybe she was afraid of Cromwell and kept it in her bedroom just in case he showed up at her home. Maybe she intended to kill him if he did show up. Somebody else beat her to it."

"Or, she shot herself to avoid talking to us," Lagarde said. "A lawyer would have been a better option, if she wanted to live. I think that little circle dance she did indicated her state of mind. She couldn't light on one way to go. She was locked up in her mind, with too many conflicting thoughts. If she wasn't the killer, I think she knew who was."

Black was looking at his computer screen. "We got a first take on what was in Foster's car. You might find this interesting."

Lagarde got up from his chair and walked behind Black to peer over his shoulder at the screen. "Make that larger," he said.

Black looked up at him and smirked. He held down the Ctrl key and pushed the wheel on the mouse. Everything on the screen got larger, including the type in the preliminary report, which said the crime scene technician had found a few drops of blood on the floor of Ms. Foster's trunk. That was it—no hairs, fibers, fingers or feet—just the blood. They had enough to run a DNA match and would let Black and Lagarde know later whose it was, if they could.

"That might be a break," Lagarde said. "Let's go see if Ilise Vander can tell us anything about the demise of Ben Cromwell."

They drove up to Martinsburg in silence. Lagarde was trying to do the arithmetic of this case in his head. He had 1 and 2 and lots of x's and y's and no idea if he should add, multiply or divide. If the blood on the floor of Evelyn Foster's car was Ben Cromwell's, that pretty much placed her at the scene of the murder. She must have taken at least some of those body parts away in her car . . . unless he was getting ahead of himself. It hardly seemed possible that a woman who was pregnant, had an abortion, and who had recently been notified that she was HIV positive would have the emotional strength to butcher a man and fling his body parts to the four winds. It would have taken her hours to get the job done. If she took only some of the parts, there were others in on the murder with her.

He remembered his idea of a coven.

There could be other reasons for Cromwell's blood to be in the trunk, like she had a flat tire and he cut his hand putting on the spare tire. Although it didn't seem like Cromwell was the white knight kind of guy who would help anyone fix a flat. It could be Foster's blood, or someone else's. Lagarde would have to wait on the match. But, if it was Cromwell's blood and Foster carted away a bagful of body parts, where would she take them? Was she the one who dropped the head in the spa dumpster? Would she have the nerve to take Cromwell's body parts to the hospital? They dispose of body parts every day. There would be a system. Didn't he read somewhere that the hospital had a permit for an incinerator? There must be some way the hospital inventories what goes into the incinerator, or whatever they do with body parts stuff they discard. There were probably federal rules governing disposal that they would have to follow.

"If she burned body parts in the hospital's incinerator, maybe she borrowed the murder weapon from the hospital," he said out loud.

"What?" Black said. "Who's burning what parts?"

"Foster, if she transported Cromwell's body parts in her car, dropping them off at various dumpsters all over creation, would she have dumped some at the hospital in their incinerator?"

Black's eyebrows went up. "Worth checking on," he said as he pulled up in front of the Kentucky Street house where Ilise Vander lived with her mother.

They got out of the car and walked up onto the front porch. Black rang the doorbell and Lagarde pulled out his credentials to show to whomever opened the door. To their surprise it was Marc Delany.

"Hey," Marc Delany said to Black.

"Hi, there, Mr. Delany," Black said. "We'd like to ask Ilise some questions about Ben Cromwell's murder."

"You can't do that," Delany said.

"Really, why is that?" Black said.

"She's not here."

"Okay, when will she be back?"

"Not for a while."

"What's a while?"

Delany looked down at the toes of his work boots, he looked over his shoulder back into the house, he looked out past Black as if there were something significant happening in the street. He ran his hand through his hair. Black just kept looking at Delany.

"Her mother sent her away to her aunt's in Florida," Delany said. "She needs some sunshine and a break from here."

Lagarde had to admit that the kid looked miserable. He was a terrible liar. But they had no warrant and needed permission from the owner of the house to enter. "Is Ilise's mother here?"

"Yeah, she's here. She's inside," Delany said without moving from the doorway, which he filled completely.

"Could we speak with her, please?" Lagarde said.

Delany called over his shoulder, "Katrina, they want to talk to you. Is that ok?"

They heard a woman's voice say, "Sure, why not? Tell 'em to come in."

Katrina Vander was wearing an outfit she probably shouldn't have, tight black jeans, tight red fuzzy sweater, black suede ankle boots. Her very curly, deeply auburn hair was piled up on top of her head. Her lipstick was a shade of red Lagarde associated with menstrual blood. He wondered if she was a witch.

The coven.

She was sitting with her legs drawn up on a purple couch. The living room wasn't large and was filled by one sofa, one orange chair, a fake walnut coffee table with an overflowing ashtray and a few empty bottles of Bud. A dining area with a Formica table and four straight back chairs led to the efficiency kitchen. The two front windows were flanked by floor to ceiling purple panels. *Some HGTV design scheme was at work here,* Lagarde concluded, *but had been interrupted before it was completed.* There was a short hall and what appeared to be two bedrooms and a bathroom off the hall. *The Vanders weren't living in the lap of luxury, but the place was big enough for two people and tolerably neat except for the smell of smoked cigarettes.*

"Mrs. Vander, I'm . . ." Lagarde started to say, showing his credentials.

"Yeah, yeah, I heard all that stuff from Marc when you guys talked to him up at Bigmart. What do you want?"

"We are interviewing people who knew Ben Cromwell to find out who killed him," Lagarde said.

"I never met the bastard," Katrina Vander said. "Glad of it, too." She crossed her arms across her substantial breasts.

"But you know that your daughter was seeing him?"

"Yes, she saw him all right, and he made her crazy. Do you know my sweet girl tried to commit suicide because of that monster?"

"No, I didn't know that" Lagarde lied. "What else happened?"

"He gave her AIDs," she yelled, "he infected her with all kinds of poxes, those things they call social diseases. He was a social disease himself. I'm glad he's dead." She nodded her head to emphasize her point.

"Is your daughter Ilise pregnant?" Lagarde asked.

"What? No way. And if she was, we wouldn't be keeping that punk's baby, I can tell you."

"Do you have any idea who might have killed him?" Lagarde said.

"Nope. Not a clue. But if you find the guy who did it, you should give him a parade. Get one of those Presidential medals and pin it on him."

"So you think a man killed Ben Cromwell."

"Who else could it be? You don't think my little Ilise who weighs a hundred pounds soaking wet could've knocked off a guy that size?"

"Do you think we could look in Ilise's room to see if there's anything there that might help us find the guy who killed Cromwell?"

"Help yourself," she said. She pointed down the hall and lit a cigarette. She inhaled and blew the smoke in their direction. "First door on the right."

Black and Lagarde walked down the short hall to the bedroom on the right. It was a girly-girl's room trending to punk, pink and black, music diva posters, black nail polish, lipsticks from pink to purple and several different kinds of makeup on the dresser. There were surprisingly no electronic devices. *She must have taken them with her to Florida, or wherever she was,* Lagarde assumed. They looked under the bed, opened the drawers, looked in the closet. Nothing of interest. Lagarde ran a hand under her pillow and pulled out a journal. He flipped through it. It wasn't Ilise's diary, it was Ben Cromwell's. He held it up to show Black, who was flipping through some fashion magazines he found on the floor of the closet.

"Might prove useful," Lagarde said. "The question is, when did

Ilise get the journal? Did he leave it with her before the murder or did she pick it up off the ground right after?"

They walked back into the living room where Katrina Vander and Marc Delany were sitting companionably without speaking. They were watching a streaming rerun of *The Walking Dead* on the five-foot wide television.

"Okay if we take this?" Lagarde asked. "Looks like it belonged to Ben, and Ilise seems to have left it here."

"Yeah, sure, get that creep's stuff out of my house," Katrina said.

"We'll come back if we have more questions," Black said. He handed his card to Katrina who leaned over to take it from him, displaying her significant cleavage.

It occurred to Lagarde that she might like younger men. Marc Delany seemed very much at home with her.

Black met Lagarde's eyes, grimaced and shook his head. "Not my type," Black mouthed.

They went back to the front door. Lagarde turned to look at Mrs. Vander, who was lighting another cigarette. "One more thing," he said. "You mentioned you worked with Marc at Bigmart. What do you do there?"

"I'm a butcher," she said, winking at him.

Lagarde pulled the door of the Vander house closed behind him and he and Black walked to the car and drove away. While Black was navigating the narrow streets in Martinsburg to begin the eighteen mile drive back to Headquarters, Lagarde started leafing through Cromwell's journal starting from the back. There weren't many entries. The guy wasn't big on words. Most of the journal was blank. He flipped to the front of the book.

There was a drawing, maybe what was supposed to be a self portrait, at the beginning of the pages on which Cromwell had written. There were a few names and telephone numbers on the first page. They would have to call all of them. Then about fifty pages of the journal were blank. Some pages had been ripped out at the binding, as if Cromwell used the front section for notes he later discarded. Cromwell's diary, sporadic as it was, started about the middle of the bound journal. Was that for secrecy? Maybe he figured he had a long time to fill up the book and something important would occur to him later.

"The guy had some talent," Lagarde said, and showed the front page with what appeared to be a self-portrait drawing to Black, who glanced over and looked back out the front windshield to make sure he was still in his lane.

"Thought a lot about himself, didn't he?" Black asked sarcastically.

Lagarde nodded. He paged through the book. Periodically, he said "God," or "Jesus" or "Holy shit."

"Okay," Black said, "looks like you're the one having all the fun. Just read some of the entries to me."

"Well, he does a good job of making it clear he was dealing drugs. He says he used pages from the journal to make little pill packets to sell. If he were still alive, we might be able to use this document to indict him for a felony or two. But the real gist of what he's writing is how little he thought of women. They were all whores or bitches to him. He used them up and spit them out."

"Yeah, like what?"

"So for instance, here's what he wrote about his grandmother back in November of 2012:

Beverly gave me this journal to write my stories and poems in. She thinks I'm a writer. Totally got her wrapped around my finger. Just took putting in a few plants for her to get all warm and fuzzy. She asked me if I wanted to come for Thanksgiving. I'm working on breaking her down about letting me smoke in her house. Once I get that, it'll be easy to let me take a drink, a little glass of wine. From there, I'm good to go. I could live there. Couldn't stand that old place she had in Burkittsville. Always thought some witch was going to jump up at me. And too damn much work all the time, every day. But it wouldn't be a bad

*thing to inherit her new place when she drops dead. That's got to
be soon. That old bastard she was married to is already gone."*

"You might be reading into it, you know," Black said. "Lots of grandkids
are irreverent about their grandmothers. They don't have any respect
for old people and they talk crap, but that doesn't mean they're evil."

"I don't think I'm reading into anything. It's all laid out right
here. The entries start in November of 2012 and go until March 14,
2014. He didn't write a lot during that two year period, but he wrote
enough. He writes about meeting Ilise, Evelyn, Lila and Violet. He
knows that Lila gets mad at him and doesn't want him around. He's
bored out of his mind with Evelyn and after a while he knows Evelyn
has had it with him. He says some vile things about how he's going to
use Ilise to make some money, not just pimping her out, but something worse than that."

"Read me that part so I can see what you mean," Black said keeping his eyes on the road as he eased onto the highway.

"December 2012, Cromwell wrote,

*"Got some X and some oxy for my little girl. Gonna see what
she'll do when she's really mellow. Don't want to put no track
marks on her pretty arms. I got some friends I've been telling
about her; they're anxious to give her a try. I figure I can get
$50 a pop from each of them. If I dose her right, she won't even
remember. I just tell her we had the most amazing night. She
won't be able to walk after, but I'll tell her that just means she
gave me all the lovin' I needed. If I train her right, she'll be good
for at least three or four years till she gets scaggy."*

"Right. Our murder victim is a piece of work, all right," Black said. "I
think we already knew that. Does the journal give us any clues about
who might have murdered him?"

For a while, neither of them said anything, as if they were trying to recover from the image Cromwell's words had planted in their brains. Lagarde continued to read to himself.

"Holy hell," Lagarde said. "Katrina Vander lied. Remember she said she didn't know Cromwell? Well, I was wondering how she knew he was a, how'd she put it, a 'guy that size'? Here's the answer. She did know him, in the Biblical way."

"Why, what does Cromwell say?"

"On December 23, 2012, he wrote:

"Got my Christmas present early. Ilise had to work late for the rush. All the women getting dolled up for the holidays, she says. Said she was doing color all day. So I'm there at the house chillin out in her bedroom when her mom bursts in the door. Her boobs are practically popping out of her top. She takes one look at me and says let's see what Ilise is all hot up about and pulls off her panties and hikes up her skirt. So I just pull her tits right out of her shirt and squeeze them and she's ready. I like a bitch who's always in heat. No wasting time hanging from the chandeliers. I fucked that woman every way I could think of, front, back, upside down, legs in the air, 69. Totally understand where Ilise gets it from now. And then, she's like done with me, she gets up, grabs her clothes, goes in the bathroom and I hear water running in the tub. When she comes out, all shiny clean and lookin ten-years-older without her makeup, she says to me, that's it, no more. And get the fuck out. So here I am at Beverly's like I just want to spend time with her during the holidays. She's making cookies. She got on the phone with Dad and told him I was there and she'd bring me down for dinner on the day. Not sure I can make it that long. I might need to take a break before that."

"It does sound pretty conclusive that Vander knew him," Black said.

"Are you smirking?" Lagarde asked, looking over at Black.

"Look, Sam, if it hadn't turned out so bad for Cromwell, and you just met him and saw his journal, would you believe that stuff? I think he made up that stuff about Katrina Vander to make himself look good. Hell, maybe he made up all of it. That journal is like his mirror. That's why there's that drawing. He looks in there, scans a few pages he wrote before, it tells him who he is. Maybe he has to keep checking back so he can feel real, just like those kids who lie about who they are on Facebook. They're making up a life they don't have so they can be more important, or more appealing, or popular because their own life is so normal and boring."

"Wow, that's pretty deep, Larry," Lagarde said. "I wouldn't have thought of that on my own."

"Just being devil's advocate here. Is there anything in there that makes him seem like less of a monster? Maybe like he's just a guy trying to get over?" Black asked. "He did write a poem," Lagarde said. "Seems very out of character, but it's timely and I don't think I've seen it in any magazine recently, at least any magazine that Cromwell might be reading."

"What kind of poem? Full of flowers, love, angels and rhyming couplets?"

"You are certainly surprising me today, Larry. Are you taking a course in poetry?"

"No. I've just always been interested in poetry since high school." Black looked over at Lagarde. "Don't look at me that way, man. Poems are made up of words just like you and I speak all the time. Each word is like a breadcrumb in the forest or a piece of a puzzle. To understand the poem, you just have to do what you and I do in real life. Follow the breadcrumbs, put the pieces together, and suddenly you get it."

Lagarde was staring at Larry Black. He shook his head.

"So read the poem to me."

"He wrote this in January 2013," Lagarde said. "He said he was watching the news on television and this is what came to him."

The Boy

The boy says without blinking
that his father, mother, aunts and uncles,
cousins, oh, yes, also grandparents were killed
in their home by mortar and gunfire.
He wears a striped t-shirt.
He shows the dark long scar on his belly
where shrapnel was extracted.
Around him is the rubble of his home.
He does not weep. He's far past that.
He says simply Assad did this. He knows the reason.
He looks straight into the camera,
afraid, now, of nothing.
He is the face of the next revolution.

"That's not bad," Black said softly. "Cromwell might not know who Bashir Assad is or what's going on in Syria, but he sure captured the deep tragedy of that civil war."

"Yeah, that's what I thought," Lagarde said. "It does kind of give you another twist on the 'who is Cromwell' question."

They were quiet for a few miles. Lagarde read the journal entry out loud that indicated Cromwell felt his life was crashing down around him, which is what caused him to stash all his loot at Beverly's house. When Lagarde got to the last entry, he said, "Here it is, here's the clue."

"Tell me, man, don't leave me hanging here."

"On March 14, the day before Cromwell was killed, he wrote in his journal that he was going to meet up with Violet late that night to get the gold ring. He also says his usual crap about 'getting a bump from that whore,' but the central point here is that the meeting with Violet was planned for either late the day before or early morning of the day he was killed."

"Now that's what I call a clue," Black said as he pulled into a parking space at Headquarters.

CHAPTER THIRTY-NINE

APRIL 7, 2014

They were sitting across from each other in a little Italian restaurant in Martinsburg on Queen Street that was known for its Eggplant Parmigianino, Sam Lagarde's favorite meal. There was a demi-carafe with fresh flowers on the table and a candle. The mood in the small place of twenty tables was pleasantly casual. It was a mom and pop restaurant, not one of those mega franchise chains that were taking up space and customers by the mall. Lagarde noticed that Beverly Wilson did not overdress for dinner. She was wearing purple slacks and a nubby green jacket that seemed to be closed on a slant, one corner jauntily hanging below the other. Her face glowed in the candlelight. *All women benefitted from candlelight,* Lagarde reflected, *but Beverly improved the entire room. If someone was rating the restaurant, Beverly being a patron would raise its Zagat score.* He worried he had gotten her here on false pretenses. He wanted to warn her about what he found in Cromwell's journal, prepare her for what she might hear. You never knew how information would fly around or where survivors would hear it from. He wanted to talk to her about what Robert, her son-in-law, said. But more than any of that, he wanted to spend time with her and it was possible that after this conversation, she wouldn't talk to him ever again.

"I found Ben's journal," he said.

"Oh, yes, I gave him one to write in. I was hoping he might be a writer," Beverly said. She was carefully picking through her salad, eating one small piece of lettuce, one olive, one piece of tomato, at a time. "Great salad dressing," she said.

"He seems to have been a pretty disturbed guy," Lagarde said. He was probing and they hadn't even gotten to the entrée. He had misgivings already that he was screwing up everything in their very new relationship.

Beverly looked up at him and put her fork down in the plate. She dotted her lips with the cloth napkin. "Yes, he was very disturbed, from an early age. His thinking was skewed."

"What do you mean?"

"He never seemed to figure out how people are supposed to be with each other. He was a narcissist—the whole world was about him—but there was something else wrong. I know this will seem absurd, or far too clinical for a grandmother to be saying, but it's as if he expected every woman he met to breastfeed him and change his diaper, literally or figuratively. He never grew out of that early stage of development where you are completely taken care of and you don't have to do anything but just exist in return. His emotional development is arrested somewhere around three years old, maybe younger."

"So you don't think he was a criminal—the drug dealing, the stealing, the highly abusive behavior with women? I'm guessing he's infected almost every woman he had sex with in the last ten years. He's the Typhoid Mary of AIDs. I think he knew that and did it deliberately."

"No, I do think he was a criminal, as you put it, but the context for that was his mental illness," she said in the same way someone else would say, pass the salt, please.

Lagarde nodded. What was clear was that she couldn't bring herself to see Ben the way he did. He had a murder victim who was a nasty piece of work, to put it mildly. She wanted to think that Ben wasn't responsible for his own behavior. Maybe that was the only way she could deal with it. But that attitude didn't help him solve this case. Lagarde had a possible assortment of killers and none of the surviving family members seemed to want him to do his job. There was something odd about that.

"I talked to your son-in-law, Robert," Lagarde said. "He said there was no point in finding Ben's murderer."

Beverly went back to picking through her salad for a few minutes. "Sarah told me. I agree with Robert. Unless you think there's some gang out there who will commit another murder like that, what is the point? This killing seems to be about Ben only. The state won't gain anything by incarcerating his killers. We, the family, don't want revenge."

She will never cease to amaze me. "Did you know he was seeing several women at one time?"

"I never asked him what he was doing about anything. Really, I couldn't bear to hear any of his stories. They just depressed me, and whatever he did tell me was intended to manipulate me in some way. I tried to stick with what was right in front of me at that moment. Otherwise, you live in regret and constant recrimination."

The waitress cleared their salad plates and placed the entrees. The aroma of the food was delicious. Beverly leaned toward her plate and sniffed. She had ordered the veal marsala.

"Oh, good, it smells exactly right. Do you think we could talk about something else, Sam? At least until dinner is over."

Lagarde nodded and smiled at her. *That was it for the difficult conversation for tonight.* Then he realized this was the first time she had used his name instead of calling him Detective. Lagarde cut into the eggplant and took his first bite. "Perfect," he said.

CHAPTER FORTY

APRIL 8, 2014, 10 A.M.

Ben Cromwell's diary put two pieces of the puzzle together for them. Cromwell had an appointment to meet Violet Gold and the ring he mentioned in his journal was found at the murder site. Those two facts meant that at the least Cromwell and Gold met either at or just before the murder. They had to talk to Violet Gold. She was either their best witness or she was in on the murder. If she was really in Europe, they would take the next best thing . . . her parents.

It had taken a few days, but Corporal Black located Violet Gold's parents. They lived in one of the very posh neighborhoods in the foothills of the Blue Ridge Mountains. Black drove slowly up the winding road, more like a boulevard than a street, as they watched for house numbers. Sam Lagarde spotted the large stone house tucked back in the trees. There was a circular drive. The plantings around the house looked professionally cared for—no weeds, lots of mulch, little drainage trenches cut in to separate grass from plant beds. There was a three car garage. The house appeared to be on two or three acres. Lagarde figured they did not do their own mowing. Black pulled onto the circular drive and parked in front of the house. They walked up the four wide stone steps and rang the doorbell. Neighborhoods like this already had front gates and gate houses, but were not yet locking those gates or staffing the gate houses with security guards. *That'll come as soon as the residents suspected any of their precious objects or lives were in danger.* He wondered if Ben Cromwell's association with their daughter would feel like enough of a theft to the Golds to lock the gates. It would to him.

The door was opened by a middle-aged woman wearing black slacks and a t-shirt. There were orange deck shoes on her feet. Not what Lagarde expected. Maybe she was the housekeeper. He held out his credentials and introduced himself.

The woman, who was letting her buzz-cut short hair turn gray and was wearing no makeup, looked at the badge and then at him and said, "Yes?"

"Are you Violet Gold's mother?" Lagarde said.

"Oh, no," she said and laughed as if anyone thinking she was Mrs. Gold was the funniest thing she had heard all day. "I'm the neighbor. The whole family has gone to Europe on a vacation. I'm just in here watering plants and taking in the mail. Did something happen to Violet? She's supposed to be with them. I think they were meeting in Venice."

"Are you close friends with them?"

"Well, close as neighbors go. We have dinner together, go to the movies, that sort of thing. I'm not a confidante, if that's what you mean."

"Do you know when they are supposed to be back?"

"The Golds will be back in late April, maybe the 20th they said. I don't know if Violet is coming back with them or not."

Lagarde thanked her and gave her his card, just in case she thought of anything. A few weeks in Europe, that took some bucks. If Ben Cromwell had known Violet Gold came from this kind of money, he might not have been so quick to mess with her. It was kind of fascinating that the guy never realized that if he played his hand differently he could have lived pretty well without having to do a day's work in his life. He just had to be nice to the women he had sex with. Either Lila Townsend or Violet Gold could have supported him without a blink. It was curious that he needed to hurt them; as if he couldn't help himself. He was addicted to causing pain just like he was addicted to taking drugs. Cromwell was complicated. Beverly was right, Lagarde's problem in thinking about this crime is that the guy wasn't a victim. He was a perp who happened to get killed.

til they got closer. The guy took off down the block holding onto his pants and Black took off after him. Lagarde ran back to the car and drove to head the guy off. Two blocks later they had him cornered in an alley that backed to a high wall near the railroad tracks.

"All right, smart guy," Black said, grabbing the collar of the guy's sweat shirt, "get on your knees on the ground right there. All we want to do is talk to you." Black quickly searched through the guy's pockets and pulled out a thick roll of cash and ten small plastic bags of what looked like crumbling sugar cubes. "Selling crack, smart guy?"

"I didn't do nothin, man, I don't know nothin about nothin," the guy said.

"We got you cold on the drug sales, I'm standing here looking at your shit, so don't give us that crap," Black said. "What's your name?"

"Duhwayne."

"Duhwayne what?"

"Jones."

Lagarde noted that Duhwayne Jones had pierced most of his face—eyebrows, nose, lips, anywhere someone could put a pin through. His face was dotted with studs. He looked like he might be nineteen, barely shaving every day, a hank of dirty blonde hair hanging over his pimply forehead. Lagarde pulled off Duhwayne's cap. The rest of his head, except for that lank Mohawk, was shaved. He had a Swastika tattooed on the back of his skull. *Pretty, Duhwayne Jones was a poster boy for united global stupidity.* His eyes were bloodshot from consuming his own product. He was rail thin. He was the very bottom of the drug food chain, someone who sold to support his own habit.

"Do you know Ben Cromwell?" Lagarde asked the boy.

"Yeah, I know him. What about it?"

"Where you're working, was that his corner?"

"Yeah, most times, but he gave it to me."

"He gave it to you."

"Yeah, he told me he was movin on to better things an I could have it."

"When was this?"

"Maybe a month ago. Said he was goin to California. Be a movie star."

"A movie star. And you bought that? Anybody after Cromwell? Did he pay his debts before moving on?"

"Word on the street, he was in hock to Jimmy Two Shoes, but I ain't heard nothing about nothing."

"In hock for how much?"

"Couple thousand. Somethin he could make up in a week of bein prosperous. Problem with Ben is he would put his profits up his arm sometimes."

"Where did you go to school?" Black asked.

"Musselman, when I went. Didn't have much truck with school. School is for lightweights."

"And you're a heavyweight?" Black said.

"Yeah," said Duhwayne. "You see me. What you think?"

"Where does Jimmy Two Shoes live?" Lagarde said.

"Up in the towers with his grandma, got him a nice pad."

The Towers, subsidized housing intended for the elderly, not their crop of gangsta grandkids. "Does Jimmy Two Shoes have a real last name?" he said.

"Yeah. He was Goodwell in school."

Now there was an ironic name. "Look, Duhwayne Jones, if I catch you back on that corner by the school selling drugs, I'm booking you and you'll do the full load. The boys up in Huttonsville will eat you for lunch. You get me?"

Duhwayne Jones nodded and scrambled to his feet, still holding onto his pants.

"Now get out of here," Lagarde said.

Duhwayne took off at a gallop away from them.

"I suppose now we go see if Mrs. Goodwell's grandson is at home?" Black said.

"Yep, that's our next stop," Lagarde said. "Jimmy Two Shoes is one of the names with a phone number in Cromwell's journal. Put Duhwayne's stuff in an evidence bag and put it in the trunk. We'll turn it in when we get back to the office. Let the drug squad know about him and his business."

CHAPTER FORTY-TWO

OCTOBER 1996

Ben Cromwell was up early, earlier than his father and Sarah. He was on a mission. His stepmother was pregnant again, which he knew because he heard her throwing up every morning in the bathroom. Other than her eyelids being spotted with red dots, she seemed very happy. His father seemed happy, often putting his arm around Sarah and hugging her for nothing. He smiled at her from across the room when she was making dinner. The whole thing made Ben want to barf. He liked it better when Sarah was unhappy, the way she was when she lost the last kid. She cried for days. She huddled in the corner of the sofa and left him alone. Then she just sort of dusted herself off and went back to work; shopping and talking to his dad like normal. They palmed him off on Beverly and went away to some island, maybe it was Bermuda, for a week. They came back tan and smiling. He *really* wanted to puke then. But now, he had a plan. If his dad married this bitch to have another kid, Ben was going to do something about that. It was hard enough getting what he needed. He had no plans to share.

Sarah always ate oatmeal in the morning. She made it the old fashioned way, in a pot on the stove. The cardboard box of oats sat in the pantry all the time. Sarah was the only one who ate that stuff. That was his opening. Ben dumped the store of drugs he had acquired from various friends' bathroom medicine cabinets onto his bed and sorted through them. He was looking for white tablets that could be ground up and would blend in with the oatmeal. Naproxen, that looked promising. Celebrex. Vioxx. That would make a nice mix. He took the stone bowl and pestle Sarah kept on the counter for mashing the herbs she grew in her garden to his room. He put all the pills into the bowl, opened the capsules, dumped their contents in the bowl and ground it all together. When the mixture was fine enough, he carried it to the kitchen and put it on the counter. He pulled the box of oats from the pantry and dumped it into a large plastic baggy. Then he dumped his pill mixture into the baggie, zipped it up, and shook it thoroughly to mix it all together. He did a little shake, shake dance to assist the mixing process. He was happy, he realized. He was taking charge of the situation. Then he poured everything back in the oatmeal box and put the box in the pantry. He threw the empty plastic baggy in the trash can. She'd never know, until she dropped dead or lost that baby she wanted. Even then, who would suspect him? He was totally innocent. He didn't touch her. He rinsed out the stone bowl and pestle and put them back where Sarah had them on the counter. His work here was done.

CHAPTER FORTY-THREE

APRIL 8, 2014, 12 P.M.

Sam Lagarde and Corporal Black got nothing useful from Mrs. Goodwell about her grandson. She would not admit that he was living with her. She would not let them come into her apartment. She had no idea where her grandson James was these days, hadn't seen him in God knows how long, but she thought he had a job over at the mall, maybe near the yogurt place. And he was a good boy, anyway, did her shopping for her and ran to the drugstore for her pills and what were they doing wasting their time going after good boys when there was all that trash out there? They asked to see a photograph of him and she showed them his high school graduation photo in cap and gown. He looked like a normal kid, not like some drug kingpin. Lagarde asked her how James got his "two shoes" moniker and she just looked at him like he had snakes coming out of his ears.

Lagarde and Black headed back to the office to see if forensics or the medical examiner had anything new for them. Lagarde thought they were about out of rocks to turn over. All they had was a body—no weapon, no prints, no fibers on any body parts, no trail that led to anything viable except Evelyn Foster, who had taken herself out of the picture. There was plenty of motive to go around, but those with good motives had good alibis. He still had some suspicions about Marc Delany and Katrina Vander, but somehow that didn't make sense. Neither of them seemed capable of planning a murder where they didn't leave a wide trail of evidence. Delany, they had been told by Sterling Townsend who repaired the kid's rotator cuff, wasn't strong enough yet to push Cromwell around, let alone tackle him and hold him down while he cut off his head. And no matter how much Katrina Vander reminded Lagarde of a witch, she was too small to have handled Cromwell on her own. He couldn't see how she'd be much use even if she and Delany went at Cromwell together. What was she going to do, kill him with sleaze?

That brought Lagarde back to the idea that it was a group of them, and maybe that was the right idea. But he couldn't prove that Violet Gold participated in the murder, only that she gave Cromwell the ring before she left the country. And truth be told, he couldn't prove when the exchange happened. He could only surmise that it happened just before the murder. Ilise Vander wasn't available to talk to, according to Delany. Lagarde wasn't sure that was true, but for now that's what he was working with. Evelyn Foster was dead. And Lila Townsend had a pretty good alibi: she was in New York City at a medical conference giving a paper on something he couldn't pronounce. Maybe he had the wrong group. Someone knew more than he did. He had to find that person and shake the facts loose.

Black checked his email. He made a call. He motioned for Lagarde to come over to his desk and put the caller on speaker. The lab had a match. The blood on the floor of Evelyn Foster's trunk was Ben Cromwell's. That was the best clue they had, and that suspect was dead.

"What about Cromwell's notation that he was seeing Violet that same night just before he died?" Lagarde said.

"The guy lied, he always lied, to everyone," Black said. "Maybe he even lied to himself."

"But the ring we found, the one that Violet bought him, that's what got lost in the body parts shuffle. Do you think that's significant?"

"My way of thinking? It fell out of the bag when Foster was stuffing bags in her car. He was obviously wearing it. His finger was still attached to it."

"You think Evelyn Foster was capable of doing all that damage herself?"

"A woman scorned, man, is capable of anything. Besides, maybe she cut him up to make it easier to get him into her trunk. You know, each bag was a lighter load to lift."

"What if all five of them did it?"

"All five who?"

"Evelyn, Violet, Ilise, Lila and Katrina."

Black looked at Lagarde like he had lost his mind. "You think the lawyer and the doctor were involved in a murder? Why would they risk that? They can just walk away from the bum."

"What you said, Larry, 'a woman scorned is capable of anything.'"

"Wow, that's some theory," Black said. He shook his head. "We are weeks away from the murder. The case is practically cold. We can't even zero in on one suspect and now you want us to nail five of them? As you keep reminding me, we have no weapon, no fingerprints and even if they have motive, they have some good alibis. What's the simplest solution?"

"I think Ilise is missing because she's the weak link. We find her and press her and the whole story will come out," Lagarde said.

"Okay, if we're going up to Martinsburg to find Mr. Goodwell, let's stop by at the Vander residence again and see if she has miraculously returned home," Black said. "I don't think she's out of state."

Lagarde handed Cromwell's journal to Black. "Better bag this for evidence before we go."

He went to the men's room to take a piss. Standing there unzipped, the thought hit him. *What if Cromwell met up with Gold with Ilise in his car, got the ring, stopped to take a piss by the stable and was jumped by his old drug buddies. Maybe Ilise hid in the car until they were done and then found the journal on the ground near the scene. She would have called her mom to come pick her up. The girl might not be talking because she was afraid the guys who killed Cromwell would kill her. Maybe Jimmy Two Shoes had a story to tell.* At this point, Lagarde was desperate to arrest someone and he hoped he could make any theory stick.

CHAPTER FORTY-FOUR

MARCH 15, 2014, 2 A.M.

It was a moonless night, a horror story night where unseen beings race across a wood, hiding in wait, determined to harm the heroine. *Except this time, I'm the malevolent one.* Unaccustomed to her role as wolf or worse, she stood in the dark next to the driver's side door of her rented Kia Scion waiting for Ben Cromwell to descend the sloping cement walk between the casino parking lot and the stables. In the dark, the stables looked like large discarded crates, unreal, detached from purpose. She could have been a player in a Minecraft game, standing still, her heart pounding, gripping her secret weapon, waiting for her moment to destroy the monster. She would need all her superpowers, if she had any, to complete this mission. She wished instead that she could just fade into the night like a whisper.

She had no trouble pulling into the stable employee's lot and parking. No one questioned her. There were a few other cars already parked here. Violet wondered if stable hands slept overnight in the horse stalls. She was the first of her group to arrive, watching as the others drove in, parked and flashed their lights to indicate they had arrived. There was to be no gathering, no talking to each other beforehand, and no talking during or after. After, they would all scatter. They would never see each other again, never communicate in any way. Violet was jittery. The last thing she wanted to do was to see Ben again. But someone had to be the bait, and the bait had to be good enough for him to bite on. She wouldn't have the courage to do this again. This was a one-time deal. She, at any rate, was not going to stick around for an encore. If they couldn't pull this off, she was out of here. Let the guy rot in hell. He was no longer any of her business.

She watched Ben saunter out of the garage, imagining he had the upper hand. In the last of the lights from the garage, she could see Ben was wearing the black leather jacket she'd bought him and that snide sideways smile that was all his own. The smile was taunt, something a child would do when he'd won an argument over who had dibs on the front seat, wiggling his fingers in his ears and yodeling nonsense sounds. She first saw this look when he failed to pick her up for a dinner date and didn't call her for two weeks. Didn't return her frantic calls. Didn't answer the door of the trailer she rented for him when she beat on it. When he finally arrived at her townhouse a few weeks later, he stood outside in the rain and called her from his cell phone. She opened her door and was flooded with relief that he was still alive. She pulled him into the house. She threw her arms around his neck, kissed his face and neck and lips. When she stood back to catch her breath, he was smiling that smile. That night, while she slept, he took two hundred dollars from her wallet, a few blank checks from her checkbook, her iPod player and left again.

It took three cycles of this behavior for Violet to get it. She was his piggybank. He could break into it and take what he wanted whenever he wanted. She didn't need to remember this sequence to hate him. The final blow to her carefully assembled idea that she was in love with him came when he staged the threesome with Ilise. That scornful look on his face when he put his cigarette out on Ilise's bare hip haunted her. Hating him was now part of her DNA. He was a virus that had wormed its way into every cell, delivered its sickening burden, and twisted her into something completely different from nature's intention.

Violet was shaking. She wanted to vomit. It could be fear; she had never killed anyone before. It could be fury; just the sight of him brought back months of debasement. Maybe it was the risk. She kept forgetting she was sick. Although they had plotted the killing with an eye to never being discovered, they had probably left clues everywhere, things they hadn't counted on. They were novices, of course they would get things wrong; possibly give themselves away. Even though they had agreed she did not have to actually kill him, she was part of the conspiracy. She was an accessory and a witness to premeditated murder. This murder was a capital crime and it carried a sentence of life imprisonment in West Virginia. She had argued with the women against killing Cromwell, asking why they would give up their own lives just to take his. Nevertheless, they were caught up in a frenzy they no longer controlled. It was as if their lives depended on killing him; as if they would be released from bondage only when he was dead. Killing him was all they thought about, just the way they once thought about how they wanted him to touch them, kiss them, fill up their bodies and breathe into their mouths. Now the only act that would satisfy that craving required blood—lust and murder were permanently intertwined in their minds. Murder was their new addiction.

Violet couldn't deter them and it seemed she couldn't extract herself, but she planned to leave the country as soon as they were done. She already had her plane tickets—first to London, then Rome, with no ticket home. She thought she might go from Italy to France and then to Switzerland. She had never been there and she had read in the news that notorious criminals had comfortable residences in Switzerland. She gave notice at Legal Aid two weeks before saying she wanted to travel a bit. She checked into the airport Hilton Hotel yesterday evening with another overnight tonight. Tonight she had ordered room service at 11 p.m. and gave the porter a large tip to give herself a verifiable alibi. She would head directly to Dulles airport after the killing. She could do the automated hotel check out from her phone at the airport when she was turning in the rental car. She would be standing in the international security check through line in her bare feet with her purse in a rubber bin and her passport and plane ticket in her hand by 5 a.m.

* * *

Two days ago she told her parents she was taking a little vacation to Europe, going with friends. It was a sudden impulse, she said. They were pleased for her. "Glad to see you rewarding yourself for all your hard work," her Dad said and gave her a warm hug. "Send us lots of photos," her mom said. "We'll meet you in Venice for a few days." Their kindness made her stomach twist. She had not told them the bad news about being HIV positive, maybe she would never tell them. They were too proud of her. She couldn't sacrifice that pride for sympathy; couldn't bear to see on their faces the desolation they would feel.

Violet made the call to Ben from a pay phone at the Food Lion on old Route 9 near the IRS complex and the U.S. Coast Guard Operations Systems Center in Kearneysville, an area in the West Virginia Eastern Panhandle she had never been to before and would never go again. This was about as random a location as she could find. She had driven the old roads that connected all the small towns before the modern highways and called from various pay phones, the few that were left, across Berkeley and Jefferson counties until he answered. She did not want to leave a message. If he didn't pick up by four rings, she disconnected. She wore gloves so that she left no finger prints on the phone or the quarters she dropped into the phone. From the pay phone, she watched people drive into the market parking lot, exit their cars and lock them, and enter the market through the automatic doors. It was mesmerizing, all the coming and going, all the normal things that people do without thinking. A woman opened the back door of her beige mini-van and helped a young boy out of the vehicle. She took him by the hand, inclining her head toward him as she talked to him. She was smiling. The child was wearing a red jacket. He looked up at her, laughing. Violet watched them walk all the way to the supermarket door.

Ben answered on the fourth ring. "Yeah," he said.

"Ben? This is Violet." She could not keep the little sob out of her voice. She hated herself for not having enough self-control to have this conversation calmly.

He laughed. She felt heat suffuse her face.

"I'd like to meet," she said. "I still have some of your things I cleaned out of the trailer to give back to you."

"I don't care about that shit," he said. "Not if I have to listen to you whine about the relationship." He said the words "the relationship" in a little falsetto voice. She could imagine his head tilted to one side in imitation of a woman, his lips twisted. She had seen the act before. "There was never any relationship."

Violet could not suppress her sharp intake of breath. It was distressing how easy it was for him to hurt her.

"You left the ring I bought you, the fourteen karat gold one with the emerald. It was under the bed. The jewelry store won't take it back because it's engraved. It's worth at least five hundred dollars at a pawn shop."

She waited while he was silent. She could imagine the calculations going on in his mind. The pros and cons, getting his hands on a wad of money versus having to face someone he had discarded. She bet the money would win . . . and maybe he thought he could get a quick blowjob if he played his cards right. She counted on his narcissism, on his thinking that women never got over him, that the world revolved around him and, that somehow, no matter what, he could always get over on them.

"Okay, where?"

"In the employee parking lot by the stables at the Charles Town race track, off Flowing Springs, near the casino garage."

He laughed again. "That's specific. When?"

"How about Tuesday, at 2 a.m.?" She waited for him to ask why the odd location and time or to negotiate with her. Her ready-made answer was the truth: she didn't want anyone to see her with him. But he didn't ask.

"So be it," he said and hung up. Violet shook for a while and then walked rigidly to her car where she collapsed into sobs.

Even now, standing in the dark waiting for him, it was possible she would not be able to go through with murdering him. She knew Evelyn felt that way, maybe Ilise, but not Katrina and Lila. She had considered suddenly warning him off, give a signal that he should run. She might do it involuntarily, a flinch of morality, the last vestige of ethical behavior she had left. She didn't know. It was one thing to hate someone, to wish them dead, to even think about killing him. It was quite another to do it. They had talked through all the methods they could use. The talking was therapeutic and was quite enough for her. They had already imagined stabbing him a thousand times. Stabbing him was the preferred action, particularly for Ilise, at least that's what she said, but Violet thought Ilise had her misgivings also. Ilise's mother Katrina was the clearest. She wanted to castrate him. They all wanted him to suffer. The downward arc of their arms, pressing through the resistance of the skin, muscle, to the bone, thrusting again and again seemed the most satisfying. Lila convinced them that stabbing him to death was not the most efficient way to end his life. It could be loud. He would have time to scream. He would thrash. It would be hard to hide the body. There were other ways, she said, that would satisfy them.

Violet's last minute misgivings held her in place until Ben walked directly up to her, invading her personal space, breathing her air. He leaned over her and she backed up to her car.

"What? No kiss for old time's sake?" he said. He smiled that sideways smile.

Violet held the ring out on the palm of her hand. "This is yours," she said. Her voice shook. "Take it."

Ben took the ring from her hand, running his finger across her palm as he did it. Violet rubbed her hand on her thigh. He placed the ring on his right pinky and held his hand out to admire it.

"You always had good taste, I'll give you that. Maybe I'll keep it instead of pawning it, to remember how hot you used to be."

Violet stepped sideways away from him. She wasn't supposed to say anything. She was supposed to get him to take her in his arms, to distract him, but she couldn't bring herself to do it. His arms where the last place she wanted to be. She did not want his breath on her skin.

"You are such a jerk," she said. "You could have had everything, anything from me. You just had to be honest."

"Oh, fuck, you said you weren't going to go over all this stuff again. It's over, little girl, get that through your brain. And anyway, you're lying about that part about giving me anything." He smirked.

"How could you treat me this way?" Violet felt her voice rising even as she tried desperately to calm herself. She clenched her teeth. "You are not worth even one minute of my time."

"What makes you so special?" Ben said. "You're no different from a hundred other bitches who want something from me."

"You think I want something from you? You're a moron."

Ben Cromwell laughed. He grabbed her shoulders and pulled her toward him. "Of course you want something from me. You want the heat. You want the jizz. You want me to love you," he said. "You're just another cunt always freaking out about love. What does love get you? You know now, don't you? Love gets you fucked up and sick."

"You're insane," Violet said, struggling to pull herself away from him.

"You think I didn't know I was giving you AIDs?" he said, leaning over her, whispering harshly in her ear. He leaned back a bit and hissed at her, his teeth bared, "You think I didn't do it bareback on purpose? You think you're more important than the toilet paper I wipe my ass with? You're the ones who are insane." He laughed and yanked Violet toward him.

Before he could press his lips against Violet's mouth, Lila Townsend moved swiftly from behind her car and jabbed the hypodermic needle into his neck. The hypo contained the highest possible dose of potassium chloride. She pushed the plunger all the way down.

"How do you like this drug rush, asshole," she said to him.

Lila gave Cromwell a big enough dose to kill him instantly from cardiac arrest. Even if it took a little longer than that, he wouldn't give them any trouble, she had told them. She stepped back away from him, watched while he grabbed his chest, tried to yell, and crashed to the ground.

Lila dropped the needle into a small plastic baggie she pulled from her pocket. She put the baggie into a large green garbage bag she took from a box in the back of her car. The needle would go into the medical waste container for sharps. Other instruments they used tonight would be returned to the hospital and sterilized in the hospital's usual manner by people who had nothing to do with this bit of surgery. It was Evelyn's task to return the surgical tools and dispose of the needle.

From a black satchel in her car, Lila pulled out the disposable footies, full body coveralls, gloves, masks, caps and plastic visors she had acquired for all of them from the hospital's surgical supply room. She had used her husband's key card, a duplicate he had carelessly left behind in the top drawer of his closet bureau when he moved out of their house, to gain access to the hospital's storage area. When they were done with them, the bloody disposable clothing would all go into the hospital incinerator to be burned with other waste. That was also one of Evelyn's jobs.

They pulled on the gloves, first one pair then a second. Each of them would leave the bottom pair of gloves on until they had thrown away all the bags in different dumpsters. There would be no fingerprints on the bags. They pulled up the coveralls, put on the booties, the hats and masks, the clear plastic visors. Had someone seen them from the garage, they might have looked like a hazmat team cleaning up a spill.

Evelyn Foster pulled a painting tarp from her car and unrolled it on the ground. Violet and Ilise rolled Ben Cromwell's body onto the tarp. He was surprisingly heavy. Lila pulled the battery-powered amputation saw, scalpel, Liston amputation knife and Satterlee bone saw she had borrowed from the hospital's surgical suite from another bag and laid them out on the tarp. Ilise opened a box of contractor-sized plastic garbage bags, double-bagged ten and placed them within easy reach of the operating arena. Once the bags were filled with pieces of his body, each bag would be placed inside another and the tops tied. The bags would be driven by each of them to different dumpsters across the area.

Evelyn, Katrina and Ilise undressed the body they knew too well, throwing the clothing and everything Cromwell had in his pockets into one of the garbage bags that would also later contain their bloodied disposable garments. While Ilise held the flashlight, Lila drew lines in black magic marker on the body indicating where cuts should be made. By then, Ben Cromwell no longer seemed to be a person. Katrina Vander picked up the battery powered saw, turned it on, and with no hesitation made the first cut precisely on the line Lila had drawn. Later, when the tarp got slippery with his blood, they got a little sloppier.

CHAPTER FORTY-FIVE

APRIL 8, 2014, 2 P.M.

This time, when Detective Sam Lagarde and Corporal Lawrence Black knocked on the door of Katrina Vander's house on Kentucky Street in Martinsburg, Ilise Vander opened it. At least, the girl who opened the door looked similar to the young woman in the photographs in Katrina Vander's living room, if thinner, paler and significantly unhappier.

The detectives were momentarily stunned by their good fortune. Just to make sure this was the girl they sought, Lagarde formally introduced himself and Black and asked if she was Ilise Vander.

"Yeah, that's me. What do you want?" she said.

Lagarde recognized the defiance, which didn't seem particularly notable. He once had teenagers of his own. He knew the tone. It wasn't personal. It was like the makeup a kid put on and the weird stuff she did with her hair intended to attract attention and push people away at the same time. He believed all teenagers should be sent to boot camp around the age of sixteen, forced to do community service by serving food to the homeless and cleaning the streets, and not be allowed to come home until they were at least twenty-one and the aliens who stole their brains right out of their heads returned them.

"Marc said you went to see an aunt in Florida," Corporal Black said.

"Yeah, well, he was wrong. Sometimes he doesn't listen," she said. She snapped her gum.

"Is your mother here?" Lagarde asked.

"She's at work," Ilise said.

"We'd like to come in and talk to you," Black said.

Ilise eyed him as if he was a stray cat that might have fleas. "No way," she said. "I'm here by myself."

"Ms. Vander, we are here as part of our investigation of the murder of Ben Cromwell," Lagarde said. "This isn't a social call. We have some questions to ask you and we can come in and ask them or take you to headquarters and ask them there. Which would you prefer?"

Ilise Vander stepped back into the house and walked away from the door. She left the door open. That was as much of an invitation as they were going to get, Lagarde figured. He and Black followed her into the house. She dropped herself down onto the sofa, pulled her legs up to her chest and wrapped her arms around them. Black and Lagarde took wooden chairs from the dining table and placed them near her. Ilise watched them for a minute and then put her forehead down on her knees. Lagarde wished he was limber enough to do that.

"We understand that you were in a relationship with Ben Cromwell," Lagarde said.

Ilise Vander nodded.

"Your mother said that you are now HIV positive because of him. Is that true?" Lagarde said.

The girl nodded again. Lagarde noticed that her toes with their chipped black toenail polish were gripping the sofa seat and her hands clasped each other tightly around her knees. She had been biting her finger nails. She was desperately holding herself together. He needed to find a way to break through this barrier.

"Ben told his father that he made you pregnant. Is that true?" Black said.

She looked up at him. Her eyes flashed. "What? That asshole. No, it's not true. He lied. Ben always lied." She put her forehead back on her knees but now her entire body was shaking.

"And Marc said you tried to commit suicide. Is that true?" Black said.

She nodded and said nothing. That line of questioning would not payoff, Lagarde guessed. He couldn't bring himself to be that unkind to this kid.

"What else did Ben lie about?" Lagarde asked.

"He lied about my being the only woman in the world for him," she said. "He lied about loving me. It's all in his fucking journal. He didn't love me at all, he was just using me." She started sobbing.

Black looked around for a box of tissues, found them in the bathroom and brought the box to Ilise. "Here," he said. She pulled a tissue out and blew her nose.

"That's right, Ilise," Lagarde said. "He was also having sex with women named Violet, Evelyn and Lila while he was seeing you . . . and your mother." That was the bomb he thought would blast through her resistance.

She said nothing. She looked as if she had stopped breathing. Lagarde waited to see if she would say anything about the women. She didn't bite. Finally, he said, "Where were you on March 15th?"

"I don't know," she said.

"You don't know where you were or you don't want to tell me?"

"I don't know where I was," she said.

Little lie, big lie. "How did you come to have Ben Cromwell's journal?"

"I found it."

"Where did you find it?"

"It was on the ground."

"On the ground where? At the stables?" Now it was Lagarde's turn to hold his breath. Would the girl actually admit she was at the murder scene?

"Outside my house. He must've dropped it there. He was always carrying it."

He exhaled. *This was another lie.* "So did you see Ben on March 14th?"

She looked confused, as if she were checking a calendar in her mind to see if that was a possible date when she could have found the journal. "No, I didn't," she said. "I didn't see him on March 14th."

It seemed to Lagarde that her strategy was to tell him part of the truth in everything she said, as if part of the truth were sufficient to maintain her integrity. Or maybe that was just too complicated. She wasn't a complicated girl. She wasn't a girl who formulated a strategy. She was hiding something and she was struggling with it. As he saw it, there were only two options: either she saw Cromwell just before the murder and she got the journal then, or she was there at the murder when it was happening or just after.

"So you saw him on March 15th?"

"Yeah, he came by here late at night, like one in the morning, and climbed in my window like he does. He wanted to fuck me, but I told him to drop dead. He went back out the window. I found the journal in the morning outside my window." She seemed relieved now that she'd told Lagarde that. She breathed in deeply and shook her hair back off her face. That look of defiance was back.

"You know that we have the journal, right?" Lagarde said.

"Yeah, my mom told me you took it," she said. "That's ok, I don't want it back. You can keep it. It's just a piece of shit like Ben was."

Lagarde was quiet for a few minutes, thinking about the girl. Defiance might be her only defense mechanism, and considering what Cromwell had put her through, she needed some defense. Reading the journal must have been a shock, unless she knew about the other women beforehand—but she couldn't have known about her mother and Cromwell.

"Do you know Violet, Evelyn or Lila, the women mentioned in the journal?"

"I know Evelyn," she said. "I met her when I was in the hospital after I . . ." her voice trailed off, muffled in her arms.

True. She knew Evelyn. A deep red suffused Ilise's neck and cheeks. "So you never met the others, the women mentioned in the journal?" he said.

"Ok, so I met them, so what?" Ilise snapped. "We met at Target and talked about what a shit Ben is and stuff. There's no law against that." She glared at him.

Lagarde sat back in his chair. So the women met before the murder. That could be evidence of premeditation, of conspiracy to commit murder. His eerie hunch about a coven might just pan out, or their meeting could be just what the kid said, a therapy session.

"Did you know that Evelyn Foster committed suicide?" Lagarde said.

"What?" The girl's voice turned shrill. "She what? That can't be. You're fucking lying to me." Ilise jumped up from the sofa, ran into her room. They could hear her in her bedroom talking on the phone, saying between wracking sobs, "Mom, Mom, Evelyn killed herself, Mom, the cops just told me about it. I can't take it, Mom. What am I supposed to do?"

She was quiet for a while except for her sobbing. They heard her say, "Okay, okay, okay."

Ilise came back into the living room holding the phone in her hand and said, "You have to go now. My mom says that unless you are charging me with something I don't have to talk to you. And even then, she told me to shut up and not say nothing without my lawyer."

It sounded to Lagarde like Katrina Vander had already talked to a lawyer. He wondered if that lawyer was Violet Gold. They were getting closer. He told Ilise they would be back in touch and not to leave town.

Lagarde and Black let themselves out the front door and got into their car. Their next stop was to track down Jimmy Two Shoes, just in case he was their real killer and the women were simply an intriguing side show in this murder circus.

CHAPTER FORTY-SIX

APRIL 8, 2014, 3:10 P.M.

It took a few minutes of walking around the mall to find the yogurt stall even though Lagarde and Black consulted the You Are Here map at the entrance to the mall. It seemed to them that the shop had been moved since that map was printed and placed under glass. The mall was practically empty of shoppers. It was, after all, a Thursday and well after anyone's lunch break, but Lagarde thought that if this was the level of foot traffic—a mother with two kids in tow one of whom by the state of the snot on his face had been crying for the last twenty minutes, two elderly people in matching powder blue sweat suits doing their afternoon lap, a knot of teenagers pointing and giggling in front of the Victoria's Secret store—this mall would soon be shuttered store windows facing thousands of square feet of ceramic tile and a few hundred dying palm trees surrounded by acres of empty parking spaces. The Sears was already gone. He wondered if any clever entrepreneurs would realize the potential for a combination of offices and residences, a kind of live-where-you-work, never-have-to-go-outdoors-at-all, no-commuting, controlled environment. Keep the food court, add in all the service businesses like clothes cleaning, shoe repair, florist, bakery, grocery store, a gym, swimming pool, basketball court, clinic and library. Hell, he might even want to live in a place like that in his old age. Maybe some new software company would see the benefits of such a clever reuse of available space. Instead of building new campuses, they could recycle the empty malls all over the country. Put solar panels on the roofs, create a common garden. Even during this short fantasy, Lagarde knew it would never happen. Pipe dreams, his mother used to call these ideas that popped into his head, nothing more than smoke.

There was no one lounging around the food court who matched the photograph of Jimmy Two Shoes that his grandmother showed them. They decided to get some yogurt and wait a while. Corporal Black surprised Lagarde by ordering something called 'tutti frutti.' The guy was just full of surprises. They took seats on the small white chairs with insubstantial wire backs at a round table where they could watch the area from all approaches. Lagarde wondered if the tiny chairs, more decorative than utilitarian, would hold Black but he managed to balance himself in one with one foot on either side of the seat.

"Used to spend a fair amount of my time at a mall like this when I was a kid," Black said.

Lagarde looked over at him. "Any good memories?"

Black grinned. "Some very good memories. The girls were very pretty at my high school."

"There weren't any malls where I lived as a teenager," Lagarde said.

Black looked at Lagarde as if he said he used to live in a cave. "You serious? There had to be."

"Nope. No malls. We had a downtown where the large stores were located along the main streets, you know, Market and High, and near to home we had small corner stores where you could find almost anything you needed. But there were no interior courtyards like this. Some really big department stores had restaurants with counter service and tables. But you couldn't just lounge there all day, you had to order food, eat it and get out."

Black shook his head in disbelief. "You missed out, man. Malls are the best place for people watching."

"Hah! I thought that was zoos. Speaking of," Lagarde gestured with his hand to indicate the direction in which Black should look, "this might be our guy."

"What do you know, Duwayne Jones is a Jimmy Two Shoes look alike," Black said.

They got up from their chairs, tossed their empty yogurt cups in the trashcan and walked over to the man wearing the slick sweat suit, a garland of cheap gold necklaces around his neck and his pants below his butt. His baseball cap was on backwards. He had a scruffy beard and a face Lagarde figured only a grandmother could love. Black positioned himself behind the guy, Lagarde stood in front of him.

"Jimmy Goodwell?" Lagarde asked.

"Yeah. Who wants to know?"

"The police, Jimmy, that's who."

Jimmy's body jerked as if to run, but Black grabbed his arm.

"Got something in your pockets you shouldn't, Jimmy?" Black said.

"Nah, I'm just here to hang with my posse," Jimmy said. His head bounced up and down in rhythm to some tune in his ear from his iPod.

Black patted Jimmy's bulging pockets and extracted little packets of white dust, pills, cubes, and grass. "Expecting a big day, Jimmy?" he said. "You brought your own supermarket to the mall?"

"Got my bidness, yo. Why you want to mess with my bidness? This is my space."

"Take out your ear buds, Jimmy, we have some questions to ask you," Lagarde said. "Let's take a little walk to our car, just in case we need to transport you over to regional. You get my meaning, Jimmy?"

Jimmy nodded, slouched, removed the ear buds. Black kept his hand on the man's wrist, holding it up behind Jimmy's back, as they walked back in the direction where they had left their car. Jimmy held his pants up with his other hand.

"So we understand you knew Ben Cromwell," Lagarde said.

"Yeah, I know him. So what?"

"When was the last time you saw him?"

"Man, I don't remember shit like that. I saw him when I saw him. That's it."

"Do you think you might have seen him on March 15th?"

"What was March 15th? I got no idea what day that was."

"Did you have a problem with Ben Cromwell? Did he owe you some money?" Lagarde said.

"Yeah, he owed me, but he's always good for it somehow. He gets money, he pays me back. Sometimes my boys got to remind him of his obligations, but, you know, he wants to play, he pays."

"So when was the last time you saw Ben?"

"I might have seen him in early March, don't exactly remember. He was always disappearing."

"Does he still owe you money?"

"Nope. He's paid up and hasn't come back for any product in a while. You guys seen him? He told my man Dopey he was goin to Hollywood. Far as I know, that's where he is."

"He's dead, man, and we think you made him that way," Black said.

Jimmy Two Shoes stopped in his tracks. "Dead? No way, man, that's not my style. I don't do dead. You got nothing on me. That what this conversation's about, I want my lawyer."

Black and Lagarde looked at each other over Jimmy's head. They had nothing. They walked Jimmy out of the mall and over to the county sheriff's cruiser conveniently or accidentally parked by the mall entrance and handed the drug dealer over to the deputy, suggesting that he search Jimmy's pockets.

They waited while the deputy extracted the evidence that might put Jimmy behind bars for a year or five or twenty depending on how many times he'd been convicted of this felony. He had way more weight and variety than anyone needed for personal consumption. They had him on intent to distribute. At the very least, they should have him on violation of probation. Jimmy stood there like he knew the drill and understood enough about local police officers not to resist arrest. Jail was safer than a few angry cops.

While the deputy hooked up the cuffs, Black asked Jimmy, "So why do they call you Two Shoes?"

Jimmy laughed, showing two gold-capped teeth. "Cuz the first time I collected on a debt someone owed me, all he had was two shoes and I took 'em both."

Black and Lagarde walked back to their car.

"That arrest should hold the creep up for a few weeks anyway. At least his grandmother will know where he is," Black said. "What next?"

"I think we take another run at Lila Townsend," Lagarde said.

"Office?" Black asked.

"Yeah. She should still be there in the half hour it will take us to get there," Lagarde said. "Take Route 45. It'll be quicker to get to Shepherdstown that way."

CHAPTER FORTY-SEVEN

APRIL 8, 2014, 4:30 P.M.

There were only a few cars left in the Shepherdstown train station parking lot when Black pulled their car into a space near the doctor's office door. Through the glass, they could see the receptionist at the desk, but the waiting room was empty. Either all those pregnant bellies were parked in examining rooms or the docs were done for the day. Lagarde opened the door, held it for Black, and they both walked up to the desk.

There was a nurse in a gaily colored smock picking up toys from the floor and putting them back in the toy box. Lagarde wondered vaguely if those smocks made women patients feel happy or annoyed. They would annoy him; too much enforced happiness.

The nurse looked over at Lagarde, seemed to recognize him, and said, "You're the detective, right? Dr. Townsend left about an hour ago. She said she needed a run. Do you want her home address?"

"That would be good, yes," Lagarde said.

The nurse called over to the receptionist, "Betsy, write Dr. Townsend's home address on the back of a business card and give it to the detective, please." Betsy did as she was told and handed the card to Lagarde.

Black and Lagarde thanked the nurse and receptionist and walked back out to their car. They consulted Google maps on Black's mobile phone to pinpoint where the good doctor's house was, then headed over there.

Lagarde's phone buzzed. He looked at the screen. It was Beverly Wilson calling him. His heart did a little jig and he cautioned himself to cut it out. "Hi Beverly," he said into the phone.

Black looked over at him and gave him a "you're getting way too familiar with her" look. Lagarde grinned the silly grin men grin when they are smitten and know it.

He listened to Beverly talk. His smile faded. This wasn't a personal call. She was talking about the case. "I'll come by later. I'll call before I come," he said and disconnected.

"Man, I hope you are not getting involved with a relative of the victim," Black said.

"Too late for that caution, Larry, but I don't know that it will go anywhere," Lagarde said.

"What did she want?"

"She has something to tell me about the case. She wants to tell me in person."

"Do you think she's been withholding evidence?"

"It sounded more like she just learned something, or got another one of those calls from one of the women Cromwell was screwing, like she did from Evelyn Foster."

They pulled up in front of Lila Townsend's beautiful home. It had the simple modern lines of a Frank Lloyd Wright, with lots of glass and stone. There were old trees on the sweep of lawn from the road up the slight rise to the house. From the wide front window you could look clear through to the back deck and the Potomac River beyond. The furniture that could be seen through the window was low and sleek and didn't interfere with the view. It looked like Townsend's home was a tranquil place where someone could refresh her mind. They walked up the flagstone path to the front door. Lagarde noted that the house had a small sign indicating that it was protected by a security service. There were lights facing out from under the eaves that would go on at night. *They might be motion sensor driven and would turn on when someone approached the house.* The door lock was an electronic keypad, not a key. There was a small camera above the front door and an intercom next to it. Dr. Townsend wasn't taking any chances about being surprised.

Lagarde wondered if these security enhancements were pre- or post-Cromwell. He rang the bell.

Lila Townsend said through the intercom, "Yes, detective?"

Lagarde realized she could see him on a screen inside the house. "We'd like to talk with you for a few minutes."

"I'll be right there."

The door opened and Lila Townsend in bare feet and wet hair, wearing black tights and a long blue shirt that seemed to bring out her freckles, stepped back to let them in. "We can talk in the kitchen," she said. "I'm making myself dinner."

She led the way down the hall to a large kitchen that looked out through a floor-to-ceiling window to a deck facing the river. The kitchen opened into the living room with no wall between the rooms and had a cathedral ceiling. Blue lights, the same color as her shirt, hung down from the ceiling over the center black granite island. Lila Townsend stood at the counter and resumed chopping a red pepper on a lime green cutting board.

This is a completed HGTV dream house. "We talked to your husband," Lagarde said.

"Really. How is he?"

"He was in Maui when Ben Cromwell was murdered."

"How nice for him," she said.

"We also talked briefly to Evelyn Foster."

Her hand paused almost imperceptibly above the pepper and then resumed its methodical motion.

"She apparently was pregnant and HIV positive . . ."

"Detective, why are you telling me this?" Lila Townsend interrupted him. "Ms. Foster is not my patient. I do not need to know her medical history. It's inappropriate for you to tell it to me."

"I think you know Ms. Foster and that you met with her."

Lila put down the knife, put her hands flat on the granite counter, and looked straight at Lagarde. "And that leads you to what conclusion?"

"Did you know that she committed suicide?"

"When was this?"

"Three days ago."

"How?"

"She shot herself."

Lila Townsend looked down at the red pepper she had been cutting. She folded her arms across her body. She looked out the wide window at the river running swiftly by her beautiful home. The late afternoon sun laid a veil of filigreed gold on top of the river. Lagarde watched it with her and waited.

"I did know her," Lila Townsend said. "She didn't seem that unstable."

Lagarde looked at Lila Townsend for a long minute. *She's one cold woman.* "How did you know her?" he said.

"We met at a Target store. We discovered we both knew Ben Cromwell. We compared our experiences. It seems she came off rather worse for it than I did."

"Did you see her after that meeting?" Lagarde asked.

So far, she had told him only the truth, as far as he could tell. She was right. She did not seem worse for wear for having allowed Cromwell into her life, however briefly. As she had told him in his first interview with her, she was short a few material objects, but it appeared those could be easily replaced. She had recovered from the experience and seemed to have her health and her sanity. She wasn't in meltdown the way Ilise Vander was and Evelyn Foster had been.

"No," she said. "I didn't."

That might be the lie, but he had no way to prove it.

"Do you know Violet Gold?" he asked.

"Yes. She's my patient. I am unable to tell you anything about her."

"How about Ilise Vander?" Black asked. "Do you know her?" Black, it seemed to Lagarde, was a little impatient with Lila Townsend's imperial style.

"Evelyn knew her. I met her when I met Evelyn," she said.

"So, you all just met at Target and had a little powwow about Ben Cromwell, did a little ritual cleansing, burned some sage and then got on with your lives?" Black said.

Lila Townsend laughed. "If only it were that easy. Is there anything else? I've had a long day. I'd like to have my dinner and relax."

Black and Lagarde looked at each other. Lagarde tilted his head toward the front door. Black nodded. "That's it," Lagarde said. "We'll be in touch if we have something else."

"Oh, and Dr. Townsend," Black said, "if by some chance you hear from your patient Violet Gold, would you tell her we'd like to talk with her in connection with the murder of Ben Cromwell?"

They saw themselves out. In the car, Black said, "She's definitely involved."

Lagarde nodded. "Let's pack it in for the day, go back to headquarters. I still have to go see Beverly Wilson. Maybe you can find out how the hospital disposes of waste. Maybe they inventory what goes in the incinerator and who brought it to be destroyed."

Without saying another word, Black drove back to the Troop 2 Command where Lagarde could pick up his own car.

CHAPTER FORTY-EIGHT

APRIL 6, 2014

Violet Gold walked along the path on the six-hundred foot high palisades that rose straight out of the sea in Sorrento above the Bay of Naples. In the distance she could see the islands of Ischia and further on, Procida seeming to float on the Mediterranean Sea. The air was soft and perfumed. A profusion of brightly colored flowers hugged the path. Palms and lemon trees competed for space in the sun and those unique Amalfi coast trees in the shape of umbrellas shaded well-placed benches along the path. *This is heaven.*

There were few Americans in Sorrento. Most Americans didn't even know this Italian city existed. She was staying in a hotel that was built into the cliff just above the sea. The walk down the stairs to the beach was steep, with so many turns, that there was an elevator. She thought she could stand in this spot at a curve in the path all day and watch the ferries and yachts come and go from the quaintly named little and large marinas. She could watch the dramatic cloud formations and the change of light that reminded her of Renaissance paintings. She became quickly accustomed to men calling after her, "*Ciao, bella!*" wherever she walked. It was a greeting that did not seem intended to harm her. She smiled to herself, but did not answer them. She was off men for a while, maybe forever.

The visit with her parents in Venice had been fine, although her mother continually commented that Violet was too subdued and that it was a good thing she had stopped working at "that place." Her father had plans for her to join his own law firm. "And high time, too," he told her with a kind smile. They bought her a stunning Venetian glass chandelier for her townhouse dining room, "And later you'll move it to your real house after you're married," her mother said, and had it shipped to their home for safe keeping until she returned. She didn't have the heart to tell them she might never come home . . . might never marry . . . would never give them the grandchildren they were planning to dote on in their old age. The entire time she spent with them, sitting in cafes watching the people and pigeons, browsing through shops, nibbling at delicious food, she could not find a way to tell them she was HIV positive, much less that she had helped kill a man. The words stuck in her throat.

"Eat something, you're fading away," her mother said. Her father hugged her shoulders as they sat in a gondola, "When you get back, let's go to the beach for a while," he said. "You always loved it there." She caught them looking over her head at each other. She was the most miserable in those moments, thinking she would never have a man in her life who understood her so completely that a simple look would convey everything each was thinking.

Violet knew it was obvious to her parents that something was wrong. But they were not the kind of people who would try to pry it out of her. They trusted her. She had always been such a good girl, there was no way for them to guess what was really wrong. Her mother suspected a man was involved—but in the way of normal heartbreak—not this disaster she had created. She knew if she told her father, he would put on his legal hat and figure out a defense for her, one that would probably work out okay, for her anyway. To stay out of prison, she would have to cut a deal, secure immunity from prosecution, provide evidence, and testify against the other women who also killed Ben Cromwell. It would be a sensational case. The papers would have a field day, many days. This was the kind of story even the *Washington Post* would deign to cover. Her parents would be shunned by their friends and neighbors, not because they did anything criminal but because their daughter did. She just couldn't do that to them. If she could just stay away, keep moving, find a simple job in Geneva or Zurich, an apartment, and build a new life for herself, they wouldn't have to go through that. They could come and visit her once or twice a year. They would adapt. She was their only child. She knew they would do anything for her.

She walked into the heart of the city, with many other people walking, shopping, eating in the cafes, savoring the handmade gelato served from small stalls all along the street. There seemed to be an unending stream of people walking on the streets except during siesta from 1 to 3 p.m. On Via San Cesareo, she went into a small supermarket, small by American standards which is to say twice the size of a roadside convenience store but large for a small Italian town of slightly more than sixteen-thousand people. There were even racks with clothing. She sorted through the blouses and found a brown silk tunic that she purchased for the novelty of buying something made in China from a store in Italy. It would probably remain a private joke forever. To whom could she tell it? She had never felt so alone. Outside on the narrow street, she walked with everyone else toward the piazza. There were small lights in the trees that would go on at dusk, adding to the enchantment of the place. The front of the cathedral would be illuminated. There would be small lights on under the umbrellas and the large canopies that covered the outdoor cafes. Sorrento, without doing anything but adding lights, was a magical kingdom.

She had discovered that she could see Mt. Vesuvius from Sorrento. The day before she took the tour bus to Pompeii and wandered through the ruins of the town. She imagined herself on the day of the volcanic disaster in the year AD 79, hot ash raining down from the volcano, running toward the sea, terrified. She could guess that there were people who said, "What volcano?" and just continued their daily activity, sitting in the communal bath, drinking wine, having sex, people who suffocated or were cooked by the heat and covered by twenty feet of volcanic ash. If life was a do-over, she hoped she was one of the Pompeiians who ran toward the sea, not one who cowered in a villa near a mural of some highly erotic sex act.

Somehow, her thoughts always came back to Ben Cromwell and that they had murdered him. She was circling the drain of that disaster. It seemed to her that the women, once his victims, had become the monsters. They had been swept up and lost themselves first in a fury of lust and then blood. They were worse than Ben. He was a jerk who just wanted to rob them and make them feel small and dirty. They had obliterated him. Standing there amid all that lush Sorrentine beauty, Violet realized she had to shake off her stupor, go home and tell her parents, talk to the police, face what she had done and take the punishment. There was no other way. She would make the arrangements to get home tomorrow.

CHAPTER FORTY-NINE

APRIL 8, 2014, 6 P.M.

Sam Lagarde rang the bell to Beverly Wilson's house and she opened the door immediately. *She must have been waiting on the bottom level of the townhouse for him.*

"Come into the studio," she said. "I brought down some tea." She walked into the room ahead of him and handed him a cup and pointed to a wicker chair for him to sit in. She was wearing a long yellow sweater she held wrapped around her body as if she were cold.

This was the first time he had been in this room of her townhouse and at first he needed to turn in circles to survey all the canvases that were propped up in various stages of being worked. He loved the colors she was using. It felt to him as if she had invented color, or at least made him see color in a way that he had never seen it before. Although there were sometimes objects that he recognized in her paintings, tree trunks could be several shades of green and their leafless branches trailed off into the mist at the edges of the painting. Bushes could be dark purple or rust orange. Snow could be blue. The sky could be any shade at all. It was as if she had transformed the world just for him. He was entranced, just wanted to sit there and stare at the canvasses. Beverly didn't say anything for a while. She let him absorb the colors. Time seemed to fade away.

Finally Beverly said, "Sam, I've been thinking about this for two days. At first I couldn't figure out what to do. I was confused. I've decided I have to tell you even though I'm breaking a confidence. Ilise Vander came to see me."

Lagarde felt an electric shock course through him. He was thrown out of the world of Beverly's paintings and back into the real world of murder and sorrow. He looked at her closely. Could he trust her? It was a question that was now open where a moment before it had been settled for all time. She had turned his world upside down for sure.

"When was this? What did she tell you?" he asked.

"Before we went out to dinner the other evening . . ." She paused and let that information sink in. Just the fact that she had kept the meeting from him for so long was evidence of betrayal of a sort. It was clear from the look on her face that she knew he would take withholding the information as a breach of trust. "She didn't give me any details," Beverly continued. "She's really too shaken to talk much, but she said they killed him, that they all did it together. She said her mother told her it was the same as putting down a rabid dog."

For the first time, Lagarde saw tears in Beverly Wilson's eyes. She wiped the corner of her eyes with her fingers. She shook her head as if to stop the tears. That didn't work.

"That's what made me think I had to tell you," she said through her tears, which had now overwhelmed her ability to hold them back with her fingers. "Ben, for all that he was, was not a rabid dog, he was a human being. Flawed, cruel, crazy maybe, but human and not deserving of that horrible death."

"Did she give you their names?" he asked cautiously.

"She said Evelyn," Lagarde nodded, "her mother, a doctor somebody, I don't think she really knows her name, and she killed Ben and hacked him into pieces." Beverly covered her face with her hands, leaned over her knees, and her whole body shook with the force of her sobs.

Lagarde waited. He wanted to take her in his arms and comfort her, but she was now a witness. She could identify one of the killers. She had a first-hand confession from one of them and, even if there was some reason it couldn't be admitted as evidence, as hearsay it would be a powerful bargaining tool for the prosecutor. He needed to keep his distance from her. The new information was that Katrina Vander was actively involved in the murder and that Violet Gold was not, if Beverly's hearsay version was accurate. She could have misunderstood Ilise. Ilise could have lied to her. But obviously, he would be arresting Ilise and Katrina Vander. If Katrina had already talked to a lawyer, they would probably make a deal with the prosecutor rather than go to trial, but that wasn't his problem. His job was done when the perpetrators were charged and handed over for trial. The tricky part was still finding a link to Lila Townsend.

"I thought you said the family didn't want revenge and didn't care about whether we found who killed Ben," he said. The minute the words were out of his mouth, he wondered why he was being so petulant. That conversation was now beside the point.

She looked surprised at his coldness. "I don't want revenge," she said, "but I think Ben deserves justice, no matter what *he* did. The people who killed him are no better than he was, and maybe they're the real monsters." She got up from her chair, found tissues on a table that was deep in paint containers, brushes, small canvases and pads of paper palettes and wiped her face and nose.

"Why didn't you tell me right away that Ilise spoke to you? Why didn't you tell me when we went to dinner?"

"I don't expect you to understand why I thought I had to keep the conversation with Ilise from you. Please let me know what I am supposed to do next."

Lagarde got up from his chair, contemplated saying something compassionate and quashed it. "I'll need you to come to headquarters and make a formal statement for the record," he said. "We can do that tomorrow. You should ask for Corporal Black."

Beverly nodded. "I will do that."

He nodded to her and let himself out the front door. In the car, he called Black. "I think we've got them," he said. "Get some back up and go pick up Ilise and Katrina Vander at their house. Tell them they are being arrested for first degree, premeditated murder. Alert the prosecutor's office that he'll need a grand jury for the indictment. I'm going to get the good doctor. I think she'll come without a struggle. But just in case, send a cruiser over to her house to meet me."

CHAPTER FIFTY

APRIL 8, 2014, 6:45 P.M.

When Corporal Black and two state troopers got to the Vander's house, the front door was ajar. Inside, Ilise Vander was standing over her mother with a heavy cast iron frying pan in her hand. There was blood splattered on the wall and Katrina Vander was lying in a pool of blood on the floor of the dining area in their small house. Her hair was matted with blood and her face looked like a truck had run over it. In her hand was scissors.

Marc Delany was standing there in the living room with his mouth open and his arms stretched out toward Ilise. "Come on, baby," Delany was saying as the police entered the house, "just give me the frying pan. It's okay. I got you now. You can stop."

Black rushed Ilise, grabbed the frying pan from her hand, put it on the table, pulled her away from the body and secured her with handcuffs behind her back. He sat Ilise down in a dining chair and told her to stay there. He bent down, careful not to disturb the body, and felt for a pulse at the carotid artery in Katrina Vander's neck. She was gone. *Murder of opportunity*, was the first thought that flashed through his mind. *One fewer perp to arrest*, was the second. He took a glove from his pocket, picked up the frying pan with it and handed it off to another trooper to bag and tag. Black called in this new murder before he said anything to Ilise. He needed the crime scene forensics guys to give this house a thorough scrub and the medical examiner's office to send a bus to pick up the body for autopsy.

Marc Delany slumped down on the couch like a puppet whose strings had been cut. He was crying. He wiped his face with his hands and looked at Ilise as if he had never seen her before.

"God, Ilise, what got into you? What's your problem? She was just trying to help you," Delany said.

"She fucked him," Ilise said. "She fucked him and then she told me he was a rabid dog so I couldn't have him anymore. She wanted him all for herself. She told me I had to kill him. She made me kill the only man I ever loved!" the girl wailed.

"You're not making any sense," Delany said. "She never had sex with Cromwell."

Black half listened to the conversation while the other half of his brain was dealing with required procedure for the new murder.

"Yes, she did!!" Ilise screamed. "He said so in his journal. She started it."

"The creep lied, Ilise! That was his trademark, he lied. He always lied. Your mom was trying to do what was best for you."

"How did she know what was best for me?" Ilise stamped her feet against the floor and threw her body around in the chair as if she wanted to leap out of her skin. "I'm the only one who knows what's best for me!"

"Yeah, you did a good job with that, didn't you?" Delany bellowed. "You really took care of yourself."

Ilise screamed at him, "You asshole. What do you know? You couldn't even half love me the way Ben did. You'll never know what we had."

Marc Delany shook his head. "He didn't love you, Ilise," he said.

"Oh, yeah? Mom said that. She said Ben didn't love me. Look where she is now. Just watch what you're saying. If I could kill her, I can kill you. If I hadn't listened to her, Ben wouldn't be dead right now."

Black thought Marc Delany might vomit right there. The kid was the color of the farina Black's mother used to make him eat when he was young. He also thought Ilise might be having a nervous breakdown or a psychotic break, but he sure wasn't a shrink and that wasn't his call to make. He was very glad he had two more state troopers along to control the situation. They made a quick search of the house inside and out to see if there were any more victims or perpetrators around, but it was clear that all the drama had taken place right there in that little front room with the purple couch and fake walnut dining set. One trooper stationed himself on the front porch to signal the arriving team that this was the house. The other stood by the back door in the kitchen, just in case the girl decided to flee.

Black turned to Delany. "What happened here?"

"Katrina called me, said Ilise was going crazy, running around the house, screaming at the top of her lungs, trying to stab herself with scissors. She was worried Ilise would commit suicide. She asked me to come over to help calm her down so I did."

"And when you got here, what did you see?"

"I could hear them screaming at each other from outside the house so I rushed in. They were wrestling each other. Ilise was trying to stab Katrina. Then Katrina got the scissors. It looked for a second like that was it, the fight was over. Katrina was trying to calm Ilise down, and then Ilise ran into the kitchen and grabbed the frying pan off the stove and started to whack away at Katrina's head. It happened so fast . . . Katrina dropped to her knees the first time she was hit. I couldn't move fast enough to stop it. Ilise was like an animal. Her teeth were bared and she was hissing. There was blood flying everywhere. I felt like I was back in Iraq, like we were hit by an IED and all I wanted to do was drop and cover my head." Delany was shaking. "I couldn't stop it. I'm sorry. I was just rooted there in one spot. I'm sorry." He put his hand over his eyes.

"You're an asshole, Marc," Ilise whispered. "What a loser. Did she fuck you too?"

"That's enough," Black said to her. "Ilise Vander, I am arresting you for the murder of your mother tonight and for the murder of Ben Cromwell on March 15th." Just to be sure he was saying this correctly, Black pulled out his credentials holder and removed the Miranda Warning card from the pocket. He read the card to her exactly as it was typed.

"You have the right to remain silent. Anything you say can and will be used against you in a court of law. You have the right to an attorney before making any statement and may have your attorney with you during questioning. If you cannot afford an attorney and desire one, the court will appoint one for you. You may stop the questioning at any time by refusing to answer further or by requesting to consult with your attorney. Do you understand each of these rights I have explained to you? With these rights in mind, do you wish to talk to us now?"

"I don't need any attorney," Ilise Vander said, her chin tilted up and her eyes defiant. "I killed the bitch because she made me kill the man I loved. She was a monster. I hate her. I didn't want to kill him. They were all like witches. They wanted to get blood on their hands. They wanted to dance in his blood. They were all into it. It was like sex for them."

"Ilise Vander," Black said, "I'm going to take you to headquarters where we will book you and question you further about this murder and the murder of Ben Cromwell." He paused, unsure whether he should be kind or just get on with it. He chose to be kind. "I suggest you wait until you have a lawyer present before you say anything more."

It's okay to be kind. He had three witnesses to her freely given confession, if you could consider being absolutely insane a state of freedom.

He put his hand under her arm to support her as she stood up from the chair. Ilise Vander tore herself away from him and ran out the front door, barreled past the trooper and out into the street just as two more cruisers, lights flashing and sirens blaring, pulled up to the house. She stood in the middle of the street barefooted, tossing her head, laughing, cackling and turning in circles, screaming, "I killed him, I killed him, I killed him. Do you hear me? I killed her. I killed him. I killed her."

Lights came on in nearby houses. People came out onto their porches to watch the girl dance in the street, screaming, illuminated by the flashing lights of the police cars.

CHAPTER FIFTY-ONE

APRIL 8, 2014, 7:15 P.M.

Once Ilise Vander was secured in the state trooper cruiser and on her way to headquarters for a formal interview and booking, Corporal Black phoned Detective Sam Lagarde, who answered on the first ring.

"You there yet?" Black asked him.

"Just around the corner, why?"

"Ilise Vander killed her mother and went stark raving mad—or the other way around. We've got her, but I'll bet she'll be ruled unable to participate in her own defense. She's going to spend some time in the loony bin. Doubtful she'll be much of a witness. Even if she tells the absolute truth, a jury will just think she's crazy and discount her testimony."

"That's compassionate, Larry. So you're saying she did or didn't confess before she went around the bend?"

"She confessed after she went off the deep end, so maybe it doesn't count. But even without the Cromwell connection, we've got her for murdering her own mother. Marc Delany was an eye witness to that. When we got there, the weapon was still in her hand. I took it off her before she could do any more damage. Our witness to this most recent murder is still sane, thank God. Delany was at the house and saw it happen. We took him also to get his witness testimony while it's still fresh in his mind. He might know something about the Cromwell murder from Katrina, something she told him before her daughter whacked her."

"What did Ilise kill her mother with?"

"A frying pan," Black deadpanned.

Lagarde was silent for a minute. "All right, then. I'm at Dr. Townsend's. The other cruiser is here. I'm going in. See you back at the corral."

He hung-up, then sat in his car for a few minutes to think through what Black told him and summarize where he was on his suspects. Evelyn Foster suicided, Katrina Vander was killed by her daughter, Ilise Vander was insane, Violet Gold was missing. That left only Dr. Lila Townsend as a possible suspect on the say-so of a girl who had lost her mind and who didn't know the doctor's name when she *still had* some grip on reality. And the information that Ilise said a doctor was involved in the Cromwell murder was second hand from Beverly Wilson. Unless Townsend confessed, he didn't have a case against her. They still had no weapon, they weren't sure how Cromwell was killed before he was dismembered. They didn't know what he was dismembered with although the medical examiner guessed it was a surgical instrument or instruments because the cutting edges made different marks on different parts of the body. She'd speculated that at least three different blades were used.

And, to top off his list of evidentiary problems, he wasn't sure that Townsend had the opportunity to kill Cromwell, given that she was in New York City prepping for her presentation at some medical conference on the same day. He had studied possible routes provided by Google Maps and saw that she could have murdered Cromwell and driven the three-hundred miles at a very high rate of speed and made it to her hotel in the Big Apple in five hours, or she could have taken the earliest train that went from D.C. to NYC by way of Baltimore, but she would have arrived exhausted and maybe frazzled looking. He found the conference website and watched the video of her presentation. She was as calm, collected and put together as anyone who had a full eight hours of sleep the night before and a good breakfast that morning. Truth be told, she looked radiant standing at the podium, talking in her melodious voice about killer infections that women might contract during or after pregnancy. If she did kill Cromwell, seven hours before her 11 a.m. presentation, with slides, on March 15th, she was the coldest person he had ever met in his life.

Lagarde got out of his car, signaled to the other troopers to accompany him, and walked up to the front door. The outside lights went on, lighting up the entire front lawn. He'd been right, she had put in motion detectors. He rang the bell. He knew she could see him on the television monitor inside the house. A few minutes went by and then Dr. Townsend talked to him through the intercom.

"Yes, detective," she said.

"Please open the door, Dr. Townsend," Lagarde said.

Two more minutes passed and Dr. Lila Townsend, wearing the same outfit he had seen her in earlier that evening plus running shoes and a hooded sweat jacket, opened the door. "Yes?" she said.

"Dr. Lila Townsend," Lagarde said, "I am bringing you in for questioning in the murder of Ben Cromwell on March 15th of this year. You have the right to remain silent. Anything you say can and will be used against you in court. You have the right to an attorney before making any statement and may have your attorney with you during questioning."

Lila Townsend interrupted him. "Got it, detective," she said. "I choose to remain silent and I want my attorney present at any and all questioning." She stepped outside, pulled the front door closed, and tapped the keys on the lock.

"We will want access to your house to search it," Lagarde said, somewhat nudged off his rhythm.

"You'll have to get a warrant for that," she said.

"You'll be able to call your attorney from headquarters," Lagarde said.

"I've already done so. He will meet me there," she said.

Lagarde wondered if she had killed before and been arrested for it. She seemed to have anticipated his every move. His earlier assessment that she was the coldest person he had ever met needed amending. Except for Attila the Hun, she might be the coldest person anyone had ever met.

CHAPTER FIFTY-TWO

APRIL 9, 2014

Lila Townsend did not confess. She said nothing during the interrogation. Her lawyer did all the talking. She either looked attentively at Lagarde, down at her hands on the table, or at her attorney. In her running shoes and hoodie, her hair loose and her freckles highlighted by the bright overhead lights, she looked more like a college student than a hardened killer.

By 10 p.m., the night they brought Townsend in for questioning, the county prosecutor, Vincent Toricelli, told Lagarde he didn't have enough hard evidence, credible hearsay or circumstantial evidence to file a complaint against her, much less secure a grand jury indictment. They didn't have her fingerprints, fibers or fluids on a murder weapon. They didn't even have a murder weapon. Here the prosecutor looked at Lagarde as if he were in third grade and hadn't yet learned to read. There were no vectors that connected Townsend to Ilise and Katrina Vander. There was no witness to her being at the murder. The "some doctor" reference that came via Beverly Wilson was worthless and tainted because it was third hand and the witness was the victim's grandmother. Ilise Vander didn't know Townsend's name and was unable to identify her by sight when they walked her by the doctor in the office. Theoretically, they should not have attempted such a casual drive-by identification, but Ilise had a tenuous grip on reality and they were hoping for something, a twitch, a sudden shock of recognition, maybe she would point and say, "Her, that's the one, she was with us when we murdered Ben Cromwell," but no such luck. The girl walked by Townsend as if she weren't there. And for Townsend's part, she didn't seem to see Ilise Vander either. She didn't even breathe in the girl's direction.

Townsend had a decent alibi. She wasn't in town when the murder took place. Black had called the conference hotel in New York City and apparently Dr. Townsend checked in on March 14th, the day before her presentation on the 15th. Someone could have done that for her and given her the key to her room when she arrived, but they had no proof of that. The prosecutor made it clear he wasn't saying she was not involved in the murder, but Lagarde had to find something he could hang his hat on in court. He at least needed credible circumstantial evidence and the fact that Townsend said she had sex with Ben Cromwell and he robbed her wasn't enough even for motive, much less means and opportunity. Lagarde felt let down. It seemed to him they were very close to solving Cromwell's murder, yet every time he came close to the finish line, someone moved it. Marc Delany had been no help. Apparently Katrina Vander told him exactly nothing about the Cromwell murder. That intimacy Lagarde and Black observed in the Vander household between Marc and Katrina did not come from sharing homicidal secrets.

Ilise confessed repeatedly and implicated her mother and Evelyn by name in Cromwell's murder. She gleefully took credit for killing her mother all on her own. *Maybe that was enough to conclude this whole mess.* Her public defender informed them he was filing a pretrial motion for an insanity defense. The prosecutor said he would ask the court to order the defendant to submit to a mental examination by a court appointed psychiatrist, but in the hallway outside the interview room, he told Lagarde that Ilise was no use to them as a witness. Ilise's attorney had no objection. The girl would likely be in a state mental institution for the rest of her life. Whether that was better than life in prison or not was never a question anyone asked. *Ben Cromwell certainly had his revenge on these three women, without lifting a finger. They had destroyed themselves as completely as they destroyed him.*

Lagarde could file his report and close the case and clear it off his desk. But he knew he didn't have the whole nut, and that bothered him.

Cromwell had been dead for almost a month and they hadn't really cracked the case. It was like not being able to find the word you wanted to say, the word that was just sitting there in the back of your head taunting you, because you knew it yesterday, and you knew you would know it tomorrow, but right now when you wanted to say it, it was hiding in the folds of your brain like a child tucked into a closet no one ever opened.

When Beverly Wilson came in to make her statement, Lagarde asked Black to take her deposition so there would be no later accusations or innuendoes that could be offered by Ilise's lawyer. There wasn't much Beverly Wilson added to what they knew except the fact that Ilise had confessed before she went off the deep end completely. It was likely this case would never go to court. It might all be resolved by a plea deal with the prosecutor. There might be a day in court where only lawyers and the judge talked, but Lagarde didn't see a trial.

Beverly looked at Lagarde from across the room before she went into one of the interview rooms for her deposition, but she didn't smile or greet him. She looked older today, sadder, as if the spirit that enlivened her had slipped away. Her face seemed to have collapsed into a hundred wrinkles that mapped her sorrow. When she was done, she left without saying goodbye. Lagarde felt a small hole open in his heart. He should never have let himself get attached to her.

The Captain said to clear the case and move on. Go with what he had and call it a day, she said. That afternoon, as Lagarde was finishing the last of the forms he had to file, he got a call from a Howard Gold, who turned out to be Violet Gold's father. Mr. Gold said he was acting as Violet's attorney and had some information to provide in the matter of Ben Cromwell's murder. He wanted to talk with both Lagarde and the prosecutor at the same time. Lagarde rocked back in his chair. This was the nutcracker moment he'd been waiting for. They set a time for the next morning in the prosecutor's office. Lagarde told Black he should be at the meeting also. Regardless of how anyone else felt, Lagarde would bet this was the breakthrough in the case they had been waiting for.

CHAPTER FIFTY-THREE

APRIL 10, 2014

Violet Gold and her father, attorney Howard Gold, seated themselves in prosecutor Vincent Toricelli's Martinsburg office across the table from Lagarde and Toricelli. The office, in an old turn of the twentieth century brick building that had been remodeled into architectural oblivion, was dark, with overhead florescent lights, and metal bookcases along three walls loaded with law books Lagarde bet no one ever looked at anymore since online services were quicker. Black said he preferred to stand. A stenographer was present to record the deposition. The transcript would be shared with Howard Gold when it was typed. Lagarde got his first good look at Violet Gold in the flesh. He could see how Mr. Chaplin, her Legal Aid supervisor, had been smitten. She was simply gorgeous, maybe thinner than in that Legal Aid softball team photo. Prior to Ben Cromwell coming into her life, she had probably been pretty smart as well. It looked to Lagarde as if Cromwell had managed to destroy this young woman's life as well. The dead guy was batting 850.

Howard Gold cleared his throat. Lagarde had a moment to think that Violet did not get her looks from her father. He remembered the neighbor's laugh when he asked her if she was Mrs. Gold. He thought he knew why now. Howard Gold leaned forward with his hands loosely folded together on the table. Somehow his posture made it clear he was in charge of this meeting. Toricelli did nothing to disabuse him. Gold made short work of declaring that he was Violet's attorney of record, that he was offering them information about the murder of Ben Cromwell in exchange for immunity from prosecution for Violet, to whom he referred alternately as his client or Ms. Gold. Lagarde started to interrupt, but Toricelli held his hand up, palm towards Lagarde, indicating he should keep his mouth shut. It was clear to Lagarde these two men knew each other from various lawyer's networks, maybe golf, maybe even that Toricelli had his eye on a partner seat in the Gold law firm at some future date when he was tired of being an underpaid public servant. Whatever their relationship, everyone listened politely to Gold's proposition and Toricelli agreed, to Lagarde's dismay, to give Violet complete immunity, regardless of her role in the murder and before she told her story. Toricelli's only demand was that Violet Gold agree to testify at trial if a trial was necessary. Gold said yes without checking with his daughter, although she looked at him with dismay. He asked her to relay her memory of the facts of the case. Violet nodded and spoke in nearly a whisper.

"Several of us discovered that during the course of our relationships with him, Ben Cromwell had infected us with the HIV virus and other diseases," Violet said, her voice shaky but controlled. "It seemed to us he did that deliberately, that he was trying to kill us by infecting us. He also stole money and goods from us and broke into our homes repeatedly. We were horribly afraid of him. Each of us felt like he might kill us at any minute. We had no control over our own lives. There was no place we felt safe." Her voice grew steadier as she talked. "We learned about each other over a period of six months or so and finally we got together to talk about our experiences with him, in a kind of support group."

Lagarde raised his eyebrows. Violet Gold lowered her gaze to the table. "When did you get together?" Lagarde asked. He couldn't stop himself even though Toricelli glared at him.

"This is not an interrogation, detective," Toricelli said. "Please allow Ms. Gold to give us her entire statement."

"February," Violet said. "We met in late February. I don't think anybody expected how far it would go, but when the conversation turned to killing him, I explained right away that I could not kill him, that I wouldn't kill him." She paused and took a tissue from her purse and dotted the corners of her eyes.

"And yet you murdered him on March 15th?" Lagarde said.

"Yes," Violet Gold said. "They did. I didn't."

"How exactly did *they* do that?" Lagarde said. Toricelli continued to glare, but he didn't stop Lagarde from asking nor did he indicate Violet should not answer the question.

"It was agreed that I would call Ben and ask him to meet me at the stables," she said. "He came to meet me and they took it from there."

"So there was a plan in advance to murder Ben Cromwell and you all carried it out?" Lagarde said.

"Yes," Violet Gold said in a whisper. "They did."

"Who are they?" To Lagarde, after the issue of premeditation, this was the key question.

"Lila Townsend." Violet swallowed hard and started to shake. "Katrina and Ilise Vander. Evelyn Foster."

"And you are a co-conspirator and accessory," Lagarde said, just to get it on the record that Violet Gold understood her complicity in the murder.

"Yes, but under duress," Violet said.

"How did they kill him?" Lagarde ignored her claim of being under pressure from anyone or anything except the demands of her own ego.

"Lila, Dr. Townsend, injected him with something. She said she was going to look into pentobarbital and if she couldn't get that easily she would use potassium chloride. I think those were the names of the chemicals. The idea was that he would die quickly. It looked like Ben had a heart attack right after she injected him, but I'm not sure. It looked like he died right away. But no one checked to see if he had a pulse or was breathing. Then they cut him up. They were supposed to put the pieces of him in plastic bags." Violet covered her face with her hands, lowered her head, and sobbed, shaking her head. Her father patted her arm. She pulled herself together.

"Did they bring the instruments they used to cut him up with them?"

"Yes, Lila got them from the hospital I think. They were surgical instruments."

If Lagarde was keeping score, it looked like he had Dr. Lila Townsend on murder one. There was plenty of premeditation. He looked over at Black, who was taking notes. Black nodded. That would be life in prison for the good doctor. Lagarde briefly wondered if her husband, Sterling, would get the beautiful house.

"What did you do with the body parts that were in the plastic bags?"

"Lila, Ilise, Katrina and Evelyn each took some of the bags in their cars and threw them in dumpsters all over the area."

"Who put the head in the spa dumpster?"

"I don't know." Violet shivered violently. It might have been the first time she heard that detail.

"What did you do with the cutting instruments?"

"Evelyn took them back to the hospital to be sterilized, or whatever they do with surgical instruments after they're used."

"What about his guts?" Lagarde knew he was being harsh, but he was thinking of poor, crazy Ilise going to a bleak state asylum for the rest of her life and pretty, rich Violet getting to hang out at a beach resort for the rest of hers. There was nothing fair about this deal the prosecutor struck with the Golds.

"They were to be burned in the hospital incinerator with the disposable cover-ups everyone put on . . . but I don't know if that happened."

"Who took Ben's guts and your disposable garments to the hospital?"

"Evelyn was supposed to but I left before the rest of them did. I left after they started cutting him. I couldn't take it." Violet was sobbing again.

Howard Gold suggested that the prosecutor had what he needed to make his case. He promised that Violet would answer any new questions that arose. Then he asked that the information provided in this interview pertaining to Violet Gold remain confidential, within the confines of the prosecutor's office.

"Sorry, Howard, I can't promise that," Toricelli said. "If we go to trial and Violet testifies for the prosecution, her connection to the murder will be revealed. Undoubtedly, she will be censured by the law board and lose her license." Then he signaled to the stenographer to stop. He leveled his practiced glare at Violet. "You're very lucky, Ms. Gold, to have found a way to be useful to us in this matter."

Violet Gold nodded, her face still shrouded by tissues and her hands. Her father put his arm around her and helped her stand. They walked out of the office.

"I don't know if you deserve the credit or not," Toricelli said to Lagarde and Black, "but that interview locks up the case against Dr. Townsend. I'll get a bill of indictment against her as soon as possible. I'll let you know when to pick up the warrant to go get her."

"Maybe we should hold her in advance?" Lagarde said.

"That's probably not necessary," said Toricelli. "She thinks she won already. She's got a practice here. She's not going anywhere."

Lagarde nodded. He and Black went out to their car. "There's still something about this that doesn't make sense," Lagarde said, once they were on the road back to their own office. "They met to talk about Ben Cromwell and suddenly they were talking about murdering him? That's quite a leap for sane people to make. The murder wasn't done in the heat of the moment. They planned it down to the last detail. What got them to that boiling point and sustained it for weeks after they met? There's something we're missing. Maybe something that Violet Gold doesn't know."

CHAPTER FIFTY-FOUR

APRIL 11, 2014, 11 A.M.

When Lagarde and Black arrived at Lila Townsend's door, warrants in hand for her arrest and a premises search, they found no one at home. The troopers they brought along for the arrest broke the door down and they ignored the loud beeping of the house alarm system while they searched for the good doctor from room-to-room, out on the deck, down the stone steps to the river. Nothing. All her personal belongings, including her car, laptop and phone were gone. Even the furniture, dishes, pots, paintings, rugs and accessories were gone. The house was an empty shell echoing with their footsteps on the wood floors. The prosecutor's devotion to dotting I's and crossing T's had given Lila Townsend enough time to flee. Lagarde guessed that when you had a few bucks to throw around, you could get pretty good service from moving companies. She didn't do this on her own.

In the kitchen that faced the river, propped up on the granite counter, was a note addressed to Detective Sam Lagarde. The piece of white paper was folded once so that it stood up like a tent on the bare black surface. It was the same stationery on which Townsend's stay away warning letter to Cromwell had been printed. Black picked up the paper and read the note. He took one step backwards and then handed the paper to Lagarde.

Lagarde held the paper in front of him, found the right focal length, and read the typed note:

Dear Detective Lagarde, don't trouble yourself looking for me. You won't find me. I'm leaving the country.

The piece of the puzzle you're missing is this: I am the older sister of the boy Ben Cromwell murdered when he was eight-years-old. I didn't know that until Katrina told us about the murder when we met in February. No one was ever punished for that crime. It took twenty-two years for my brother to get justice. I am not sorry.

A life for a life . . .

She had usefully signed the note in her own hand, "Lila Townsend." He hoped they would find her fingerprints on the paper so they could verify that she had handled the paper. It was possible that the printer, had she left it behind would still have a ghost copy of the note in its memory, but they didn't have the printer. Anyway, all that would prove was that someone had typed a note on a computer that was no longer in evidence and printed it out on that piece of paper that she would likely have handled at any other time. And at this point, what did it matter anyway? The murderer had fled.

Lagarde read the note again, and then another time. He looked at Black who shrugged and held his hands out from his sides in a "what are you going to do" gesture. Black had plainly had enough of this case. Lagarde shook his head. He didn't want to go any further either. This note was as good a confession as they were going to get from Dr. Townsend. There had been enough death. It was time to wash their hands of this case.

"Let's let the Captain make the call on whether we pursue this or not," Lagarde said to Black. "If she left the country, finding her is way beyond our resources, and what's the point."

Black nodded. "I think we've done all we can with this case," he said. "I'll be glad to go back to just plain vanilla murders after this."

Lagarde had one last thing to do on the case after filing the paperwork that would send the body to the funeral home designated by Ben's parents. He had to tell Beverly Wilson what they discovered and give her back Ben's belongings. He wanted to see her and he was dreading the meeting. How would he tell her this final piece of devastating information?

CHAPTER FIFTY-FIVE

APRIL 12, 2014

Sam Lagarde called in advance to make sure Beverly Wilson would be home. He had the duffel bag of Ben's things in his car. He had heavier baggage in his heart. He still did not know how he would tell her what he knew. He rehearsed various ways of telling her on the thirty minute drive from his office at the Troop 2 Headquarters to her home in Falling Waters. He still wondered if he should tell her at all. How much sorrow can a person take?

He parked in the spot marked Visitor, pulled the duffel bag out of the back of the car and walked toward her townhouse. She was waiting downstairs for him and opened the door before he rang the bell.

Simultaneously, they said, "I'm glad to see you, so sorry I was so . . ."

"Wrongheaded," Beverly said.

"Callous," Lagarde said.

They smiled at each other and relaxed a little. Lagarde offered to hand her the duffel bag but she shook her head and pointed to the door from the foyer that led into the garage. He took the bag into the garage and put it in a corner. He wouldn't want to deal with the contents now either. Beverly, it seemed, didn't even want to touch the bag.

"I think I'll give it to Robert," she said. "There might be something in there he wants to keep as a memento of Ben."

Neither of them mentioned the thousands of dollars in cash stowed in the three shoe boxes. It was up to Robert Cromwell to decide what to do with that. It was beside the point, anyway. Lagarde guessed that after the duffel bag sat in Beverly's garage for a few months, it would occupy a similar spot in Robert Cromwell's garage, probably for years.

Beverly looked unbearably sad to Lagarde, as if she were a moment away from weeping. In his assessment, her grandson's death had been difficult, but finding out why and how he was murdered were worse.

"Come up stairs and have some coffee," she said, and led the way.

He walked into the kitchen with her and watched her prepare the coffee in the same red mugs in which she had given him coffee the first time he met her. It felt like millions of years had passed since then. Then she had a grandson who had been murdered in a grisly way. Now there was only a grisly story to replace him. He needed to tell her the end of that story and he knew she was waiting for him to find the words. *Start anywhere*, he told himself. They went into the living room and took the places they sat in the first time they met.

"You know we have Ilise in custody," he said. She nodded. "She will be in a state mental facility for the rest of her life, I think. I don't think I had a chance to tell you that she killed her mother."

Beverly gasped. She looked at him as if, after Ben's death, this might be the worst thing she had ever heard, but Lagarde knew there was more and that it was worse than this. Katrina's death was like an appetizer to a smorgasbord of horror. He had to plow on and get it done.

"Evelyn Foster, the woman who called you on the phone, she committed suicide." He looked at her. She had bent her head down. She put her hand on her cheek.

"Violet Gold turned state's evidence, that means she told us what happened and she agreed to testify in court, if it comes to that, but it won't."

"I don't know about Violet Gold," Beverly said.

"She's a young lawyer that Ben was seeing." He didn't tell her that Violet Gold would not serve any time in prison for killing Beverly's grandson.

"So they were all in on it together, like Ilise said?"

"It seems that way."

"What about the doctor somebody that Ilise mentioned?"

"She got away, fled the country."

"You mean she just got away with killing someone and no one is going to do anything about that?"

Sam Lagarde sighed audibly. Beverly had come a long way from thinking 'what is the point of arresting someone for Ben's death,' as she had said earlier in the month.

"If she ever comes back into the state, there's a warrant out for her arrest," he explained, "and in all the states that have a reciprocal relationship with us. She could be arrested in Maryland and returned to us for prosecution, for instance. The warrant will never expire. If she comes back in fifty years, she can still be arrested."

"But you're not going to do anything about finding her?"

"She left us a note saying she was leaving the country. She emptied her house. She told the doctors at her practice she was leaving. She emptied her bank accounts. We don't have the resources to track her."

He had known this wouldn't go well. Beverly had the look of a wild woman, as if she were going to jump up and start searching for Lila Townsend herself.

"What about the FBI? Can't they find her?"

"They don't really have jurisdiction in this crime."

Beverly shook her head. Lagarde knew she was thinking the law was beyond her. Even to him, it looked like the two centuries of jurisprudence the country had amassed couldn't do anything to prevent any crimes and barely did anything to provide justice to those who were harmed by the criminal class.

"Why did they do it?" she asked.

That was the question Lagarde was dreading because it was really unanswerable. All murders were mysteries at their core, even when you knew who did it and how. How does any human being bring himself or herself in this case, to destroy the life of another person? There's a natural stopping point where the normal person pulls back, appalled at their own behavior. *You have to pass that point to complete the job.* You have to pass the point where you care about anyone but yourself, or your orders. Even trained soldiers have trouble with killing. They have to tell themselves they're killing the enemy to protect the guy next to them, because they've got his back, because it's their job. Ordinary citizens killing other ordinary citizens; that is bizarre behavior that can never be understood. Even all the social research showing how easy it is to give a person power over others and how they will abuse that power couldn't prove to him that killing was normal. You needed fear, frenzy, superhuman strength, and a glacial emotional coldness to do it. Perhaps all killers are insane. They passed the normal stopping point and kept going. Something in their brains derailed. But how could he explain this to Beverly? He couldn't really explain it to himself and this was his job.

"They all seemed to have gone crazy at the same time," Lagarde said. It was the easiest way to explain what happened. "They wanted revenge for the harm Ben caused them, but that wouldn't have done it, tipped them over into murder. None of them alone would have killed him. Even together, they needed a stronger motive than the harm Ben did to each of them. Do you know about the incident," he stopped for a moment and checked the word he was using, "the time when Ben killed a boy when he was young?"

"What? What are you talking about? Sarah has never said anything like that to me."

"When Ben was eight, before his mother died in the car accident, so I'm guessing before Sarah knew the Cromwells, a young boy died in a swimming pool accident in Ben's back yard."

Beverly was silent, waiting, barely breathing. She was staring at that weird glass sculpture on her coffee table.

"Although the incident was filed as an accident by the Springdale police, they were suspicious that it was deliberate. There were gaps in

Eileen Cromwell's statement that led them to believe she was lying. The dead boy's parents told the police that Ben did it, that he had been doing strange things to their son and that he was afraid of Ben. It's all in the record. But it was all inconclusive; there was no prosecution. Ben was never charged, not even as a juvenile."

Beverly was weeping openly now. She wasn't even trying to wipe the tears off her face. She shook her head. "What does that have to do with these women murdering Ben?"

"The boy who drowned was Lila Townsend's brother. Her maiden name was Greene. She lived a few blocks away from Ben Cromwell. She was a teenager when it happened. Her parents died in a car accident when she was in medical school. She never put it together until Katrina Vander told them the story about the drowning."

"I'm lost," Beverly said. "Why would Katrina Vander know this story?"

"It turns out Katrina was Eileen Cromwell's half sister. You know that old saw about six degrees of separation?"

Beverly didn't respond to Lagarde's attempt to lighten his explanation.

He plowed on. "Well, Eileen told Katrina about the drowning before she died. Katrina told the women in February. Violet Gold told us the story Katrina told them. We checked it out. It seems to be true."

"It's too much, it's too much," Beverly said.

She stood up. She paced the living room. She walked into the kitchen and then the dining room and then came back into the living room. She looked out the window. She walked over to the coffee table, picked up the blown-glass sculpture in both hands, lifted her arms and threw it at the wall. It hit and shattered. Pieces of it clattered on the floor and broke again.

Lagarde was startled. He didn't expect this violent gesture from her. He sat and watched while she paced again. Then she went into the kitchen and took a broom and dustpan from the pantry and swept up the glass pieces. She dumped them into the trash bin in the kitchen.

She came back into the living room, sat on the couch, crossed her legs and folded her hands in her lap. Her cheeks were flushed. Her eyelashes were still wet from her tears. Lagarde wanted to get up and sit next to her, put his arm around her, pull her close to him and console her. But he didn't. There was something in her posture that told him she was pulling herself together and she needed to do it by herself. It looked to him like she knew how to do this from experience. She had practiced. There was so much he would never know about her life before he met her. They were quiet for several minutes.

"Will you tell Sarah and Robert this story?"

"Only if they ask me," Lagarde said. "Otherwise I will tell them we know what happened, who did it, and have made an arrest."

"That's good," she said, "don't tell them. It's too much to know. They need to bury their son and grieve for him. That's all that should be on their plates now."

Lagarde nodded. He stood up. Beverly stood. "If there's anything you ever need from me," he said.

She nodded. "Thank you, Sam, for telling me everything. You've been very diligent. I appreciate your effort." She walked down the stairs.

Sam Lagarde followed and at the front door took Beverly Wilson's hand in his, turned it over and noticed for the first time the sprinkling of age spots across the back of her hand. They spun outward, like a constellation of stars and planets spiraling out from an explosion of matter and light. He placed his other hand over hers and saw the intimation of a similar universe on his. He would come to the place she was, he would learn what she had learned about solitude and self-sufficiency. He wasn't there yet. He still thought he needed someone to complete him. He still wanted that someone to be her. Her eyes were kind, even as she pulled her hand away.

He touched the soft skin on her face with his fingers, the first moment of intimacy combined with the knowledge that it would never deepen. He would have to live the rest of his life in this moment, in the time she allowed him to share the air around her, to stand in her aura, to learn that love was not taking something or giving something, it just was. Beverly Wilson had unraveled that mystery for him.

"Goodbye, Sam," she said. "Be well."

He would play that benediction over and over in his mind in the coming years until it became both blessing and command.

ACKNOWLEDGMENTS

Many thanks to my writing group Karen Robbins, Tara Bell, and Millie Curtis, for their endless patience and encouragement. To my husband who is the best sounding board for character and plot development, much gratitude. Thanks to my first readers, Dr. Gregory Mestanas, artist Patricia Perry, counselor Carmen Procida and photographer Carolyn Bross for their insightful feedback and advice.

ABOUT THE AUTHOR

Ginny Fite is an award-winning journalist who has covered crime, politics, government, healthcare, and art. She was born in Los Angeles and raised in New Jersey. She studied at Rutgers University, Johns Hopkins University, the School for Women Healers, and the Maryland Poetry Therapy Institute. She previously served as a press secretary and a district director for a governor and for a member of Congress; a spokesperson for a few colleges and universities; and a media director at General Dynamics Robotic System, a robotics R&D company. She is the author of five novels: *Cromwell's Folly*; *No Good Deed Left Undone*; *Lying, Cheating, and Occasionally . . . Murder*; *No End of Bad*; and *Blue Girl on a Night Dream Sea*, in addition to three collections of poetry and a humorous book on aging, *I Should Be Dead by Now*. Many of her stories have also been published in literary journals. She currently resides in Harpers Ferry, West Virginia.

THE DETECTIVE SAM LAGARDE MYSTERIES

FROM OPEN ROAD MEDIA

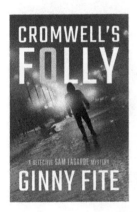
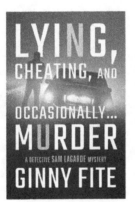
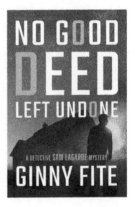

OPEN ROAD

INTEGRATED MEDIA

Find a full list of our authors and
titles at www.openroadmedia.com

FOLLOW US
@OpenRoadMedia

CPSIA information can be obtained
at www.ICGtesting.com
Printed in the USA
JSHW040044011122
32383JS00001B/12